World War III: Corona

Dr. Sam Swapn Sinha

Preface

This book writing is an act of fiction. Wang Wei and Zhang Wei are fictional characters who have nothing to do with real life people or situations. The conception that Chinese government said this or said that- is just an imagination. Although it has been researched well and thoroughly investigated, correlation cannot be established or guaranteed between events with perfect accuracy. The author of the book will not be responsible for any deviations found. Readers are free to make their own conclusions based on several assumptions. Any resemblance to real life is just a coincidence. Chinese government or anyone else should not feel offended. This is just fiction. Author is not liable for any damages to any party including the Government of China. The purpose of writing this book is to create an awareness amongst the readers that the global good and saving mankind must be the prime concern of human endeavors and any sinister designs must be stopped, discouraged, and not accepted by people, governments, and institutions internationally. It is also designed to create a learning opportunity for Chinese government to look at and understand what the world might think of them in the current scenario. China is trying to be belligerent and reactive right now, instead they can be sorry for what happened and make amends.

The writing and content in this book sometimes shifts from the author to the Chinese CCP person suddenly and abruptly to create a twist. I hope readers understand it and enjoy that, it is intentional. Mr Wang Wei and Zhang Wei are the guys from the Chinese Government. Why I chose Wang Wei is because it is one of the most popular names in China as we have in America- John Smith. Wang Wei and Zhang Wei are fictional characters who resemble and represent Dr. Sam's understanding of how Chinese government feels, thinks, and articulates their thoughts. This may be done in mandarin or Cantonese but Dr. Sam's interpretation is in English. Often in the book when I say "America" I mean "The USA". I use this expression as most people when they speak about the United States they never say US or United States, instead they will America, meaning America is USA. So I found it more interesting and colloquial. Also, this book is written in simple colloquial language and English that we speak in America. It has not been designed to look ornamental and flowery in nature but flows like ordinary Americans speak on a day to day basis. It is informal, casual, and nonchalant vernacular fashion.

World peace is very important and all nations should come together in promoting that. This idea of destroying the world is wicked and should be fought through dialogue, peaceful means, and mutually beneficial systems should be worked out to save human beings. Billions of people in the world from Africa, South America, Latin America, East Europe, some parts of India, etc. need support to grow out of poverty but governments worldwide are spending billions of dollars to augment their armies and defense budgets. USA, China, and now India spend 100's of Billions of dollars each year to feel that they are stronger. This has become an ego fulfilling game. Whom are they trying to defend themselves from? This must stop. This desire to rule the world must end. I am going to give my life for this cause. Corona has been designed for the last two decades to help some countries boost their ego and create fear and kill ordinary people. I will not let that happen. We need a new global system. We need disarmament, reduction in defense budgets, scaling down military warheads, and want to leave a safe, secured, peaceful world for our kids. We need to create new organizations as global agencies have become defunct and have failed to deliver again and again.

Thanks to all who helped become what I become!

I want to thank my family Monica Sinha, Eva Sinha, and Eti Sinha. I am thankful to my elder sister Neel Kamal Darbari, my brother in law Tribhuvan Darbari and niece Ritwija Darbari. Ritwija the idea and writing this book all happened in your room- so thanks a lot. I also want to thank my younger sister Rimjhim Sinha, her hubby Dr. Ved Prakash and my niece Devina Prakash & nephew Divyansh Prakash & his newly married wife Manisha. My family has been the main anchor and my main support of my life. My daughters Eva and Eti are the reason I exit, live, and thrive. I know they will not believe this when they read it but it is true- this is coming straight from my heart. My daughters will say "Papa you have no time for us", my answer is "dear because I was busy thinking about and writing this book". While all these years I have been busy working in the company to grow it to a multi-million dollar business or following my passions of writing, travel, exploring life- -my family has always supported me.

I want to thanks Professor Ahmad Banafa, from Stanford University, #1 Tech Voice to follow and influencer on Linkedin, award winning Author and a writer. Speaker on Cybersecurity to the Pentagon. Expert on IOT and Blockchain. A Member of MIT Technology Review, has been Interviewed many times on CBS, ABC as Technology Fortune Teller, for agreeing to be on the back cover of the book. I have been teaching courses at the same university for the last five years and enjoyed learning from him. He has a depth of ocean in him and continuously challenges the status quo His profile can be seen at https://www.linkedin.com/in/ahmedbanafa/

I would like to thank Karl Mehta, CEO Edcast who is Karl Mehta, CEO Edcast -Future of work platform. Karl and I are working on some initiative together. He has tremendous energy and

5

is a constant problem solver. Once When I was interviewing him on my Radio show "Tech Chai with Dr. Sam", I asked him tell us the secret sauce for success, he replied "success is nothing else but an eventual outcome of a stream of continuous failures, when nothing else is left, you will get success". These words still resound in my mind and heart all the time. Karl's company is funded by Stanford University Ventures Funded, he is a Serial Entrepreneur- at a very early age he took an exit for a Quarter Billion Dollar by selling his earlier company to Visa Card. Karl is a co-Author of the book-Financial Inclusion at Bottom of Pyramid. He is the Board Member for California Workforce Investment Board. He was the Technology Advisor to President Barack Obama- Ex Chief Technology Officer. He has been awarded by Prime Minister India, Hon'ble Narendra Modi under his Code for India initiative. He received an award from The President of India for being a leading global Tech Advisor, https://www.linkedin.com/in/mehtakarl/

I want to thank my family friends in America, Amit Goyal, Ajay Dubey, Sid Jaitly, Ajay Jaitly and their respective families. I also want to thank my childhood friends Ajay Gupta & Ajay Singh and many others who were there in helping me and making me what I became in life. I also want to thank Ravi Yadav, my friend from Delhi who has always helped me and supported me in pursuit of my dreams. This list is endless as I am one of the very few who has been endowed with a vast group of family and friends who consistently shower their love and affection to me. I also want to thank my wonderful students- now in thousands all over the world, who have motivated me to get up each day and live my life with passion and excitement. I want to thank them for seeing the 'guru' in me. I want to thank my fans, thousands of them all over the world who look upon me to solve their problems. I am just an ordinary guy next door. But I want to 'put a ding in the universe', as Steve Jobs said, and leave this place with slightly more stock of happiness and world peace.

About the Author

Dr. Sam- Swapn Sinha, is a California, United States based Professor, CEO, entrepreneur, investor, trainer, life coach, mentor, philosopher, and a social activist. After getting his MA, MBA he joined IndianOil and worked there for more than a decade, after quitting his life-long permanent well paid Government public sector job in India, to explore his passions, he embarked on his journey to pursue a Doctorate degree in International Business from the United States from Golden Gate University in the beautiful city of San Francisco in Silicon Valley California. In his own words: " I wanted to know what I was born for, why do I exist, who am I, and what is the purpose of my life, I set out on my global journey?. He teaches courses at a local university in Fremont. He has been in America for more than 17 years. His wife Monica Sinha and wonderful daughters Eva Sinha, Eti Sinha live in Fremont, California, with him. He loves to read a lot, sing, play guitar, run half a marathon, and play Chess, Sudoku, and drive cars like crazy. His best friend is his pet Elon for the last 3 years.

He is a very well-known trainer and coach in Silicon Valley and a very popular Agilist & life coach in the United States and globally. His corporate career spans more than 30 years across Fortune 500 and start-ups. He likes to travel, wander, be a lifelong learner, and explore the world. He wants to continue his " globe-trotting" and someday scale Mount Everest. He loves reading, writing, coaching, video teaching, and has his own You tube Channel Dr. Sam Swapn with close to half million views and thousands of subscribers.

He has written several articles and books. He is a keynote speaker, writer, author, youtuber, presented in several conferences, a corporate trainer, a part of a think tank. He is a member of Forbes Technology Council. He is one of the best sellers. His first book was published in 2007 on FDI and Emerging markets of China and India by Universal Publishers. His article on China and India- A comparative study was published in prestigious Financial Times in 2007. Dr. Sam's second book on saving the environment - Green Business was published in 2010 by Author house. His other 4 books are under active writing and preparation- Agile, Project Management, The Country Inc., Equality & Equanimity.

He has taught thousands of professionals and his students love him for his teaching and coaching style. He has a highly unique style- interactive, engaging, thought provoking, visual, action oriented, colorful, peer to peer, captured in his patent on his "Smarter Learner" platform. His contributions to the growth of teams, corporate leadership, governments, international business, and the global world are significant and noteworthy. His courses on Strategy, Project Management- Agile, Business Analysis, and latest technologies such as AI, Data Science, Blockchain are very well received. He is invited as a guest lecturer and a team coach at several Bay Area companies.

He has been following China closely for the last many years as his Doctorate work in San Francisco involved study of China and India in 2003-2006, and when Corona happened suddenly at the end of 2019, It all just came together. Why now? Who did this? What is the motive- all these questions led to the research, discovery, and some eureka moments that led to the building of this book: Corona- The III World War.

Dr. Sam was a student of Biology and Chemistry in his early years and studied these two subjects at the Bachelor of Science level. He spent hours with his microscope that his doctor dad bought for him to study biology and zoology- looking at viruses, amoeba, paramecium, bio cells, mitochondria etc. to understand how they are formed, replicate, mutate, etc

After completing this book and working on some of his videos, he wants to travel, watch, write, help humanity in bringing social justice, and help create an equal and peaceful world where everyone is happy and he will help to achieve balanced growth and global happiness. His nonprofit 'Sabla' is devoted for that purpose only and he wants to contribute the rest of his life for the next 20-30 years towards 'not profiting' but giving it back to the world.

He can be reached at sam@strategisminc.com or called on his USA number 415-377-7536. His India number is 9650014333. Your feedback will be greatly appreciated. I love you all. We all need to fight for world peace. We are all together in this.

Table of Contents

Abstract- Summary

What the hell is this Corona? How did Corona go Viral? It is more prevalent than the US Dollar today? Corona- Most spoken word in the world, ever on earth, in the known times, modern or ancient, we do not know? This F**cked up the whole world. Who made it? How did they make it? How did they manage it so selectively that it did not destroy local highly populated lands but spread it globally? How millions will be impacted and how will it kill people in hundreds of thousands globally? How will it Destroy economies, in some cases, permanently and structurally? What will happen in the Future? How life will change after Corona? Will Corona ever go away? It has been there for two decades now? Will people go to watch movies in a hall anymore, will they ride buses, catch trains, board planes, stay in hotels, eat at restaurants, and watch their favorite game in a stadium on a large scale? Has anything like this happened before? When? The flu of 1918? Something similar happened 80 years ago- World War II- so is this worse than that? Yes, of course. So is it World War III?

This is World war III- Corona- and the attacker is invisible and no one can catch it, shoot it, or put in a cage or in a concentration camp. It is many times smaller than the 5 tons nuclear bomb that created an impact of 15000 tons of (TNT) Trinitrotoluene, that killed 80000 people and destroyed cities of Hiroshima and Nagasaki in Japan. Corona has already killed three times more than 80,000 killed by bombing in 1946. More than 350000 people are already killed and many more are dying as on May 20th. It is expected more than 10 million people will be directly impacted by the virus worldwide.

The most people killed initially were in the G7 countries but now Corona is changing direction and color and going to other lands. It will keep changing till this book goes into print. It appears that the countries attacked initially are the richest countries, is it because they used to control 70% of the world economy when this idea of bio warfare was conceived, even now they control almost half of 48% of global GDP.

It is suspected that US taxpayers paid for the development of this virus which eventually killed close to 120000 Americans as on June 20th. The US based Universities and their Chinese lab connection is under huge suspicion right now. The Education Department in the US on May 1st asked the University of Texas System to provide documentation of dealings with Chinese Lab. It is suspected that the University funded via grants, gifts, contracts research to Wuhan Institute of Virology and its research with the popular 'Bat Woman' Shi Zhengli. She worked extensively on 'Zoonoses'- meaning on diseases that passed from animals to humans. Some noted scientists from Top universities such as Harvard were arrested by the US government for their alleged involvement in conducting clandestine research in foreign land, taking huge sums of money from Chinese government, and not informing the US government about it at all.

The department also asked the University to explain in detail its financial ties with CPC Chinese Communist Party, 24 Chinese Universities, Huawei Technologies, CNPC- China Petroleum, also gifts made by Zoom CEO Eric Yuan. The Chinese government and Dr. Shi have denied that the virus leaked from the lab but some believe it did. Universities made $6.5 billion dollars funding that were not articulated to people earlier but now in the current circumstances it needs disclosures. Universities are required to disclose any foreign funding made for more than $250,000. The department has asked to clearly explain the relationship between UT Galveston National Laboratory relationship with Chinese government run Wuhan lab. The system did disclose $13 million in gifts etc. but the department wants more information. There are strong doubts that some people for their vested personal interests in America, China, etc cheated the nation and are traitors to be tried for treason and are responsible for deaths of ordinary Americans and killing people globally. Do Professors who were supposed to keep our intellectual property safe, sold it for a higher sum of money? Has greed taken over once again leaving ordinary people at the mercy of the big, mighty, and the rich?

There is a sinister design being discussed in this room. Mr. Wang Wei is shouting on the top of his voice in a thick mandarin accent, talking to his thousands of party workers and henchmen gathered to attend this annual meeting- "We lost face in Hongkong totally and America influenced it badly- the lady there supported Americans". Wang further goes "We have lost face with the world in 2019 that we are #1 Superpower. Why does America not treat us seriously and see that now we make more contributions to humanity than them?". Zhang Wei, head of the party, reports to the high command " Our manufacturing is down and debt is building. Have we reached the stage of creating another 'pearl harbor'? Wang says- "We cannot take it anymore, we must declare decisively but intelligently that we are global leader #1 in the whole universe". He goes-" Let us drop a virus bomb and kill the world economy and then rebuild it, that will bring our economy back into full swing and declare us as the world SuperPower #1 as people die in mighty America like insects". He ends the speech with "That day will define us without even speaking a word. The world will know that China has happened."

The new world order strategy is being concocted with champagnes and vodka in this room dominated by leading CPC members only. The economy of this nation is crumbling under debt and over investment. The greed and desire of Mr. Wang Wei to dominate the world is increasingly being felt in the room. The currency melting and the debt rising is not helping much to showcase real domination. One day this whole dream of CPC and its constituents might just collapse under the debris of real estate debt and over investments in 'ghost towns'. The sleazy slimy designs are being concocted and articulated to save the world- the only problem with that was that the Chinese are seeing this as a only solution to save the world and see themselves as saviors from American onslaught and their brazen supremacy.

So, they all got together and plotted this game. This was a setup. Yes- Wang Wei set it up. To destroy the whole world. Once the world is destroyed a new order will emerge. Wang goes-" We will be the winners. Our currency and our economy will rule the new world post World War III". Wang Wei: The head of State says " Ha Ha Ha they cannot stop us from being the king of the new world- their days are over, they ruled the world for over a century, now it is our time". We are 1.3 billion people, we are present in every nook and corner of the world, products made by us run America. We manufacture everything they need and still they rule us-why?. Even the iPhone they sell for $1000 in America is made for 100$ in China. We make it, they brand it, and make tons of money. Our military is better than theirs. Our fighter planes and submarines are smarter than theirs, why should we lead a life of playing the 'second fiddle' and be subjugated to America- Europe's supremacy any more. We deserve to conquer this world & we shall".

Wang's desire seems to have no ends, he further continues- "This world needs us. This world belongs to us. For centuries it has been like this only when China had the 'silk route' till in modern times America and Europe stole the show in just the last one or two centuries. That is how it was always the case in olden times before America happened and England went out to attack countries. Last century, these guys came and created World war I and World War II and then dominated the world for the whole century. The world now should be our baby and it needs a new style of parenting and leadership. The next war World War III will be created by us and will establish us as undoubted global leaders. Because it is our baby and we will own it. When we will create World War III, we will do it in an even smarter way than them, no battle tanks, no guns, no planes, no missiles, no drones, etc- that is all old school. We will do it with something that they cannot even see, touch, and feel. And then set the reset button for the world for the 21st century and beyond. This will have a bigger impact than World War I and II combined. World war III is coming by 2020 so be ready- All".

The bioweapon idea is planned, executed, and checked continuously to see the development of the plan. The story moves on from the implementation of the idea to the accident that creates havoc. The plan seems to be failing, in a hush-hush, the Chinese government contain the spread of virus locally, and export and transport the virus through a meticulously executed strategy that takes Corona to New York and Europe but not to Beijing and Shanghai- the most populated cities in the world. America and Europe are badly affected by the virus. The world is devastated and most economies destroyed, something similar happened in World war II- but this has a bigger scale, impact, and adoption than the previous war. Everyone in the world knows the word Corona- 7 billion people speak one word with scare and awe- Corona- "please do not kill us".

Very few economies do not see much negative impact and see a better future as a substitute of China- for example India, consequently, in the long run. World War III has destroyed the world- $10 Trillion is lost potentially from the world. America with aging baby boomers and Europe with an older retiring population are now forced to take a back seat. America and Europe's world domination is over. In the new world order China becomes the world leader #1 as America struggles to survive and fight the virus and its after effects. America is in big trouble. Even though after sometime it appears that America and Europe are back but the truth is the change is irreversible, an internal damage has been done. China sets the new global standards- the new basket currency-Renminbi and Yuan, new culture of Yin and Yang, the Dragon is the new symbol of power and strength and replaces the Statue of Liberty as the major force of world power.

For the benefit of our readers for this book, even if Corona mellows down now, It is going to happen again after sometime, maybe again and again. Studies from John Hopkins University suggest that. So read this and understand it. And be prepared for it. What are the next steps- how do you get ready for it? How do you prepare yourself, your family, friends, and colleagues to get ready for this never changing reality Corona that the human race has been struck with in this 21st century, with this new biowarfare World War III race to an unfinished line. What will you do? How will you survive? We must all understand and chalk out a strategy to win the game instead of being a victim of it.

Chapter 1

Beijing gets This sinister Idea

"There cannot be two suns in the sky, nor two emperors on the earth." Confucius (Chinese Philosopher)

In the modern times, China was a poor country until very recently, around the 1980s. It had the largest population of humans or 'homo sapiens' on the face of the mother earth and had to feed a billion people. China adopted one child policy in 1970 to control its growing population. As a result, each family could have only one child, by 2017 the population aged in 40 years and started retiring leaving extreme pressure on China for survival. Imagine you were 20 year old in 1980 and by 2020 you are 60 going to retire if not already retired. By 2020 China faces many problems such as an aging population, shrinking workforce, dropping revenues, reducing exports, higher wages due to growth for the last 30 years, now slowing economy, increasing costs, environmental degradation, and lack of a well-defined social welfare system. China is also losing manufacturing to its neighbors such as Vietnam, Philippines, India etc. It appears that China is losing steam and will never be able to achieve its long term dream and ambition to become the largest economy in the world and world's Superpower#1.

Even before Corona dawned upon us, The World Economic Outlook published by the IMF in October 2019 predicted that Global manufacturing will experience a downturn and the Trade war between Chinese Premier Xi Xinping and United States Donald Trump will escalate in 2020. Trump is not giving up on his demand of higher tariffs on the import of Chinese goods to America. Policy uncertainty from the USA is putting pressure on Chinese economy. Geopolitical tensions are there and Chinese economy is becoming more vulnerable. Trade disagreements and distortionary barriers are hurting the Chinese economy. Even in Europe similar problems are there. The world is becoming more nationalistic and more inward oriented and the China that thrived on the concept of exporting to a free 'globalized world' is currently under tremendous pressure. Once again things are going back to square one from where we started- it is becoming a conservative 'localized world.'

Michael Pillsbury, Director of Center of Chinese Study, at Hudson Institute, in his book, The Hundred Year Marathon "China's secret strategy to replace America as the global superpower", states that while America helped China grow its economy by allowing manufacturing to move to China, China clandestinely waged a war to replace America as the world leader much like in their eyes- America did and replaced Britain 100 years ago. This time China will do it, unlike America, even without 'firing any shot' or having any bloodbath. Mike who has studied and worked in China for decades has been a national security expert for US President Nixon and Henry Kissinger and speaks fluent mandarin. He says that "Chinese view Americans as Satan and barbarians who will be the architect of their own demise". Mike also suspects that America has unknowingly nurtured this dragon that will kill it one day.

If you understand this Chinese strategy you will get to the bottom of what they perhaps did during the Corona crisis. Michael explains this very nicely with minute detail and proper references as he expected heavy scrutiny of his work and book from intelligence agencies and the Chinese government. The Chinese Warfare strategy comes from the ancient Chinese literature, what China does comes from ancient times when the local states in China were at war called the "Warring States' ' taken from the classic of SunTzu ``The Art of War' '. Another popular fable "Stratagems of the Warring States" is behind the current Chinese strategy. The Nine principles of Chinese strategy and how they were applied to create the current World War III are as follows-

1. *Induce complacency to avoid alerting your opponent* (till last moment no one should know what is going on- during Corona crisis no one in the world had any idea of what is happening in Wuhan in China, even when people asked, they said do not worry it is a 'local seasonal influenza' thing and has no chances of "human- human" spread.) (They called it a flu of unknown origin)

2. *Manipulate your opponent's advisors* (China convinced WHO that everything is alright and made WHO the spokesperson for China globally; WHO appreciated China throughout this apocalypse; China won over the US based professors from Harvard and other prestigious institutions)

3. *Be patient*- for decades, or longer- to achieve victory (China has waited patiently for 31 years from Tiananmen Square crisis to reach this point of trampling America and becoming world leader #1)

4. *Steal your opponents' Ideas and technology for strategic purposes* (most Chinese companies such as Alibaba, Tencent, Baidu are replica of American companies. China copied American companies business model but did not let any American company Facebook, Google, Amazon become successful in China. China

competes to stay ahead in innovation and patents. China bribed American Professors and experts to steal research from Top universities such as Harvard and MIT. Univ. of Texas worked with Wuhan Lab on American taxpayer dollars- and many professors are suspected to be involved in stealing technology from US and selling it to China)

5. *Military might is not the critical factor for winning the long term competition* (China did not grow its military as much as America did to keep its cost under control and move away from traditional physical warfare, in 2019 by reducing its military budget, that America mastered over centuries; Corona is non military bio weapon with worst consequences, if you kill a soldier it does not hit the economy but if you hit the common man, it puts a break to the economy.)

6. *Recognize that the hegemon will take extreme, even reckless action to retain its dominant position* (The Trade war with US is a reckless action from Trump to reduce China's power and attack the balance of payments situation; US retaliation of China over last 4-5 years since Republicans came to power, action in Hong Kong, Taiwan etc- China trying to exert force and keep power with them)

7. **Never lose sight of 'shi'** (talk to personator, deceive others till very late to take maximum advantage- China hides Corona from the world till the last moment so that they can take maximum advantage by creating confusion and maintaining lack of transparency)

8. *Establish & employ* **metrics** for measuring your status relative to other potential challengers

(China does not go by hearsay, they keep measuring themselves on a metrics where they stand- they look at all macroeconomic factors to assess the success of their strategy- see how China is growing vis-a vis America- The Belt and Road initiative, The GDP growth, Exports, The Technological advancement- AI/ Blockchain research, Patents filed, number of researchers, and more specifically in current situation how Corona is spreading and how many killed across the word, these numbers are closely watched every hour by Chinese Government- Wang Wei is not sitting idle even for a minute)

9. *Always be vigilant to avoid being encircled or deceived by others*. (Right now everyone is circling China and they have a strategy to get out of the blame game, make it appear as if they did not create Corona and are themselves victim of it, yet they are totally focused on their goal to dominate the world economy, buy cheap global assets at throwaway prices, Wuhan is back in business, Casino is running in Macau. China is fighting a border issue with India, Nepal, Pakistan, etc instead of helping reduce the impact of the virus; there is no virus guilt.)

The project "Destroy Old World Economy" and "Create The New World Order" was actually in its phase II that was initiated in 2015 when the decision was made to start the BSL Lab 4 in Wuhan. There are 70 BSL 4 sites in the world and these are engaged in bio engineering. Bio engineering and bio genetics is a hot area of research in the space of bio warfare. It appears everyone wants to build the latest and most powerful bioweapon to destroy human beings. The last phase of this project is chartered in November 2019 to engineer a lethal strain of virus that can kill humans and grow that virus globally very quickly so that China starts it but does not get caught into the spiral of downturn. Time decided for the last phase to declare China the world SuperPower#1- Six months from

November 2019 to April 30th. This would be the Fastest attack the world would witness for the first time. Wang Wei says" The whole humanity would have never spoken one word with such consternation that they will do now- Corona and bow in front of China".

The time duration of World War II and World War I was pretty long and it went on for 5-6 years, "..... but you know what, we will be quick", Wei says. The longer the war the more it puts pressure on the aggressor as per Chinese centuries old Strategy this should be avoided. The United Kingdom lost in World War II because they could not sustain the cost of that war. In our case 'Not a shot' will be fired. There will be no cost on us. No soldiers will die. Even the money we spent on the lab came from the USA taxpayer- what a smart move, No blood will flow on streets, still we will have a bigger impact than World War I and World War II combined could have. It is like 9/11 when the smart people took the enemies planes, their resources and blew their assets 'Twin Towers' and killed many people. The World In its history never had 7 billion people on earth- all will now speak one word Corona even if they cannot speak Mandarin. Corona all said & done, will have a $ 10 Trillion price tag on world resources. The world will pay for it & China will earn it.

In the modern times, as stated earlier, It is not a smart strategy to gain in a war by using equipment, missiles, drones, ships, nuclear heads, etc anymore. Do not kill people by battle tanks, guns, missiles, drones, submarines, or the military foot soldiers. That is what America did in World War II. That is where they went wrong in planning warfare in the 21st century with tools of the 20th century. You cannot win tomorrow's war with yesterday's technology that you are so proud of. We are smarter than that-we will kill by waging biological warfare. Other techniques could be 'cyber warfare' by closing their bank websites, government websites, taking away money from their counties and banks. In biowarfare we will create a new strain of deadly virus that will kill America and Europe. It will not only kill Americans and Europeans in large numbers but also destroy their economies for significant times to come, due to their aging populations and current dislike for immigration, with a bigger impact than World War II had. It will be hard for them to match up against us ever.

Once their economies are destroyed, then we will first provide them with medicines, masks, equipment to fight that virus and make money even if the quality is poor, so what, if they need to live and survive, they must buy it. They will buy it because their own products will be very expensive and the people will not be able to afford it due to economic pressures. We will also buy their companies at 'peanut prices' as their economy struggles, and sell our products and services to them. We will be much more intelligent than them and become number one in the world and dominate the world by our intelligence and economic strength. We will become the king of the market system that Adam Smith propounded and the UK and America enforced on us and on the world for more than a century. Wang concludes "Now it is our turn and we'll use their system only to make it work for us".

Why do you guys think Corona spread from Wuhan to London and New York and not to Beijing and Shanghai? In real time there might be more travelers from Wuhan to their own national capital and financial hub than some place outside in the world. Would not more people travel from San Francisco to New York and Washington DC than to London and Beijing. Do you sense there is a strategy in place here, a design to deceive? A master plan to annihilate the homo sapiens race only at certain places. Millions will be killed by this virus. Even the masks sent from China are substandard and do not meet quality standards so that people continue to die and China still keeps making an exorbitant amount of money by selling PPE at 5-10 times the cost.

There is someone who looks at all this and probes the deeper questions on the way China behaved during this whole Corona crisis. Danielle Dimartino Booth in her interview" Why did we lie to the American people", with Valuetainment, Patrick Bet David interviewed really went into details to figure out what really happened, Danielle is the CEO and Chief Strategist from Quill Intelligence. Late November 2019 the world came to know there is a virus in Wuhan. Dec 15th US Trade deal was signed, six weeks later there was an 'out clause' added if there is a pandemic in China they do not have to buy items committed as per the trade deal from the USA-why would they add this clause after six weeks? What happened in those six weeks? What is it they knew but did not want to share with the world. CIA- how could they not tell what is happening in Wuhan? Was the CIA not present in China and in Wuhan to see with their own eyes what is going on? They claim to know everything in the world and how come they did not sense such an important episode. How come Chinese knew six weeks before they told the world that they put in the contract? They used this time to structure it the way things were happening or was it that they were making it happen? No one knows the truth for sure.

Danielle also asks this probing question why did WHO not make China accountable for the mishap from the start. The World Health Organization seems like they sided with China in their game plan. South Korea reported the first case the same day as the USA reported the first case, South Korea shut the country down that day only, why did the US not take action for six weeks? Did the US have the right information to take that decision- probably not? Was the US duped into staying ignorant till the virus flared, killed its people, and destroyed its economy? There are some serious questions that Chinese agencies need to answer to American people. Was it that the Chinese government knew the rate of spread of Corona and waited for it to reach maximum people in the United States before declaring publicly.

Ever since Donald Trump became the President of America in 2016, he has communicated in very clear terms that he will not let China dominate and create hegemony over America. For years now, there is rising political tension and trade tension between The US-China. In recent times, trade tensions have been increasing continuously between America and China for the whole year of 2019, one after the other, hurting business sentiment and confidence globally and indicating signs of global recession. The US President, a businessman by background, carries his balance sheet, wherever he goes- how much we export and how much we import from your country, and wherever he sees it is a negative number, he is tough on that country and pushes them to make deals and increase American exports to that country or increase tariffs for their products to enter America. China does not like this at all and is very concerned.

The nation that was perceived to be a claimant that will destroy enemies and the world by clicking a red button from "The White house" has been subdued, humbled, and tamed by an unknown invisible enemy- a virus. Gone are the days that China is scared of America. Gone are the days when China looked at America with awe. After joining the WTO in 2000 China's ambitions are unparalleled to none. Since China becomes the second largest economy its confidence grew many times, now it can see who is their direct enemy #1- The United States. Now they want to look their enemy directly into the eye and as Wang Wei says- "You wait and watch we are coming", and "when we come you will have no idea what we did and how we did that". You think you are smart but we will outsmart you many more times. We will play so smart that you and your top research institutions will struggle to find answers but there will be -none!! China not only wants to topple The US as #1 country but also wants to grow its influence over the UN Security council and have more say than America in deciding global conflicts. It does not recognize America as the global leader anymore. If you read the Atlantis report it states this fact clearly.

China is concerned towards the last quarter of 2019 where it wanted to do around $4 trillion in GDP but because of the world economy, as per World Economic Outlook from IMF for 2020, which was projected to reduce to 3% growth rate only, and that was the least from 2019 and moving into 2020. China must do something about this quickly and create a 'reset button' so that after everything is over, the major beneficiary of the reset is China itself. The time has come to quickly move into the final phase of the project and execute the plan so that benefits can be reaped faster than normal. There is a hurry and there is a sense of urgency.

China has a big problem to solve. China is suddenly 'in 2019' not relevant to the world anymore as the world focus is shifting. China benefited for the most part due to Globalization between 2000- 2015 but since Donald Trump became the President all the leading countries in the world are becoming inward looking vs opening up globally. United States President Donald trump- won the national elections on the major agenda to "Make America Great Again " and bring back manufacturing along with bringing capital back to America. One of his major initiatives is to curtail Immigration by building a wall with Mexico, renegotiate NAFTA with its neighbors Canada and Mexico to suit American national interests and get things done within the country. He has increased tariffs on foreign goods to enter America, also increased focus on exporting American goods to China, etc than just acting as a market for cheaper low quality Chinese goods. America is no more a humble dumping ground for Chinese products that China did for decades and off course Chinese Mr Wang is not happy with that at all.

In Europe, England wants Brexit as it feels it needs to be concerned more about its own people than opening up to the world charity. Car production has dropped in Germany, German bonds are in negative for the first time forcing Germany to look inwards, and the advanced world is expected to grow only 1%.Brexit is creating a different picture in Europe where UK had major trouble with immigration and terrorism on their soil making them break out from EU and focus internally. France and Germany want to reduce immigration and focus internally to save their economies.

In India the dynamic leader Mr. Modi invites all countries in its Defense Expo in early 2020 at the City of Lucknow and requests them to " Make in India". World over Chinese supremacy is being challenged and the world is now either 'looking inwards' or 'looking towards India' or Vietnam, than depending on China. Some economies are finding it hard to survive in the new carbon economy- OPEC, Russia. Oil is hovering at its lowest prices. America is exporting more oil than it used to import and the world wants more renewables than ever before. These countries will have less revenue and cannot afford Chinese consumer products as before. This lack of investment capital has also created a situation where countries are required to find solutions internally rather than opening up globally. World over there are problems that does not help China a bit.

Qiao Liang and Wang Xiangsui, both military strategists, way back in 1999 declared, in their book- "Unrestricted Warfare: China's Master Plan to Destroy America"- write that America has a basic problem in thinking about warfare. Whenever they think about war, they think about technology, they think they can keep creating better technology and stay ahead of the curve and the game forever. Technology restricts you and puts a limit to what you can and cannot do. The authors argue that China understands this 'blind spot' and gap in American thinking. In the modern world waging a war with war planes, tanks etc. is not only costly and kills the army man more than creating significant economic or political impact. There are alternatives that can be tried in today's world- economic warfare, terrorism, economic policy, digital infrastructure and network war that can have a wider impact than just constantly gaining technological supremacy in the warfare by making huge investments. The authors did not explicitly discuss and go into 'bio warfare' by introducing a virus as a form of attack but came very close to it. They said in modern times even a small country can kill a large economy such as the USA by adopting these " Unrestricted Warfare" techniques. It appears China applied this strategy with Corona warfare. President Trump got so frustrated and confused with this enemy that his sophisticated drones and missiles cannot kill and therefore he calls it an 'invisible enemy'.

China's insatiable desire and greed to build the Corona Virus in Wuhan and to lead the world is so profound that it is not leaving any stone unturned to even steal the latest technology from the USA to desperately conquer the world quickly. Harvard University's Nano scientist Charles Lieber apparently lied about his involvement in China's Thousand Talents Plan. He was arrested by FBI for leaking US information to China. It appears Chinese government hires professors and scientists who are working on leading futuristic technology and pays them for the same work to be done in China. They can work part time for some time in China and travel between China and the United States. Lieber was involved in research with China between 2012-2017 and paid 50,000$ a month, 150K living expenses in China, and paid $1.5 Million dollars to set up a lab in Wuhan in China. It appears, as per NPR report, he did not tell all this to Harvard at all. NPR states that he set up the Wuhan University of Technology "WUT- Harvard Joint Nano Key Laboratory" in a clandestine way and usurped the American technology and sold it to China. On the one hand, he was taking a grant of 18 Million dollars from NIH from American side, and on the other hand, he was sharing that with China to profit & benefit personally in millions of dollars.

Many other people are arrested or accused of similar crime. NPR also reports that NIH is investigating 180 other scientists on similar grounds. We will come to know the truth after some time once America recovers from Corona slaughter. Who knows some of these folks have already given up their US citizenship and taken Chinese citizenship?

The Chinese government traditionally believed in mass production of goods that are cheapest and they even often lack quality. World over there is a sudden resurgence of quality focus and denouncing Chinese goods. Even during the Corona crisis Chinese companies are creating masks and other equipment that are failing the tests of quality world over. The world does not like China anymore and its domination by providing substandard inferior products that are pushed into global markets and supply chains through its companies. Modern China understands this very well and wants to be perceived as a "Technology giant & innovation center" and not as a 'world's cheap factory' anymore. It desperately wants to move up the value chain rather than being perceived as a supplier of cheap bad quality products. China is investing in cutting edge technologies- patents, AI, Blockchain, biotechnology, Cyber Warfare, Virology research, etc.

Income and expense dynamics are shifting Chinese balance sheets by the end of 2019. China is experiencing growing problems in reduced aggregate demand and reduced exports due to rising tariffs from all over the world. The debt is growing. The world is becoming careful of China and wants to stay away from China. There is going to be a decline in working age population due to One Child policy. Within China there is another problem of convergence of per capita income restricting consumption. Labor is not the cheapest anymore in China. Trade is shifting to neighboring countries of Vietnam, Philippines, and also partly to India. China needs to address this issue.

Has China created the Third World War? How is it different from the other two wars? Why do we call it a World War? During the First world war 40 million lives were lost, it created an economic downturn for Germany, and increased unemployment, etc. First world war was fought in 1914 to 1918, more than 8 million soldiers died in the war, more people died as a consequence of war, a lot of people went missing never to be seen again. Central powers dominated by Germany fought Allied powers- led by the United kingdom, France, Italy, Japan, USA. The war at that time was unprecedented due to the number of people who died because of wounds, disease, slaughter, carnage, and destruction. Something similar seems to be happening now.

Corona is the Third world war. Everything has come to standstill. China has planned well and created this Third world war. America has been dragged into this world war as it always happens and this time the losses are happening in American land. Earlier, America would create havoc in the whole world but nothing will happen in their main land, this war is completely opposite, there are more people dying in their Top #1 city New York than any other part of the world. The invincible America has been tamed by this war. The world is in tears, sad, isolated, marginalized, and there is more instability than ever before. Most people have never witnessed anything like this before. This scenario is very similar to two previous World Wars I & II.

There are rumors that America sent this virus to China in 2019 during October games in China. The Chinese Premier, to divert the attention of the world away from China, recently claimed that actually America got the virus into China during the military games held in China in October 2019. If America created the virus and sent it to China then they would have known it and would have been prepared for it but most lives and damage has happened inside of America. Right now close to 120000 dead and more than 2200000 or 2.2 million people infected with the virus as on June 18th 2020.

The way events have unfolded it appears America was not prepared for this crisis and did not have much idea about this. If you look at China, the highest population in the world- 1.3 billion people and had only 35000 deaths and 80000 people infected vs a country 1/4th or 25% of its size America- has 1200000 infections and close to 100000 deaths- if the virus spread was natural- these numbers do not make any sense. The Chinese government curtailed internal virus spread by force. It wants to establish its hegemony over the world even at the cost of its own people's dislike. China does not worry about its reputation and does not care about ordinary people's lives as evident during the crisis- China arrested innocent people, doctors treating corona, nurses helping patients, and came hard on whistleblowers to scare people and prevent information from spreading globally.

Trade war is going on between US and China and now China sees that the chances of Trump coming back to power in 2020 is increasing, so China will have to either shelve its plan to be #1 Superpower of the world or do something drastic to change the game quickly. In China Mr Wang Wei is debating whether the virus should be built there or it could be bought from Canada to China to change this game. Another theory is that China can produce it locally but camouflage the truth by stating that it originated from outside of China- in the USA or in Canada. This theory was more popular initially around January 2020 but now it seems to be dying down. Anyways, China has dominated the world manufacturing for the last three decades but now their economy is crumbling and crimping as it does not provide cheapest labor and cheapest capital as people are aging and retiring. The world needs a new factory-cheaper, younger, and logistically better located. Silk route is going to be replaced by the "Spice Route," In a hurry they want to create a new world order where they rule the world by shifting the game.

Trump on the other hand has his own desire to rule the world by building the best economy in the world. Trump is a business man who not only understands business very well, and has built business relationships throughout his career spanning the last four decades. Trump wants to lead the world with his theory of Adam Smith style of Capitalism. He wants to bring manufacturing back to America. He reduced corporate taxes, he also reduced the repatriation taxes rules so that American companies can bring in more capital into America. He wants to defend his borders so that he can get more jobs for his own people. But little did he realize that even with the highest Dow Jones stock market capitalization of 30000, lowest employment rate of 3% in 50 years is not enough, inflow of capital into America, the highest labor participation rate- one small virus can kill it all and change the game forever, in the long term, and that too in just a couple of months.

Dominating the waters is a modern strategy due to colossal global supply chains. Every country wants its navy to have control on the sea. But China has over ambitious plans there too. China has gained control of the South China Sea. In World War II part of American success was its navy and fleet. In World War III China does not want to leave any stone unturned. It wants to dominate the seas also. The South China Sea has roughly one third of shipping lines and around $3 trillion trade, it is rich in fisheries, and has huge oil reserves in it. Even though as per international law a country can claim only 10 miles into the ocean from their land's end, China claims to own 100 miles deeper into the South China sea. China does not respect maritime laws. It wants to get 11 billion barrels of untapped oil hidden in the sea. There is 190 trillion cubic feet of natural gas in the Sea bed. China does not even respect the 'Nine dash line'. The policy of bullying and intimidation continues. It claims ownership of Spratly Islands as well as Scarborough Shoal. China is out for expansion- land, sea, air- everywhere, and as nations feel weak and loosen their grip due to a virus attack, China has more opportunities to pursue its ambitions.

Leading Chinese companies were not allowed to grow in the US and even internationally creating problems for China. Companies like Huawei, etc. And many other Chinese companies faced stiff competition and backlash in the USA. They were even barred from doing business with the US market. They were forced to focus on the local market only. The growth of the Huawei company in 2019 was the least as compared to 2018 and before. Huawei experienced only 19% growth in revenue to $ 121 billion, and 6% growth in net profits, the slowest in the last three years. Most growth came from the home market and 59% of revenue came from China only. Getting new markets is harder and with the new US President they are putting more pressure on Chinese companies and not letting them expand in America. Many companies are facing this issue currently and China needs to do something about this and fix this problem quickly. How does China get business for its companies globally?

The Second World War in 1942 was fought and it redefined the new world order- America became the undisputed leader of the world for almost 80 years now. Europe was destroyed - Germany, France, England were all in doldrums and it gave America an opportunity to sell products and services and grow its economy. After World war II the whole world was destroyed. A total of 75 million people died in that war- including 20 million military and 40 million civilians. A world war typically is supposed to create a mass Genocide, massacres, mass bombings, disease, and starvation. World War II was fought to shift the fulcrum of power from Europe to America. As a consequence of World War II, In Hiroshima and Nagasaki more than 200000 people were estimated to have died as discussed earlier. World war two's precursor was economic depression much like what we are seeing in early 2020. US unemployment was around 25% before the war, and after the war, the US became the de facto leader and dumped products all over the world to rebuild the world.

There has to be III World War- Corona. Why do we need to use so many army and military personnel, war planes, battle tanks, shed blood, spend fuel, drones, missiles when we can create a bigger impact by biowarfare- the virus will do a bigger harm and that too silently, it will kill lesser people than WWII but have a bigger geographic, political, social, and economic impact world has ever seen. Wei says- "Let us create a hybrid strain of virus". This virus will come with a price tag of $5 trillion immediately and another $5 Trillion as a repeatable impact for next year and send it to America and Europe. So Corona was born. World War III seems to impact the Christian world more than any other world especially in the beginning. Bible says love one another- corona says hate each other, stay away from each other and engage in social distancing. Has anybody thought why only four-five countries had 93% of the deaths in the beginning and now close to 70% of deaths in the world from Corona are from- USA, Italy, Spain, France, and UK- is this a race war? Is this a culture war, will a new culture or new race ethnicity dominate the world after the war is over? Who knows the answer?

Congratulations!! The new world system has already been launched. After World War III when the whole world will be devastated- millions will have been impacted, hundreds of thousands will perish but the greater impact will be felt in their economies than just loss of life. World over more than 100 million will be pushed into poverty. America and Europe economies will be shattered with huge pending bills. It is time for China to sell goods all over again and become the largest economy in the world. If America witnesses a 5% drop of $1 trillion and from 21 Trillion becomes 20$ Trillion. Next year it further shrinks 5% and becomes $19 Trillion. China on the other hand experiences a 10% growth in 2020 and 2021, within 3-4 years China will overtake America and be the largest economy of the world growing from $14 trillion to $20 trillion. Then they can dictate terms with companies, suppliers, brands, currencies, nations, culture more than anyone else on earth. China will be the kingpin or the pivot around which the whole world will revolve in just a few years for next many decades to come.

"Let your plans be dark and impenetrable as night, and when you fall you move like a thunderbolt".

From SunTzu, The Art of War (Chinese Philosopher)

Chapter 2

Wuhan - The Virus idea is implemented

Viral outbreaks in China are common- SARS, MERS, and many smaller ones- one wonders why of all the places on earth the viruses are born in China. Like China is the world's factory for producing goods, is it also a factory for viruses also? China got into viruses after the SARS 2002-2004 outbreak from China in which 8000 people got impacted globally and 700 died. SARS was more lethal than Corona Covid19 and killed 10% of the cases. It spread globally and the United States also had 29 cases but no one died. Why did they not make a vaccine for SARS and why it disappeared- no one knows? China got concerned about this virus. Now there are two theories: did China want to save people from dying in the future or China realized the potential of this SARS virus, if worked upon, can create better strains that can kill thousands and impact millions of people worldwide. If you are wanting to engage in biowarfare you do not criticize a weapon because it can kill more people, you actually appreciate it. If we buy a gun for the army- we will question how far a bullet can go and how many enemies it can kill. Likewise, China found a gun in SARS perhaps which could have been built into a better gun to kill more people.

After SARS, China continued its research and found out In 2005 at The Wuhan institute of Virology that the horseshoe bats from Wuhan have natural stock of SARS coronavirus. Then they tested thousands of these bats and isolated 300 sequences. This was a remarkable discovery because now the source and origin was found, which was very close to the Wuhan lab and thousands and thousands of bats were studied in the Yunnan caves. The next question was to inject it into humans and grow it. Decades of research went into this and millions of dollars were spent in understanding the way to take the bats, dig the virus from it, implant it into another animal, and from there put it in humans and spread it to thousands to kill them.

In 2015 with an investment of $44 million this First BSL-level 4 lab Biosafety lab was built with French help. It took more than a decade to build this lab from scratch using the latest world class equipment. The US molecular biologist Richard Ebright expressed concerns over the speed and scale of the China BSL - Level 4 lab establishment research program and the previous escape of SARS from Beijing lab in 2003. Ebright called this facility world class and latest in virology and immunology but showed concerns about the threat it can pose to the US and the world and the fact it can potentially kill human beings. This Chinese lab funded by Chinese government has an extensive relationship with The University of Texas- Galveston National Laboratory discussed elsewhere in the book.

During the 2015 Conclave of its top leadership, China got serious with the virus and wanted to scale it to humans. So what is the plan? How will we do it? How will we infect so many without arms? Let us do it. This is biowarfare. Wang Wei says "We will nurture viruses like SARS which will be more lethal than SARS or Ebola in terms of speed of spread". We will engineer it. We will do it far away from Beijing and Shanghai so it does not create unnecessary risk or impact on our financial and political centers and does not impact a large population base. No one will come to know of it. It will be a closely guarded secret- if anyone asks questions, we will tell them to keep it a secret as it is in the interest of national security. We will get the virus from Canada- they have it this will show that we did not develop it internally otherwise the world opinion might become negative against us and kill our export markets. Our goal is to destroy America and also Europe. Wang ads- "In America if you destroy the top five cities of New York, Los Angeles, Chicago, Houston, San Francisco it will automatically travel to other places and the boomerang will destroy themselves".

One of the most controversial has been the 'hybrid virus research' conducted by China in 2015 when they built the 'Chimera' by combining elements from two viruses one of them was like SARS. The mutated virus that emerged was found to be capable of infecting human cell. That is how it became useful for the research but on the other hand became dangerous for survival of human beings and possibly led to eventual crisis in 2020. The 'Gain Of Function' 'GOF' became the main concern by global scientists that 'what if it escaped the lab' and infected local populations. Then it could reach devastating proportions. The staff that interacted with this virus in the lab put themselves at high risk.

Mr Trump on being asked in the congress- do you have any evidence that the virus came from the Wuhan lab reported- "yes I have". David Relman microbiologist from Stanford University states that human beings have a very high chance of making errors and they can cause viruses to leak from the lab. Yuan Zgiming, a chief scientist at Wuhan, states that the cost of having trained people to deal with stringent conditions to avoid leaks is prohibitive and maintenance is hard and most labs do not have the biosafety managers and engineers. Scientists say such accidents happen dozens of times in the most developed labs worldwide including in the USA. There are 40 papers published in the last 2-3 months to understand the link between Wuhan lab and the spread of Virus on human beings and none of them rule out 100% that the virus did not leak from the lab.

There are so many theories that support that this Corona virus came from the Lab which can mean it was manufactured by the

Wuhan lab. Some of the noted ones are as under. Lancet, the reputed peer reviewed medical journal on January 24th published a report that only 27 of the total 41 cases in Wuhan had exposure to the wet market. Jonathan Eipstein, VP Ecoheath, who studied the wet market samples says out of 585 swabs only 33 were found positive for SARS-Cov2 came from Wuhan Market meaning a lot of them were from outside. Actually, Bats hibernate in December so chances of bat being found in the market are less. The bats are not even allowed to be sold in the market.

Another report from one researcher states he was bitten by the bat and got infected. A report states that the graduate student at the lab was 'patient zero' as he was working on bioweapons for Chinese laboratory and it probably leaked from there. In 2018 Washington post reported that the lab was not safe and could lead to a disaster. A researcher from "Five Eyes Nation" told CNN the virus 'could have' emerged from the lab but at the moment we do not have any 'theory' to prove it, does not mean they can deny it with guarantee. Another research study published on January 30th indicated that out of 99 patients who tested positive for Corona only 49 had access to the Wuhan market- meaning almost 50% came from somewhere else- where?

The Chinese government kept the creation of Coronavirus far away from the political and financial center of China, at Wuhan only to keep it away from glare of media and interest groups. They had approval to have BSL Lab 4 a total of 6-7 labs in China. If we do it 6-7 places and distribute the work nationally the problem of integration might happen and potentially it could be more dangerous if virus leaks- especially knowing the kind of work they were doing and being aware of the risks involved, so they focused on Wuhan Lab only although so many labs were approved to be set up. Also, not only putting all the work together is the problem but it might explode over many demographics and put us under threat. There is too much risk involved in making it in many factories for our people. Wang says "We will make it one factory. The place where we make it there only we should be able to do "beta testing" or proof of our concept. Prototype effectiveness must be tested before we commercially manufacture it and sell it all over the world". The Chinese government did not take any chances on that.

It is important to have a city which is comparable to New York in human population and dynamics- which city is that in China? Wuhan in Hubei province. Wuhan is one of the most modern urban city and it resembles New York. If it spreads herein a controlled population of 100-200 people it will spread like fire in New York. The issue is speed as this Virus like B52 bomber is fast but not as lethal as SARS which had a higher death rate. How fast these 100 people get impacted. How do we keep this as a secret and not spread it? Even if there is a casualty it will not spread to Beijing and Shanghai and not impact our economy. Wuhan has a sub-provincial city of 11 million people, urban 9 million people, and a total close to 20 million people. An urban area of 590 square miles has 9 million people, so we can be safer here in Wuhan.

The Chinese government Mr. Wei said- "Our nation's top scientists will be involved in this". Our army and military will also help to contain it and keep it a secret affair. We have to bring the best brains together to engineer and design this virus. We will build it in the level 4 top biosafety lab we established in 2015. We will manufacture in our lab/ factory and then propagate it. We will also take help from top American professors from Harvard, MIT, and other top Universities and from all over the world on the pretext of saving human life by creating a vaccine eventually. We will get the latest equipment, latest minds, latest research, latest technology and build something iconoclastic. We will use their money, their talent, bribe their top minds and spoil them- and get the technology and research out of them, and then use it against them only.

The research facilities should be the best so that we are able to build and test a strain which replicates at a very fast rate. Several gene sequences can be tested, several combinations, mutants can be tried, to engineer the most desired one. It should be a strain which replicates more in colder temperatures. The strain should be able to withstand lower temperatures and can even spread from a longer distance. It can jump off from one person to another in less than seconds and can stay in an individual for a very long time. The success rate should be higher than 10 % which is more than SARS meaning if 100 people are infected- >10% must die. It should stay dormant for some time, even weeks, and then when it finds a weak person, or an old person, or a pregnant woman, it becomes active again. Wang proudly narrates" The virus should replace the best missiles and drones that America can send to our place".

An article was published three years ago, in Nature, International Weekly Journal of Science, in Feb 2017 that China is getting this latest Lab, the article was titled- "Inside the Chinese Lab poised to study the world's most dangerous pathogens". This was a part of the plan to build 5-7 such labs all over China by 2025. The cost was a meagre $44 million, very cheap as compared to building a rocket or drone launching stations. It states that the Chinese scientists were excited to be a part of the elite group of researchers to join this important activity as mentioned by one real scientist named George Gao. In 2017 only, scientists outside of China were concerned about the pathogen leaking out and creating an outbreak to humans. The CNAS looked at the infrastructure, equipment and management of the lab and approved it as BSL 4 lab. These labs are controversial- one was created in Japan in 1981 but till 2015 worked with only lower risk pathogens.

The USA and Europe have more than 12 such labs and it is feared why so many labs were created. The Wuhan lab is WHO's 'reference laboratory'. This was to be made in 2003 but got delayed till 2015. The first such project implemented in 2017 was a BSL 3 virus that can jump to humans from Crimean Congo livestock prevalent in Northern China. The Chinese government was happy and wanted to conduct research on primates- monkeys, close relatives of humans, as in the West it might be difficult to do so. Ebright, a researcher we referenced earlier from Rutgers University, said that this is not a good sign- it appears creation of labs in China to be a reaction to creation of labs in USA & Europe and they can be used for 'dual purposes' and the governments might use it is being done to build bioweapons. There was more danger than good to get out of these labs. It was suspected that the evil will take over the good one day.

The team will work together over a period of time and create the strains that are potentially capable of damaging larger populations of humans. The team will work for four five years on building the latest lethal strain of CoronaVirus. In 2015 the team of virologists conducted research on the bat coronavirus that can be made to infect 'HeLa' cells. The team engineered a 'hybrid virus' that can infect mice and create human diseases. This was the turning point. It also coincides with Chinese convention of 2015 where 'Made in China 2025 Dream' was unfolded. This year 2025 it was planned that the dragon will be the most powerful symbol in the world.

In 2017 scientists found that in the Yunnan cave, which is only 1 mile away from Wuhan lab, which has a large population bat coronavirus- has genetic pieces similar to SARS Coronavirus and can spillover to human beings and can create huge multiplication like 2003 SARS virus outbreak. So now we can sense the connection between Lab and Wuhan- "oh the bat is found here so that is the reason". Now they do not have to go looking for horseshoe bats in Guangdong area, where the earlier ones mostly came from. The population of bats at Yunnan cave is huge and can be easily studied in their natural habitat than transporting them to the lab artificially and simulating conditions. This was a major breakthrough and within 2 years China built the competence to lodge a global warfare based on these bats from the local cave in Yunnan just a walking distance from Wuhan lab.

In 2019 it appears they had to put the final phase into action and to release the virus. They planned to do it right after Christmas time so that the products manufactured in China and created there get sold in America, Europe, during Christmas time and sales do not get impacted negatively during the peak demand period. Most Americans and Europeans buy products made from China during this time even if they are not very rich, and it creates 30% of our exports for the whole year. After the peak in December the sales go down for more than a month and is the best time to launch the virus as it will not impact our factory outputs as much. If there are economic output losses internally in China Q1 due to any lockdown or potential accident, as a risk management strategy, we can make it up in Q2 and still be fine as far as GDP is concerned.

Research on viruses was going outside of China as well and many nations were involved in that effort. Some of them were positive in nature but some others had a wicked mind behind it. It is like World War II- the technology behind the atom bomb could have been used for positive purposes for nuclear fission to generate electricity or used negatively to destroy large sets of human populations. In 2015, Pirbright Institute, British Government funded and obtained the patent for Coronavirus antidote - to create a vaccine and prevent respiratory lung diseases such as contagious bronchitis. As late as Dec 2019- Bill & Melinda Gates Foundation discussed developing a vaccine against Corona, they feared if the virus is let loose it can kill 65 million people- the foundation ran simulations as late as in early Dec 2019 and included the CIA as a party, and they found that this lethal virus could be very dangerous for the world and lot of human lives can be lost. They kept China away from this research, meeting, and its findings. Why Did they keep China out of this meeting because they feared China is the perpetrator- this report and minutes of that meeting should be shared with all. So we knew this could have happened just less than a month before it actually spread.

University of Minnesota CIDRAP- Center For Infectious Disease Research And Policy on April 2018 published an article on their site- "New SARS like Virus from bats implicated in China pig die-off", states that in 2016-2017 in four farms in Guangdong 25000 piglets died from a virus and that came from 'horseshoe bats'. They tested if the 35 farmers who were in contact with pigs and bats- did they contract the virus in real life or not, it was found that 'animal to human' spread was not there. It appears from this article that research was going on from many years between United States and China's research institutions to understand the determinants of virus spread from animal to humans, what was the purpose of all this research, if these virus can kill 25000 pigs potentially they can kill 25000 human beings as well, the only missing link was how it jumps from animals to humans or in other words- "if we can make it jump from animals to humans we can kill thousands of humans". Why were US universities involved in such research along with Chinese research institutions and funding it like friends working on the same thing together? Is it that two guy friends are trying to date the same girl and then one guy cheats the other guy and gets the girl, but the girl is dangerous and kills one of the friends, in this case China cheats the friend USA and uses the same virus to kill its people? This is what I am reading in between the lines when I am trying to understand what is going on here. In any case the intentions of Chinese government seems dubious.

In 2014 Ebola virus outbreak happened that died quickly- This was based on research conducted by Soros & Mr. Gates in Africa- Kenema Sierra Leone. Other viruses are not as strong as Corona- where mortality can be there very quickly. The virus burns through many hosts and mutates as it creates destruction whenever it goes much like the atom bomb or the missiles. Corona group of virus was found to be suitable as a bioweapon, because it was highly contagious, had a prolonged incubation period, had respiratory implications reducing the immunity of the patient, and had a massive impact on its prey. It was found in the research that 2019NCOV came very close to SARS and MERS, but not as grave as SARS that could kill more people in terms of %age but the speed of activity of Coronavirus was the killer point as it covers more people, faster, creating more destruction than SARS and probably that is why the Chinese government decided to focus on Corona than other types of viruses.

Virus could be very damaging for certain Industries. During the African Swine flu of 2019 the virus jumped to the pig farms and a whole lot of farms just disappeared- this badly devastated the pig industry. It reduced 40% of the pig population and 350 million pigs were gone leading to a drop of 50% in pig population. If Swine flu can work with pigs so effectively, Corona can have a similar impact on human populations if they were able to replicate the virus fast via human- human interaction.

There is another theory that Chinese scientists did 'biological espionage' and stole Corona from a Canadian lab, as stated earlier. The Chinese agents from the Biological Warfare Program Team were involved in this effort, as per the investigations from- The Great Game India. These agents made at least 5 trips in 2 year's time trying to steal the virus. It was found that a mysterious shipment smuggled corona out from Canada. Corona came to Winnipeg lab in 2013 and they tested on many animals there and were trying to find out on which animal does the virus grow. It was March of 2019 in the National Microbiology Lab (NML) in Canada that the scientist couple along with their team of interns were at Canada and they stole it and it ended up in China, this virus and others were a group of lethal viruses and capable of 'biowarfare' Chinese agents were successful in replicating it in Wuhan lab. It is said that China got this virus from Canada to 'weaponize' it to impact humans. The Chinese virologists released from Canada many types of virus - Ebola, Corona, SARS, etc. Was it that Chinese government was testing which one is more effective bio weapon- the Coronavirus from Wuhan based Yunnan caves or the one that came from Canada so that they can build the best one and send it all over the world? It appears that the missing link- 'human to human' transmission was being aggressively researched and studied.

The Chinese warfare program at the last quarter of 2019 is at its advanced stage now. It does research and development, production, and has 'weaponization capabilities'. Its current inventory includes chemical and biological agents with delivery systems in rockets, bombs, missiles, sprayers, etc. PLA is at the forefront of biological warfare preparedness. In fact PLA is focused now around Biological agents and its interfaces with Brain science, AI, supercomputing. The Army now talks about the strategy of 'genetic weapons ' and 'bloodless victory'. Wuhan Institute of Virology has worked extensively for the last 15 years on several viruses- SARS, MERS, H5N1, influenza virus, Japanese encephalitis, and dengue. From 2016 onwards the CMA (Central Military Commission) funded projects on military brain science, advanced biomimetic systems, biological and biomimetic materials, human performance enhancement, and 'new concept biotechnology'. China is all set to hit the world with the latest biowarfare whenever necessary.

Almost 1 year before on March 2, 2019 before the Corona virus actually erupted and destroyed the whole world, there was a research paper published by NIH- National Institute of Health: National Library of Medicine, National Center of Biotechnology Information, PubMed.gov. The research paper was titled- Bat Coronaviruses in China. The research was conducted and the paper published by four leading scientists including Zhi Shengli, the 'Bat woman' of China. the SARS (Severe Acute Respiratory Syndrome) 2003, MERS (Middle East Respiratory Syndrome) 2012, and

SADS- (Swine Acute Diarrhea Syndrome) 2017. All these three pandemics caused huge loss of human life. All these 3 outbreaks in which thousands of human beings died, have a common characteristic, they all originated from bats, and were found to be highly pathogenic. It was concluded that the future outbreak will most likely and probably be from bats and from China. Therefore it was found it is of utmost importance to study this virus and its cross-species transmission potential. This paper kind of proves what happened one year later in Jan-Feb 2020.

China's preparedness and readiness to launch a world war of bioweapons can be understood by what happened just a few months ago as stated earlier. In Dec 2019 only there was a meeting on Corona from the World Economic Forum, as stated earlier in the book, and the three parties joined the meeting- John Hopkins University, Bill Gates Foundation, and the American military, the Chinese were not purposely invited to this meeting. Bill Gates, found a pandemic of Corona was building in the world. They were very concerned that if this pandemic hits the world 65 millions are going to be affected. What is important to mention here at this time is that the world already knew that China had a seemingly sinister design and were actually ready to destroy the world by fully developing the virus as a bioweapon. There were active discussions to avoid that situation no matter what happens. Nothing was done. Two months later it hit China. It appears the writing was on the wall and China was ready to implement their most powerful weapon on the world stage. The stage was all set up by China to take this global- the US Government should have taken action then only.

If we closely follow the preparation that went on from 2003 onwards till early 2020 it clearly shows that there is some correlation between what happened finally in Jan 2020 and what was going on behind stage. It appears that China was patiently waiting and getting ready in these 2 decades to not only make themselves stronger from an economic standpoint but also build an arsenal of bio and other types of weapons that can challenge the mighty America and Europe.

Chapter 3

The scheme is working out- Virus is replicating

Well at this time, since we already talked about the Coronavirus idea being conceived by Chinese government and implemented to grow it in the labs possibly. Because we are discussing replication of viruses, let us understand what is a virus and how it grows. it is important to explain for the novice reader the word- 'virus' as some of our readers may not understand it well enough. As a layman's definition to make everyone understand in two lines- "Virus is a non-living thing that cannot survive on its own without someone so it gets into the body of people or animals and then grows into many viruses inside only, kills that cell, and then moves on to the next person".

A scientific definition of the word 'Virus' would be that virus is a parasite, made up of nucleic acids- RNA/DNA, that needs a host to grow, it invades a human cell, and then replicates itself inside the cell, and then kills the cell in the process, to move on to another host cell or another human being. That is how it keeps growing. In the process as cells die due to virus attack, the human beings lose immunity and get infected by the virus and might die in 2-5% of the cases, if the body is not able to produce antibodies on its own or antibodies are injected from outside. How do we stop the virus? Well, we build antibodies that fight against the virus and stop it from spreading in a cell. A vaccine is something that prevents the virus from replicating itself in a cell. The best is to fight it internally by building a strong immune system by eating healthy food, exercising, and avoiding alcohol and smoking etc.

It is also conjectured that the virus did not go via mice in the lab but came from Snakes and there was a 'snake flu'. Wuhan wet market sells snakes that people eat. Snakes are a popular food in China including in Wuhan. From time immemorial Chinese have been eating snakes, dogs, bats, etc as a part of the food. In Chinese culture eating snakes is considered a good thing. I actually find it impressive- because when I think of snakes I get scared. If someone told me this guy eats lions- I would be impressed because in my case i will be scared to even go close to a snake. In order to spread from bats to humans, it is researched that corona needs an intermediate animal as a host. It is possible that from bats it went to snakes and not to rumored pangolins before it came to humans. Or it is also possible that Corona went from Bats to Snakes to Pangolin to humans. It is also possible that all these experiments were carried out in Wuhan lab only to see virus transmission in different animals. In any case the virus was to be injected into humans then only it could grow in the human population, if possible.

More research is required to test the hypotheses of snake vs mice etc. My theory is that Chinese government was testing it on snakes during the January timeframe and were not sure if it can spread to humans from snakes. The Corona Lady was working to find out if it can reach humans from snakes, if yes, then that route can be taken if not, then we need some other host, maybe a pangolin. Because humans are primates it is quite possible we need some animal that is mammal as compared to a reptile, and the reason is that, more Chinese eat snakes than theyeat Pangolin, so spread will be faster as a wider population will be exposed to test the virus capability.

Pangolin, Manis Javanica, mammals are the most trafficked scaly mammals in the world. They are endangered species that look like anteaters and half million are poached each year. It is small, 12 inches to 39 inches long and about 1.5 kg in weight. It is well known for its meat and medicinal value, because it is an endangered species it is not legally allowed to be sold in wet markets, but it is rumored that they are sold clandestinely in Wuhan and smuggled into China, as reported by The Guardian Newspaper. It is rumored that Corona came from Pangolin. It is thought that for the virus to spread from bats to humans it needs an intermediate animal and it could be Pangolin. Corona later being found in a Tiger in New York Zoo, confirms that the Corona virus is interspecies in nature. So it is possible that pangolin served as an intermediate host to the virus to find a way into humans eventually.

In the 2002 SARS virus it was found that the virus spread from an intermediate host animal- cats like civets before it infected humans. My theory that needs more research but it cannot be ruled out that the Chinese government was testing Corona frantically on different animals to see if it can quickly spread to humans, in other words- they needed the Virus to work on humans, and using Pangolin was another attempt from Chinese government to understand how to take this virus and infect homo sapiens primates or human beings. So the Pangolin spread that was circulating in the news media may not be completely untrue, pangolin were selected so that they can replicate it on humans because Pangolin are mammals like human beings.

On Jan 21st 15 health care workers in Wuhan were confirmed for Coronavirus. This confirms that the virus can spread from 'Human- human' versus earlier claims by Chinese government that it does not transfer from human to human, meaning all those people who ate the snake, bat, pangolin might be impacted due to 'animal-human transfer directly' and it cannot travel any further. It was not even discussed till this date that people can be asymptomatic carriers. On the back end it appears Chinese government was excited that they found the missing link, the 'animal - human' link, while they were testing Corona from Bats to Snakes vs Pangolins, it appears around this time they found, that if they want this bio weapon to spread to humans it is better to use Pangolins than snakes. This was the major breakthrough in research and establishing the outcome of the research via 15 health workers.

It was a big challenge initially how to grow the coronavirus in an intermediate host. Several such hosts were tried. It appears the Lab even might have got animals from Wuhan wet market also for test purposes, they will never tell us the truth, but it is quite possible that they tested Corona on several hosts as we discussed- snakes, dogs, pangolin, civets, cats, etc. Then it dawned to the team that if the end goal is to get to humans the intermediate host should have some history of replicating in humans. Then experiments were done in mice because mice are mammals. A lot of experiments on human beings were first done on monkeys and mice to establish if it can grow in homo sapiens. The experiments were not successful initially. But when they kept varying the virus gene structure it was able to double and then multiply eventually. The success of the mice experiment explains the probable reason to the Chinese government that their 'Business case' is working out and one day soon they will see it replicating at exponential speed in humans. With this the Design and engineering work was complete and time was ripe to test on its real enemy- homo sapiens.

The virus is working as per the wishes and designs of the Chinese government. The Horseshoe bats tests are successful, decades of work has been successful and 40 research papers are published only on the fact that this virus can spread to humans. The Wuhan lab has been able to extract the virus from the bat and inject it on mice and from mice it went into human cells. The virus is not dying in the human cell and neither in the mice cells. It is responding well and doubling itself quickly in the mice cells in a similar fashion as it did in the horseshoe bats. Similar pattern is noticed that was seen in Horseshoe virus expansion trends between the bats when it spread from one bat to the other and so on. It appears the lab is achieving its mission of making the virus jump on humans through meticulous strategy and execution by making it grow in human cells.

On the last day of the year 2019 before the world could even celebrate the New Year Eve, Dec31st it was reported by WHO that there is a mysterious pneumonia spreading to dozens of people in Wuhan, the 7th largest city in China with 11 million population, these people went to the animal wet market but there is no evidence it can spread between humans. It appears that these people contracted directly from the animals there. It was called a local flu.

On Jan 11th first death was reported in Wuhan China, a 60 year old man who went to the animal market. This was the first example to the Chinese government that the virus designed by them has some promise and can create damage as expected. From bats to mammal animals and then finally into human beings, and that too creating fatality. It is possible that this person was 'patient 1' and contracted this virus from the Wuhan lab researcher lady who was "patient Zero". There are many theories around this patient Zero and patient One- and a lot of them are inconclusive. From the warfare perspective this was an 'eureka moment' and successful completion of the last five years of research. A major breakthrough after SARS 2003 and MERS 2012. Wang Wei secretly meets his close coterie from the party and shares this great news with them- "We have done it, it is replicating, we will see how it does further, but as of now it can grow from animals to humans, we do not know how many and we do not know human- human piece". All these appear to be close controlled tests to contain the virus in a limited population to fully understand it before we grow it globally.

The moment news travelled to the USA, from January 17th airports in Los Angeles, San Francisco, and New York started screening passengers and each passenger was being checked from potential arrivals as three places received a direct flight from Wuhan, later CDC added two more airports in Atlanta and Washington. In all 100 people were urgently dispatched and engaged in this activity. Maybe China needed to wait a little bit for a couple of weeks as authorities in the USA became aware that something is happening? if they could wait a little bit the spread in China can be further observed and its impact can be seen locally before it goes out and creates the havoc that is designed to create. Wang wonders- "how did they come to know so early, we need to slow it down". They should get a shock and not the news about the virus and its potential threat.

When episodes of Coronavirus spread in Dec 2019 the scientists tested in China and found that the virus was 96% similar between human patients and horseshoe bats which confirms that the virus in humans most probably came from bats. Researchers are trying to test infected patients to understand the genetic sequence of the virus, they have sequenced several strains of the virus. In Feb 2020 Shi Zhengli from the Institute was the first one to identify, analyze, and name the genetic sequence of Novel Coronavirus- (2019-nCov). In Feb 2020 only the Institute filed for a patent for "Remdesivir" from Gilead, a vaccine it claims has a cure for the virus for Chinese market. Filling a vaccine at this early stage also can indicate that some folks expected that it will spread significantly in China and there was a rush to get the ownership to fix it for local populations outside of Wuhan to earn profits. This was another landmark milestone achieved and confirmed by the Chinese government. Mr. Wang Wei quietly whispers and states to his party's close coterie in a quick meeting organized to tell the committee is there any danger to larger populations to human life at this time. "This research will help us in opening doors to new vistas but we still have one last missing piece- human to human spread".

If you watch or read the Atlantis Report it talks about Biowarfare being waged. There is a lot of mystery surrounding this. The First case is reported by the Medical Journal Lancet on Dec 1st 2019. It says this all started from Wuhan fish market. The virus that was engineered at Wuhan Bio lab- the scientists there were experimenting with modified SARS virus for military purposes. This was a very closely guarded secret from Beijing. There are three countries that have already done this for military purposes- USA, Russia, China did this earlier. In 2014 two countries China and France did research in their Bio labs. Earlier also research was done on viruses in China Wuhan on Ebola and its variants. It appears the report is trying to establish links between the origin of Corona and the first few cases and its relationship with the Chinese government. There may be substance in this report but credibility of such claims must be confirmed. Its You tube video went viral and attracted a lot of attention from the public in early February of 2020.

For the virus to spread globally there have to be a few initial cases and they have to be studied closely to see the impact on humans there. The local population in China is not the same as in Seattle. There might be some demographic constituents and even cultural dimensions. For example does the virus spread only in Mongoloid or Caucasian or Africans equally or it does not matter which race you are. There are close to 8 billion people on earth- are there any dimensions of culture and race in the spread of Corona? On Jan 21st a man in his 30's from Washington state was diagnosed with Corona, he had travelled to Wuhan. On Jan20- Japan, South Korea, Thailand reported the first case on Jan 20th. These cases give confidence to Chinese government that the virus is not only successful in exporting but also adapting to local conditions and not dying or losing steam with different types of human races. It is still little early to observe and analyze the expected to see some fatalities to see if bioweapon is working effectively or not.

The scientists reported that the first 4 cases in China at the hospital of Wuhan came from Seafood markets on December 29th, and had pathogens that could be compared to 2003 SARS virus sequence. The patients were suffering from pneumonia of unknown source and were not responding well in five days of treatment. The researchers and doctors conducted field tests to understand the bigger picture as where all cases came from, where all they went, and what they did when they experienced sickness to isolate conditions. The virus was compared to SARS and MERS based on WHO guidelines from 2003 and 2012. The researchers found that the growth of the virus is exponential, testing was not done extensively. The researchers also found 89% of people went for a check on day 5 which is not a good sign. The scientists found that it doubles every 7.4 days. This explains the initial spread theory in favor of the market as all 4 came from the wet market but we need to know more about the relationship between these four cases to make other conclusions.

Around the same time locally in China on the Jan21st 15 healthcare workers are infected in Wuhan this confirms that the virus can spread between humans faster as opposed to earlier thought that it can be implanted only in animals. Scientists are now expected to share genome sequences. This clears the second hurdle. If the virus replicates human to human then it is not required to use bats or intermediate hosts and it will automatically reach the gigantic human populations locally and through export globally. The experiments so far confirm that everything is going as per plan the weapons are expanding like the bomb from World war II, though not in the same proportions. What is now understood is that it can travel from one human being to another, and we do not need to go back to bats or monkeys to get it, anymore. The human to human transfer confirms transferability of the virus and shows it can grow quickly as this health care worker's case confirms that. The next challenge is speed of spread, and the quality of spread from a bioweapons stand point.

It is now time that the virus is converged and channelized into the right direction- ie globally and stop local spread in China. On Jan 23rd there is a lockdown announced in Wuhan- all travel to and from Wuhan is suspended. Wuhan has 11 million people and now they cannot go out. Planes and trains leaving the city have been stopped. Buses and the city's subway have also stopped running the same day. Ian Mackay a virologist at University of Queensland Brisbane has a very important observation on this- will this stop the virus from spreading or will it become the hotbed and swamp where everyone gets impacted here in Wuhan. He worries that maybe the government has helped "just create a large cell culture dish where people will be all stuck here and create more cases in Wuhan transmitted through one another" but in reality, eventually, why did that not happen? Why Wuhan (less than 4000 deaths) did not become New York (400 Thousand deaths)- Why Wuhan was not worse than New York? This is a very important question to ask and to be answered by Chinese authorities and global virologists need to probe this incidence.

The plan was working well and was also evident as the Cruise Ship Diamond princess in Japan had to evacuate 3711 passengers off the coast of Yokohama Japan, as the number of confirmed cases on the ship exceeded 700 cases, largest outside of China. It appeared that 330 people were found asymptomatic, 40 were admitted to ICU and 12 died of Corona. These numbers indicate that the virus was not only working in Wuhan but showing its magic and danger outside of China as well. On Jan 24th the ship had left Wuhan China and then made several trips in the ocean to neighboring countries. It appears the ship became a den of virus and around one third of the people on the ship were impacted in some way. That was a very high percentage in a very small but concentrated population of people in such a short time and around the same time as the Wuhan local outbreak. This clearly indicates that global population is getting impacted quickly and large concentrated high density population gets influenced faster- something similar to New York-similar in structure of the city and demography present there. But there is one important question here- New York (18 million population) and London (9 million) are similar, why London did not see as much devastation?

The first case of Corona, in New York, the worst impacted place on earth where most people got infected and died, was reported on Feb 2nd. So if we notice the spread in China and New York, it is quick. It appears the Chinese government planned and waited for the virus to grow a little bit so that it reaches some proportion. They might have said, as Wang Wei would put it " We will watch the virus go out after a month of being local in Wuhan". It appears it got sent out Feb 2 first case of Corona found in New York City. China could have possibly done this by stating that all foreigners must leave now as Wuhan is closing down, only following flights will be going to New York and London and other parts of USA and Europe. If we look closely, this could have been designed to control the flow and export of Virus to a particular part of the world, this was evidence that virus is able to reach foreign defined destination, and sustain itself. It appears that the game plan of the Chinese government was working out and it was getting the results they expected and had planned meticulously.

Several scientists from New England Journal of Medicine researched and studied the early Transmission Dynamics in Wuhan, China, of Novel Coronavirus–Infected Pneumonia patients in January and published an article on Jan 29th to explain the 'how and why of the virus' and how it was growing. The researchers studied the first 425 cases from Wuhan. The researchers studied the illness time, exposure time, and demographics as on January 22nd. The researchers also studied the doubling time and reproductive number for the virus. They reported that the median person from the sample was found to be of 59 years of age, male 56%, more than 55% of cases were linked to the Hunan Seafood Wholesale market, mean incubation period was 5.2 days with a 95% confidence interval of 12.2 days to cover 95% of cases, the mean was found to be of 7.5 days, and the sample was of 2.2 reproductive number. The scientists concluded that human to human transmission occurred between 'close contacts' in the middle of December 2019 only. This can mean between family and friends as opposed to colleagues who work together in more formal settings. This study also confirms that more than 200 people did not contract it from the wet market, how did they get it? Where from? Close contacts? This is an important step as most people when they get scared about a pandemic will restrict their meet and greet to known circles of family and friends only, and it appears this is where the virus spread initially before it became global.   It appears the Chinese government was waiting for the right time to grow and export this virus and manage that whole life cycle effectively and efficiently. Wang Wei says- " we got to do this right. Right timing and right directioning', Studies from Axios have shown that if Chinese government acted fast and acted three weeks earlier 95% cases could have been prevented. So why did they wait three weeks? What was the exact reason? Was it deliberate or unintentional- no one knows, but supports my theory as an author.

The government tried to control the flow of communication and stopped people from interacting on social media therefore we could not know the exact spread of the virus as the government will never tell us the truth. On Dec 10th Wei Guixian was the first patient reported as sick. Dec 16th he was admitted to the hospital with infection in both lungs but he was found resistant to anti flu drugs. Ai Fen, a top doctor at Wuhan hospital posts information on We-chat and was reprimanded not to do that and asked not to spread the information. Same day Dr. Li Wenliang posts information on We-chat and after sometime he is called by authorities and rebuked. On Jan20th, Zhong Nanshan, the top Chinese doctor, tells everyone that this virus spreads from human to human. The Chinese President Xi Jinping publicly and officially got involved on January 7th, then some information started coming on national media about the spread of the virus problem. Why did the premier get involved so late when he knew these viruses are known to have killed 35000 pigs in China itself? It appears somewhere around his time Mr. Wang Wei states that "the right time has come for the virus to be shot as a missile and achieve its target thousands of miles away".

The virus is growing very fast, it hops from people to people, family to family, groups to groups, communities to communities, etc. it can stay in the air for some time, it can even stay on surfaces and not get killed. If someone sneezes or coughs it can get transmitted. Sneezes and coughs produce droplets that can spread the virus. Chinese government knew this as they spent years building this strain. A handshake can transfer it. If you come 1 meter close you can catch it, the way it has been concocted it can spread like easy and like wildfire. This Corona has a higher RO which means it can spread from 1 to 2 to 2.5 Persons quickly. More asymptomatic people will spread corona than people with symptoms. Studies indicate that some people have the virus in their throat or nose and when they sneeze it passes on the virus. The virus is quickly able to find a new host and have a party there and leave for another one. Many trends and mutants are seen growing as the virus keeps hopping on from one human to another. Interestingly, Americans are very touchy- feely people, they hug a lot, shake hands a lot. The virus seems to have cultural dimensions & can grow more in America.

The Chinese government says "Virology Lab is doing a great job at Wuhan and the virus is replicating and growing as planned". Later it came to the market but initial growth was internal only to the lab. Lancet reports that the first case was not from the Wuhan market, it happened much before that. Vox states that more than 1/3rd of the first few cases had nothing to do with the Wuhan market. Only 27/41 cases were reported to have gone to the market, which means others had no access to the Hunnan market. Dr, Daniel Lucey, a professor at Georgetown Medical Center, suggests that this might have happened as early as October of 2019. This confirms the spread of the virus from the lab only. The only question unanswered here is was it deliberate or was it an accident.

It appears that the coronavirus Culture was first grown in the lab. When the Chinese Government tested the virus there were initial problems and not much was happening. They tried very hard on different animals. Even the researchers were changed to get the right team of people. One researcher who was there for 15-20 years was now actually supervised by a much younger but powerful lady to make sure that the wishes of the Chinese government were achieved and they had direct control. The fact that the lab posted ads on their website that they were looking for researchers and in those ads there was a sense of urgency that we have found something very interesting and we are wanting to work with people who understand this and are excited contributing to such an important piece of work that is very prestigious for the human race and might alter future course of human race. Is the power in saving people's lives or building a capability to destroy human life?

The Chinese Wuhan lab is successful in creating the virus and successfully creating ' Hybrid growing strain' this is the link between bats and humans. Why would research be conducted to be able to create a virus that can now instead of only animals, also impact humans. The scientists travelled all over the world and brought samples of viruses, they also brought horseshoe bat- thousands of them from all over China- to test which ones can be shipped from the bat to another host. It is not necessary that all bats will be having such viruses in them. Many other animals other than

63

bats were also tested but it was found after several years of research that Horseshoe coronavirus only seem to have the capability to turn into a bioweapon. They managed the whole flow from bats to humans to replicate the virus in humans. An article published in The week: "Novel coronavirus is human-made, says Australia study-New study finds evidence of a sign of human intervention in COVID-19 pandemic", Web Desk May 20th as per the article Dr. Nikolai Petrovsky, Professor Of Medicine at Flinders University Australia states that there is a "remarkable coincidence or a sign of human intervention" in the creation of the virus. Professor states that the virus was created as a recombination event in the lab that happened inadvertently or consciously and not a result of Wuhan wet market. He says the alarming and remarkable affinity of the virus towards humans being more than animals its original host, indicates that it was engineered in a lab. There are some highly unusual features of Corona virus including optimal human adaptation points in the direction of human intervention at some point of the evolution of the virus. Professor goes on "The virus shows signs of being 'cultured' to evolve over time rather than being rapidly genetically spliced and mutated." he states - There are easily recognizable and hence clear signatures of human intervention in the creation of the virus.

Wang Fang from China or popularly known as 'Fang Fang' published 60 posts and her diary came online on how the Government of Wuhan did nothing and innocent people died one after the other, they kept underplaying the outbreak. "Diary from a Sealed City". The diary states- One resident who was separated from her family for two months read the diary daily and called it "Manslaughter organized by Chinese government". Complete failure of the government. In one friends family his father died, mother died, and wife all died, and then he himself died. The question is why would the government hide such a catastrophe and not seek help from the outside world. Was there something they were trying to hide? Maybe they did not want the world to investigate that the government was behind all this Corona devastation and did not care about Chinese people at all. It appears Chinese government engineered and manufactured Corona for mass production at Wuhan and distributed it to the rest of the world to spread without caring for the fact that thousands of Chinese people could have died from this experiment if it failed. Wang Fang articles stand as a testimony that the virus was replicating in the city and the metropolitan area creating panic, fear, sickness, and death among innocent hard working Chinese people and the government was a mere spectator. What were they watching? why?

Chapter 4

Wuhan Accident: The Frankenstein Monster

The Accident theories regarding origin of the virus and its getting out of hand or control can be categorized into four types - the possible leakage in the lab, deliberate transmission into researchers in the lab, leakage in Wuhan market, leakage from bats to humans directly. In this chapter we explore this important aspect and other related aspects, on the origin of the virus and its whereabouts.

What China had originally planned and wanted perhaps was to test the virus if it is doing what it was initially supposed to do, infect and establish spread from 'humans to humans', let some people die to test 'fatality' or 'mortality rate' and then let it spread globally. Unfortunately, It started impacting the mass scale of people locally in China itself. "How did that happen?" Said Wang Wei, No one had any clue. It was like a Pandora's box unleashed. The controlled test suddenly went uncontrolled and out of hand. Viruses by nature are highly unpredictable and they evolve and mutate as they move from body to body as per research from virologists and scientists globally. "The big problem has happened that was not thought of". Wei Goes, "We wanted to test it and then export it to America and Europe Italy, London in the United Kingdom. It in fact started impacting our own people". Very few cases are reported globally than in China which means for some reason it is growing internally than externally. People are not the main concern for the government, the main problem is that this will destroy our economy as we know this is a dangerous virus- we tested on pigs in 2019 only and 35000 disappeared, we tested two decades ago in SARS and thousands around 10000 disappeared. This is bad that the lethal virus will now freely circulate in our country. We must act fast and protect our economy. We cannot lose this battle and must come out still as world's #1 country. Wei sums up these discussions with Zhang Wei and his other accomplices.

It appears, as some evidence suggests, that the Chinese government created the virus in the lab, and tested it on a controlled population internally at the lab as well as Hunnan wet market was probably their 'human-human test' but they did not realize it will so quickly spread like a wildfire and an inferno impacting cities and communities at many times the speed of Ebola or SARS did. Wang goes "This gene is 10 times faster than the old virus we created almost 20 years ago". The virus leaking to the common population seems to be beyond the control of the Chinese government. A controlled test on humans to see 'human- human' spread is important to see whether the gun you bought from a company is going to kill multiple enemies when your soldiers use it on the border on the enemy's soil, likewise the virus has to kill the people you want to be killed and as many as you want to kill. It is a bioweapon and there is no sweet talk here- it is pure business and pure warfare tactics

In less than a month of the first discovery of the virus outbreak, the cases in China spread from none to lots. Initially in January by the 2nd week of January only 100 people died in China and 37 were infected globally from people who travelled outside in a natural market. By January end thousands had died and actually the number grew from 2744 to 4515 very quickly in two days. In just two days by January 26th more than 100 people are dead. The Chinese government is now in a big problem, they have to fix this man- quickly or end up in a big soup having millions of Chinese people dying creating a big dent on Chinese economy, creating an internal recession in China, and earning an extremely bad situation in global markets.

One single family in Shenzhen has five people impacted, one child in the same family is asymptomatic. Can you imagine the whole family is infected and 2 people died in the family. In another family the whole family disappeared. Families, communities, and counties were getting severely impacted. Think about the emotional trauma the families would have gone through. Think about the fact that these families disappeared due to no fault of theirs and family members were separated for no reason. This seems inhuman and cruel and disturbs social fabric only possible during a war scenario where people go through unprecedented hardships. The social impact of this is going to be huge and it will be very difficult for Chinese government to contain unrest and a potential uprising. I personally see the chance of that at 70-80% at this time. Another Tiananmen Square is brewing. Who knows America- CIA, FBI might create it

There are allegations of bioweapon research by the Wuhan institute of Virology. Weaponization of the virus is one of the major themes of the lab research which is very closely guarded by the Communist Party in Beijing. Some US virologists deny it saying that there is no evidence of genetic engineering and this is purely a mutating and evolving virus but others do not think like that. Trevor Bedford, a noted virologist and expert on Coronavirus said the virus mutation could be a part of natural evolution. Some virologists claim it is possible that during the previous experiments of creating CoronaVirus in the lab the virus might have 'leaked' asymptomatically into a researcher and led to the accidental release and created an outbreak. Ebright a noted researcher on virology, quoted often in the book, from the USA, said in one of his talks that he 'cannot rule out' the possibility that the virus got out by accident and leaked, creating this big problem. This accident is putting China in a very tight spot and it is facing dissent all over the world including internally. Was the accident deliberate ?

An estimated 4,3 million people travelled to and from Wuhan during the Chinese new year and just before the lockdown. Imagine how many people could have been impacted if things were not controlled in time. In Fact more than 80000 people got impacted in China in a short time and more than 3500 died in just 75 days from start to end. In just one month between Jan 15th- to Feb 15th China saw most expansion of the virus activity internally. Even these numbers are conservative as per some estimates it is claimed that millions died but Chinese government has hidden that fact from the people and the world. It is very hard for anyone to know what exactly happened in China as neither there is free media there nor people are allowed to congregate or interact freely personally or on social media sites. It appears Corona was designed to be quick- it took 28 days for Corona to spread to 262 cities, as per economic times, as opposed to H1N1 took 132 days to reach the same number of cities in 2009.

It appears the missile is getting smarter and improving in its speed and distance to kill enemy battle tanks. Before Chinese government could even understand what was going on, the Frankenstein Monster had spoiled the lion share of the Wuhan's social and economic fabric, and altered it forever for decades to come, as people died in thousands. Families will never see this scar going away as they lost their loved ones as kids, parents, brothers, sisters, etc. Frankenstein did the job it was supposed to do as per its masters' orders but added another dimension to it on its own. Evil designs have evil outcomes, often unplanned, and different from the course of action, and take you in completely new directions, unseen, unfathomable, and that is what is happening in China right now as we speak. Another Tiananmen square is in the making and might hit like a tornado does suddenly.

There are many other interesting theories, as some have been already stated earlier, some will come later, on where did the virus originate from? Wuhan market, lab, direct from animals, or from somewhere else outside China? Is Wuhan market the real and actual 'ground zero' and 'patient zero' is the shrimp vendor in the market? Or was the Virus engineered in the Wuhan lab and the person from the lab lady named Huang YanLing researcher, suspected that she was 'patient zero'. We all know that the Lab removed her picture from the Virology lab website. Has Frankenstein killed her too? Is she alive? If she is alive why does she not surface? What does she know that if she tells the whole world can put the Chinese government in a big embarrassment globally? Has she been hidden in some concentration camp by the Chinese government? We challenge her family to come and report to the global agencies. Why did they do that?

This Wuhan 'market theory' has some challenges- On Jan24th in a research they found that only 27/41 people went to the market so 14 people or almost 35% or one third did not go to the market- where did they get the virus from. In another research it was found that on Jan 30th 49/91 went to Wuhan Sea Food market- study indicates that not all cases even visited the Wuhan market and in this case it is close to 45% that did not go to the market but were positive- how and from where they got Corona?. In any of the above scenarios, as stated earlier also, the accident has not only created credibility loss for China but also impacted its future global relations. In either case the accident has caused considerable damage globally

Wuhan lab has been involved in Corona virus research for more than 20 years now- almost two decades after SARS 2002 study. As recently as In Nov 2015, a 'hybrid virus' was developed in Wuhan lab from bat Coronavirus, which could get into humans. The 'Spike protein' that was added on to the Corona virus from horseshoe bats could infect mice in 2015. That means the research has come close to the fact that the virus can potentially infect a human bio cell and create an outbreak accidently or in a planned manner. Five years ago they came close to impacting humans from Coronavirus, then why did they create this accident now? timing? Why did they wait for so long? Was it that Donald Trump and Boris Johnson were talking about conservatism impacting Chinese exports and cash flows ? Is that the reason both countries got the most virus? We all know it is nothing new, it has been there for a while- is it to declare that in 2020 China is #1 superpower in the world? The intentions of the Chinese government are becoming clearer. It is like a small kid stealing something and then telling the mom " I didn't do it, please believe me", now that it has gone out of boundaries and become uncontrollable, it is like an atom bomb, and hurting the Chinese global reputation for the next decade or so.

Two years ago, in 2018 the US Embassy people had visited the Wuhan lab multiple times and reported back to Washington that it was an unsafe place and it was conducting some virus studies on bats that could be dangerous and can create a potential pandemic in no time. The methods and safety levels adopted at the lab were highly inadequate and many messages were sent back to Washington to intervene and solve this problem before it becomes acute and leads to an accident of a potential outbreak. Why did the US government not pursue it aggressively? Why did the world let China continue on this path and not intervene when there were so many indicators? This accident could have been avoided much like the atom bomb that was dropped on Hiroshima could have been stopped. The crippled kids would not have been born today after 75 years in Japan, these kids could have been saved. This accident could have been avoided- the role of the UN and WHO is in question, and is overstated, several times in this book, and possibly the world needs a new agency to replace a defunct body created in the 1940's. G7- G10 can take that role.

Before Corona Ebola had hit the world in 2014 -2016 when 28000 people got impacted and 11000 had died and it created significant losses and deaths in Africa. Exact origin of Ebola has yet not been established till now in 2020 after 6 years even though the first human case was reported way back in 1976. Was Ebola the silent test done by China much like Kim does in North Korea with nukes? Same way with Corona we may not be able to know all about it ever for sure. Even the facts might have been altered and most evidence destroyed if not all. The biggest question that is most important is whether Corona is a natural virus like Ebola or was it manufactured by humans to kill humans in a biowarfare. Or was Ebola itself also manufactured by China or some other country and exported to Africa.

Newspaper 'Buzz feed news' reports that there is strong evidence that Corona is not an engineered bioweapon but it 'cannot be ruled out' that there is a possibility that it escaped from a research lab. There is some set of people who think it came from Hunnan market, others say it escaped from the lab from 'patient Zero' when it was extracted from bats and hybrid form was created with humans. In any case It gained huge proportions and eventually touched 80000 people in China and 3500 died because of this accident in less than 75 days. Most research from top scientists and researchers published in several papers like this one- has a similar tagline- " While we are not sure what happened exactly, we are not sure if it started from Wuhan lab, but we "cannot rule out" it is possible. This tagline seems inconclusive and does not give answers to those kids whose parents died in the crisis and they became orphans forever.

In China between January 16th when there were only 80 cases reported and Feb 16th, in one month, from a few cases it reached 80,000 active cases and so many people were infected. Likewise from 4-5 deaths on Jan 15th, by Feb 15th China reached 3500 deaths in just a month. Globally as on Jan15th there were very few 4-5 cases but in less than two months the numbers globally surpassed China and on March 15th Rest of World (ROW) exceeded China. The deaths also globally surpassed China between Jan 15th from a few people 4-5 to about 3500 by March 15th. The killer virus globally created the same impact in one month alone just as it created inside China in one month. The spread was working for the Chinese government. To control it locally -Jan 23rd Wuhan was already closed and neighboring city Huanggang about 70 miles from Wuhan with 7 million population was shut down. Same day Ezhou, the third city, was quarantined and train service stopped. Top cities Beijing and Shanghai interestingly did not see much impact of Corona at all.

The trend of spread in China as well as globally, is alarming to see, and has never been seen in human history. On Jan31st Virus seems to have gone out of hand in China as per journal Nature and close to 9700 cases reported in China alone when the outside world globally had not seen much of Corona till now. As on Feb 3rd the numbers of infected people doubled to 20,000. In just one day 3000 new cases and 65 deaths happened in less than 24 hours. By 7th of Feb. the infections increased to another higher level of 31000 and a total of 600 were dead in China. By feb 10th this number in China grew to 41000 infections and more than 900 people were dead, this was more people killed than SARS 2002-2003 had done. On Feb 11th the number increased to 43000 infectious and death crossed 1000 people dead in China in such a short span of time. On Feb 12th there were 6400 cases active and dead were 1300 in China. If you notice the trend indicated above, the numbers were growing exponentially and going crazy and no one had any idea what was happening. The accident had created weapons of mass destruction.

Global spread has similar patterns when we compare it with virus spread in China. In China, on Feb 14, first time, it was reported that 1400 Medical workers got infected and 16 of them were dead while working hard to treat corona patients. By Feb 18th the virus peaked in China. As on Feb 20th there were 7400 active cases and the world now exceeded China with 7500 infected cases, 2100 were dead in China whereas world over it was 2128. By Feb 24th there were 7700 cases worldwide and dead people were 2500. The WHO did not declare it as a 'pandemic'. By the 28th feb a total of 26 countries were impacted and on March 2nd there were 80000 cases reported from China. As on March 17th a total of infections in China totaled 81000 and there were a total of 3200 deaths in China, World had more than double numbers of 180000 cases and by now 7500 global deaths, now more deaths had happened outside of China. As on June 18th there are close to 8.5 million cases positive cases and almost half million dead. This number may cross 15 million people infections and total more than 1 million deaths.

The Hubei province had a total of 65000 infected cases out of a total for China standing at 85000. In China total people dead were 4600 out of which 4500 were dead in Hubei only. It is surprising to note that a country with 1.4 billion people had only 150 cases outside of Hubei as dead. Big cities like Shanghai had only 650 infections and 7 people dead and Beijing had close to 600 infections and only close to 10 deaths. This number is unbelievable as world over people are dying like crazy but Beijing and Shanghai did not seem to be impacted at all. How is that possible? Also even outside of Wuhan there is very little talk about the virus in China? Is China hiding something from its own people and the world? Are there millions of people dead there? No one knows? Or was it that communist government controlled the flow of the virus deliberately?

Even though the Chinese government is desperate and wants to claim to the world itself as Superpower #1 in 2020, the New year 2020 started as a bad omen for simple hard working Chinese people- Hunan market was closed on Jan1st and on Jan 2nd itself a total of 41cases were declared positive out of which 27 had visited Hunan market, as stated earlier several times, to look for same data and offer different perspectives. This spread to the common man in Wuhan and to other parts of China. On Jan 3rd itself it was named '2019-nCov", and Wuhan got 44 new cases. A guy who wanted to save lives was stopped from doing so. Why? They wanted people to die? Dr. Li Wenliang, a doctor, quoted often in our book, was reprimanded as he texted that there is a 'mysterious virus' spreading all over the place killing people left right and center. He was asked to remove the content. A lot of people went missing including researchers, doctors, nurses, etc. who tried to act as a whistleblower were silenced by the Communist party. Were they silenced so that it does not create bad publicity or was it silenced so that the virus keeps growing and eventually expands globally?

Frankenstein was spreading its tentacles globally very fast. Outside of China the virus grew very fast and in no time it reached many countries in a short span of 10 days. It reached Japan on Jan16th, France on 24th Jan, Germany reported first case on 27th January, India declared first case on 30th Jan, and on same day ie 31st Jan three countries reported cases- UK, Spain, and Russia. It is alarming to see the spread worldwide in such a short span of time. In human history, in modern times, this is an unprecedented accident causing irreparable damage for decades to come.

In the USA the 1st case was reported on Jan 20th and in Korea the same day- Korea could control it but the US could not. How is that possible? How come the US is one of the most advanced countries in the world, technologically savvy, equipped, takes quick action in face of disaster, could not fight it initially and Korea controlled it so well. Korea adopted a lot of testing and quarantine in the beginning itself as compared to America that came in the game much later. Korea is a smaller country in terms of population and that could be the reason. Another reason could be the fact that New York has a very high density of people as millions live in just few square miles, that could have been the reason for the disaster, and once it came in, it created a cascading impact on entire population in the city, state, and finally in the country. In a smaller size city with high density if you throw a bomb from skies, more people will die as concentration is higher, likewise New York acted as an inferno and from there it gained critical mass and gained everywhere else in America. Or was it that the rate of inflow was less to divert American mind to this problem, till suddenly it blows exponentially one day?

Is it that the Chinese government wanted to get rid of President Trump so they timed it so that America was caught in Presidential impeachment proceedings and debate when the virus landed into New York airports and before anyone could get a hang of it or get serious about it had already created its impact. While the nation was busy debating whether President Trump should remain in power or go, the virus was already playing its game in America. Maybe China wanted Trump to go as he was putting too many tariffs and trade restrictions, stopping China from growing in the USA, first time since WTO creation around 2000, that they thought they must send viruses which will help remove him. That also could be a strategy from the Chinese government. We do not know.

Internally in China the government was not ready to accept that there was a problem, till things went out of hand, or the government purposely made it go out of hands. When the outbreak started people started getting sick badly and suddenly people started coughing, have fever, and experience uncontrolled breathing problems. The accident happened and things started getting out of control. The Chinese government was not able to control it at all. The accident happened and it created panic and chaos in China. The government did not seem to be in control at all and for significant time had no idea on what was going on. This led to explosion of the virus.

The virus is so smart that it gets into people, even doctors, nurses cannot avoid it and kills them at a similar rate as it does with ordinary men. In America a father and a daughter, both doctors of Indian origin, died from Corona while treating patients of Corona. If the doctors cannot stop it, how would ordinary people do it? If the rich people cannot stop it, how would middle class people protect themselves? If rich countries like America cannot stop it then how would poorer countries in Africa save their people. This virus has confused everyone alike and shaken the whole world. It appears there is a huge conspiracy behind it. Someone has studied all these features of the virus even before it came into being. How is it possible that the virus grew so fast in New York, London, Rome, etc but not in Beijing, and not in Shanghai ? How ? why? These questions will come to our minds a hundred times till we get some clarity.

In Wuhan it is a very sad story and a tale to tell, for the next century, like people in Hiroshima and Nagasaki did, after the bombing in 1946, that brought World War II to an end. Mortuaries are all lined up with dead bodies. There is no place in the mortuary where people are dying like crazy suddenly and the mortuary has never handled so many volumes of dead people in such a short span of time. Hundreds of people are being buried at the same location and mass burials are happening. There is sudden panic and total confusion, it appears no one has control and even Beijing has no idea of what is happening and how to control it for a couple of weeks. There is total pandemonium.

People are entering the hospitals with cough and high fever, waiting in long lines to get treatment. Some people from the hospital only tell their relatives 'do not come to hospital, the situation here is worse than your home' so lots of people are seen treating the virus at home by inhaling hot water vapors frequently. It appears doctors, nurses, and paramedics lost confidence in their own system, and could not trust to save human life. It is reported that such people who took continuous 'hot steam' are able to save themselves from onslaught of the virus. Hospitals are turning down people as there are no beds, medicines, masks, and they are not ready to deal with the volume of the problem and the emotional impact it created on hospital staff. Ambulance after ambulance is rolling into the hospitals and not even enough doctors are there to treat them- nurses are acting like doctors in some cases. The register for dead persons is growing thicker each day, each day a new book is required to have names of all people that are dying. One place ran out of the book for recording the deaths and had to refer dead people to another place. Situation is very grim. Family members are dying. In some families the whole family is wiped out. In some families only old people are infected and a lot of them are dead.

There was so much commotion and confusion that China did not allow international inspectors to enter Wuhan to understand what was going on. The accident has taken place and it appears China does not want anyone to know that, it is not being transparent, security is very tight. The police have orders to 'shoot and kill' on slightest provocation. People are scared and do not know what to do. If they go home, there is someone sick, if they go outside, the environment is very hateful. They are lost in their own land and are in loneliness. One Chinese student reported on social media in mandarin- " my mom died due to fever and coughing, my father went missing, and I am going to also die as no one tells me what to do"

The Virus is spreading at a phenomenal speed never seen before. Though researchers and scientists have their own metrics to measure Corona and its impact, I have calculated from a business and economics perspective my own metrics to understand the impact of the virus on humans.

Rate of spread is R, Impact is I, then K is a function of - RXI= Killings K

We can calculate the Killings by the speed of travel and impact Virus created in terms of infections. We can even add a 5% as the rate of death from people infected and found active. There are many indicators calculated by MIT, John Hopkins University and many others virologists to study the impact and deadliness of this virus which is considered less lethal than SARS but a bigger killer than SARS or EBOLA due to its speed of spread and the number of people it has reached quickly. More than 7.5 million people are active cases as on June 11th, 2020.

In a hurry Remdesivir vaccine is patented in by Wuhan lab on Feb4 th , usually it takes time but suddenly the Wuhan institute of Virology is trying to compete with Gilead so that they cannot sell directly to public for getting the vaccine patented in China and can save some lives from 20,000 people who died till now in China. There are some concerns that how come they have a vaccine ready if they did not know this a month ago, it takes a lot of time to even think about a vaccine for a virus, but here in less than a month of getting outbreak and spread, the Wuhan lab is busy patenting a vaccine. Some researchers and scientists, globalists found this very strange. Is it that they knew this will happen, and it will create huge destruction, maybe not internally but outside of China, and they already built it earlier, and now suddenly trying to patent it to make quick money globally.

The original outbreak is reported from the 'Community spread ' as more and more people who shook hands with one another, hugged each other, or came close to a person who had contracted the virus but was asymptomatic, led to spread of virus in geometric proportions. The virus is spreading like wildfire from one community to another. After some time the patterns were zig- zag and not even related. Researchers who tried to understand lost track as numbers exploded and went out of control. More than 100 papers were written globally in the last 100 days to understand it but no one seems conclusive. At the end it appeared everyone got impacted by someone they met. Community spread exacerbated the impact and created an accidental spread to thousands of people.

A lot of Family members started getting the virus from the other family members. The worst part was that they did not even know if they were infected or not. Not a lot of people went to the hospital initially till they developed some symptoms so they were caught off guard and killed as suddenly in a few days their condition deteriorated from being completely well to completely unwell in 3-4 days' time. In one case, a brother said- " my sister was perfectly alright 3 days ago, where she is now, I do not see her, but the hospital call later confirmed that she was dead".

The Chinese government before they could even act, the Metro system was acting like an inferno and was severely impacted adding more cases wherever the metro went to. Same thing happened with buses and subways. Airlines were also transporting Corona internally as well as externally from International airports. Corona went wherever the transportation system took it even though it did not have any legs and was invisible. This led to the accident and explosion of the accident impacting millions of people. The Railways and the freeways were also not helping at all and adding fuel to the fire as it spread from Wuhan of 11 million people to neighboring counties with significant populations of millions of people in those communities. Suddenly life came to a stop in Wuhan and 70 miles around it.

Larry Clayman an American attorney and his group Freedom Watch with a Texas company Buzz Photos has filed a lawsuit against Chinese government stating Corona is a bioweapon 'designed' by Chinese government to destroy American economy of around $20 trillion GDP per year. The three parties sued are the Chinese government, Army of China, and Wuhan Institute of Virology. People named in the lawsuit are the Major General Chen Wei and the Director of Institute of Virology Shi Zhengli. The allegations made are - aiding and abetting death, provision of material support to terrorists, conspiracy to cause injury and death to US citizens, negligence, wrongful death, and assault and battery. The lawsuit also mentions this is a 'terrorist act' in history and they engaged in 'international terrorism', biological weapons were banned in 1925 and using them is participating in a terrorist activity that China did, to kill innocent people. The attorney argues that 'Why was there only one microbiology lab that was working on advanced viruses in China and Chinese government instead of telling the world, hide it as a 'security concern' till the world came to know about it? The doctors and researchers who raised the alarm as soon they learnt about the potential disaster, why they were purposely 'silenced' by the Chinese government? Major General Chen was so scared of the virus that she and her six team members injected themselves with the virus vaccine that was not even proven and was under trial. Why was she so scared- what did she know or do that she did not tell the world? We are all curious to know.

The 'accident theory' has many supporters and many viewpoints. We can go on and look at each study to understand some piece of the jigsaw puzzle. The definition of the word 'accident' is also a matter of perception. The accident is the creation of the virus in the lab and spread to humans or the Coronavirus spreading to uncontrolled proportions. Two researchers Xio Botao of South China University of Technology & Lei Xiao from Wuhan University of Science and Technology, as stated earlier, these researchers found that the origin is not the Wet Wuhan market but Wuhan Virology lab. There are many theories that revisit these two locations again and again to reconstruct and understand what exactly happened. Earlier the Bat Woman Shengli already published multiple papers on creating 'synthetic virus' in the lab so the theory that creation in the lab was an accident does not find support here. Another research was The Epoch Times- Dr Sean Lin Judy A Mikovits who gathered enough evidence that the virus did not come from the market, so where did it come from? Even Sheng Li was found quoting in a conference "did the virus come from the lab"?. The fact that the two job ads were posted on Wuhan Lab in December, wanting to find scientists to work on viruses that can transmit to humans, clearly establishes that that the virus was already found replicating in animals and could be transferred to humans, for that they needed the scientists- so it cannot be stated as an accident.

Handling bats is difficult and Scientists have been attacked by bats, bat blood, and bat urine has been found- this can support that there is a history of leaks from labs all over the world and maybe in China and in Wuhan possibly. Was it that the virus came directly from bats to humans? How can we be sure when people were not allowed to openly communicate? Yan Yi Wang was made the Director of Wuhan on Jan 2nd of 2020 and everyone was told and informed via notice board an Important Notice on Prohibiting Disclosure of Information on 'Unknown Pneumonia'. The Top Military Expert put as in charge. The Researchers gone missing. The name of the Huang YanLing who is probably the 'patient Zero' was removed from the Wuhan site, the patient zero, she even disappeared and went missing- so no one knows what exactly happened there. UK scientist Dave Makichuk says we cannot 'rule out' virology lab as the source of the virus accident and spread.

The article "Wuhan Virus lab leak no longer discounted"- from Cobra was published in Asia Times, on April 6th. The USA based top researcher Ebright quoted many times in the book, showed concern towards this potential accident. There is a lot of missing information- on Jan 2nd the lab sequenced the virus, the official website of the lab published it on Jan 8th, but the world came to know on jan12 why did they take 10 days to tell the world, there is something being hidden here -at best American people are funding $3.7 million to liars or to people who did not know how to handle the lab and gave birth to this virus that destroyed the whole world. There is a lot of skepticism around this accident and not conveying information about the spread globally.

America's Secretary of State Mike Pompeo says there is a 'enormous evidence' that the virus came from the Wuhan lab and not the Hunan Wet market as per article published in the Economist in May 10th, he calls it 'Wuhan virus' and says "China has a history of infecting the world", what information Trump and Pompeo have that they are not sharing with the public? What have the intelligence companies told them that is hidden from the world? We should know. Chinese media calls Pompeo 'insane', 'evil', and 'politically motivated', there is a fear of war between the two countries and expectations are that Taiwan could be attacked economically by America and taken away from China's control. Even President Trump said he has evidence against China on this issue. If you notice how Trump is reacting to China for the last 2 months, you will clearly sense that they have some knowledge from the intelligence agencies that you and I do not have and as Mr. Trump is a very intuitive guy who does not control his emotion, his wrath is showing everywhere- delisting Chinese companies from NYSE, stopping Chinese companies from doing trade with America, threatening to cancel flights from China to land in America, increasing interference in Tibet, Hong Kong, Taiwan, etc.

The 'Five eyes agreement' that was signed during World War II and has been there for almost 75 years is an alliance of five countries- United States, UK, Australia, Canada, and New Zealand. This is a secretive arrangement to cooperate in case of emergencies of common interest. It is like spying to get information about other countries. It is 'for eyes only' and cannot be shared with governments. The alliance has become active recently in the last few years against the Chinese government and a company from China- Huawei, it helped in banning Huawei from many countries. During the corona crisis this alliance has become active in creating an economic front to understand what China is doing and how to create a front to block that effort from China. Japan has been helping the Five Eyes country and supporting from Outside. Even India has been involved in some of the activities of the alliance from outside. The importance of the alliance is that they are not obligated to publish reports etc to the world like the UN or WHO does. The leaked dossier of 15 pages from 'Five Eyes' comes to the same conclusion that the US intelligence report did- China intentionally had hidden and destroyed information about Coronavirus. Virus could be transmitted into humans, doctors silencing, destroying evidence, refusal to provide samples to scientists from the global community- all leads to conclusions that China was up to something very dangerous and purposely hidden it from the world. A total of 70-75% of American Intelligence unit thinks Virus came from the lab and therefore is 'man made' and not 'animal made'.

The impact and devastation that the virus could have caused if the world did not react quickly and come together to fight its masks, social distancing, cleaning hands, sanitation, ventilation could have been huge. The lockdowns might have impacted the economies severely and created recessions that would go on for the next few years but evidently has reduced the number of deaths it could have caused. The SARS killed more than 10% people. Nature magazine reports that Corona pandemic could have killed 40 million people globally if no proactive action was taken. It is lethal and comparable to 40 million people that died in World War II. The study indicates that potentially It could have infected 90% of the Global population. Imperial College London reports that this could have impacted more than 6.5 billion people on the face of mother earth if timely action was not taken and the world came together and created a global lockdown. To some extent the Frankenstein was contained by global governments' joint cooperation and collaboration.

Chapter 5

Post-accident Panic

As the virus was spreading internally China had no idea what to do there was constant panic and miscommunication, Government was hiding information, military operation was going to control people, some people got killed as they protested, people were not shared details as to what was going on, family members, friends kept worrying about their kith and kin as lots of people went missing never to be seen again. We are not even sure if they are dead or alive. There was no communication with the outside world, academic research groups were not allowed in Wuhan, global scientific community was not told anything, the samples from lab were destroyed , researchers from lab disappeared, global media not allowed to enter Wuhan, the doctors, the whistleblowers were all curbed and army made arrests recklessly to curtail unhappiness against the government. Either they did all this on purpose to divert attention from the main issue or they did not know how to manage it. Both are not good situations for the second largest economy in the world and for the country that has the highest population of human beings and claims to be Superpower#1. The Super power doesn't lie in killing innocent people but lies in enabling the weak to stand and grow.

We talked about it earlier briefly, Li Wenliang, an ophthalmologist doctor, who was aware of the virus and its deadly impact on humans. He created a lot of noise and spread the word around on social media and got a report that there were 7 cases of

SARS virus from Wuhan seafood market. He spilled the beans and was a whistleblower who informed people from the outside world what was going on. Very quickly his post on chat went viral and had millions of views in a few hours. This enraged the government. The Chinese government reprimanded him for spreading rumors on social media and threatened to arrest him if he did not stop spreading the rumor or even correct information. By spreading the word around, he helped save many lives of victims of Coronavirus and eventually died on Feb 7th as he himself got engulfed with the virus. There are rumors that he was silenced by the government. It is suspected that the government did the same with many other people there. He was survived by his wife and two kids. His parents also got the virus probably from him.

The way events happened, It appears that the Chinese government was trying to manufacture Corona in Wuhan lab, test it in the Wuhan market, and then mass produce it to export to America and Europe much like they did for last 30 years with their products and service but this time it appears there was vengeance and an evil design against the countries that helped them build China. The Chinese government thought they would control the flow of the virus within China and quickly export it but somehow things went out of control and it started circulating within China. Now they were stuck in the situation where they had to face a tough time with local people and once the word spread on this on We chat, Weibo, Baidu, and globally on Facebook and Instagram, the government could not control it. So there was panic and for a few days, it seems, no one knew what to do. The government was caught in a dilemma and a twin scary objective- how do we stop it locally and then think about growing it outside of China? The big question was according to Wang Wei -"How do we change the direction of Corona from Wuhan to New York". Wang asked his deputy "How do we stop local spread and divert it to America & Europe who are blocking our business by tariffs".

Poynter, a digital daily from China, published an article on January 23rd, "China Government arrested 8 for spreading hoaxes about what is known as the Coronavirus: What happened to them?" Agence France Press on Jan 3rd wrote that the Wuhan police arrested a group of eight people for publishing and spreading false information on Weibo chat (comparable to Facebook in China) on the internet without verification and are comparing it to SARS. These folks were not to be found even after searching for them for 20 days. Chinese government had tried very hard to hide the SARS virus in 2003 and eventually earned a very bad reputation, till Yang Yong Jiang a physician broke silence in 2003 on SARS and people came to know about it. So comparing the Corona to SARS is not at all right as this is a very small thing as compared to SARS. The journalists from Poynter kept searching a lot for the 8 people that vanished into the thin ari and then after lots of efforts they came to know from their sources in the high command communist party government that those' misinformed 8 people' were never arrested and they spoke about virus even though they were not experts in the area. We just talked to them and let them go with warning.

The local people will not travel outside Wuhan but only global people will travel and they will have to be asked to leave, ideally they should have been put in a quarantine but in this case the government waited to understand what next to be done so that the virus does not spread locally but goes globally. Asking people to leave Wuhan was also not the best thing to do as it created a global problem that could have been easily contained and avoided with international cooperation. If America and Europe knew they would have brainstormed and come up with solutions to save China from current crisis and bad reputation that they earned. No International flight should have been allowed to leave Wuhan much like trains and buses were not allowed to go to Beijing.

The Chinese government wants to hide from people and global media the real story of how they concocted and spread this virus themselves. China government is behaving like a child, as stated earlier, and not taking responsibility for the disaster that impacted close to 10 million people worldwide. Imagine a child who is engaged in stealing a chocolate, telling a lie to the parents because the child does not want to get caught stealing and wants to keep his reputation and credibility intact. They do not want people to know what all was going on in Wuhan. They are not allowing global inspectors to come and inspect the lab. Media reports indicate that the Wuhan lab is closed down and samples have been destroyed. The researchers were asked to leave and some disappeared. Creating panic and living in panic mode is a sign of childishness not expected from nations, especially if they want to rule the world & be #1 Superpower.

Suddenly millions of people are leaving Wuhan and going back to Beijing and Shanghai after attending Chinese New year holidays on Feb 12th. Let us stop movement out of Wuhan towards Beijing and Shanghai. As discussed earlier, there are 20000 cases reported in China by 4th February. By 10 th February more than 900 people have died which is more than SARS killed in 2002-2003. Infected people are reported as more than 40000 in China. All these people who are now active and positive are known, what about symptomatic people, they will board planes, trains, trams and carry the virus all over the country, so China wants to stop that urgently in desperation not knowing how to proceed and what to do. The communist party clique is meeting in the night to figure out a strategy in a closed door meeting. Wang Wei says- " we have no idea what to do?"

We cannot rule out a possibility that the Chinese government masterminded the exodus from Wuhan, when there was panic and confusion, it appears the Chinese government Wang Wei might have said to Zhang Wei, "Let us have all foreign people leave our country- once they leave they will take the virus with them if they got asymptomatic virus lying latent into their bodies and is just sitting there, no one will know, till they reach their motherland and after few days only it might explode". Not all cases develop fever, coughs, etc only a few do so it can remain inside for a considerable time till it finds a weak host to grow. The virus atom bomb will blow in their own countries. It will save our lives locally.

The Chinese government it appears sent instructions ``Tell the lab to destroy the evidence". The doctor gets killed or eliminated or can leave peacefully without any harm done. Tell the media to hide it or in other words local media is not allowed to post anything as it is against national interest and if it compromises the national security of the country, they will be punished. Was it really true? Was the national security being compromised or people were reporting facts that they were seeing. The telling tale of Fang Fang in her 60 pages diary is a glaring example of government apathy. She reported daily that Chinese government is doing nothing to save lives; it appears their focus is on something else- they are trying to hide something rather than protecting their own people. We lost valuable time in this and thousands of lives could have been saved globally if China told the truth. Was it deliberate, intentional, or a confusion, lack of strategy no one will ever come to know, as evidence has been destroyed and no one is allowed to enter Wuhan labs etc.

The Chinese government was so scared that people will globally come to know what happened in Wuhan that they strictly prohibited people from meeting and talking. Anyone who spreads the rumor will be arrested. The Internet was closed down so people could not communicate. People got scared and kept quiet even though they saw in front of their eyes what was happening. Congregations were not allowed to happen. Curfew was imposed and movement of people was restricted. Scare and fear was created to keep people away from one another so that human communication chain was broken purposely.

The Chinese government shutdown places, websites, labs, trains, transportation, etc not only to curb spread of virus but more importantly tried to contain the flow of information so that there is no evidence left for the international community and America to come after them later. It appears this was meticulously planned and executed. The government went and arrested people left, right, and center. When a pandemic is happening and thousands of people are dying should the government come hard on their own people or try to soothe them. The Chinese government did just the opposite and acted like they acted 30 years ago at Tiananmen Square.

If the Corona virus came from bats and bats are not sold in wet market in Wuhan then how it spread. There are many theories, which will never be confirmed. It appears the 'Bat lady' knows the answer as she was working on creating a 'synthetic virus' as discussed earlier in details, and the Chinese government has given her many awards. She is a celebrity in China. Another theory is that it spread to an intermediate host Pangolin, as stated earlier in details, that was illegally sold in the Wuhan market but global scientists do not seem to support this view. So how it spread- the only possibility left is it was made from bats in the lab and tested on primates, and escaped from the lab or was made to escape from the lab. The Chinese government has to come clean with facts and disclose the correct sequence of events and allow international experts to go back in time and recreate reality and allow intelligence agencies such as the FBI to go to China and figure out exactly what happened and must be provided full information, full access to labs, full access to records, full freedom to communicate with people, scientists, doctors, nurses, ambulance drivers, mortuaries. It will take tremendous effort and resources to reconstruct the reality and no one knows China will allow that. Six months or more than half a year is gone but they did not say once- everyone is welcome to come and inspect, why?

The Chinese government suppressed the information. Even today the origin and source of Virus Covid is hidden- some say it came from Hunnan wet market and some say it came from the Wuhan lab. Some say it came from cats, some say it came from snakes. There is another conspiracy theory discussed earlier that the Chinese government created it in Wuhan Virology Lab and purposely diverted the attention of world media to the Wuhan market. They did this to create confusion and to Camouflage reality from the Chinese public and global media. The Chinese government it appears spent years to create this and spread it and confused people by saying it originated from Wuhan wet market. Or is it that they created it in the lab and tested it in the Wuhan seafood market from where it was leaked to scale as per defined plan. Let Chinese government make a categorical statement to the world media about where the virus came from. Then global inspectors can do their research to support or disprove that official version. It also appears that Chinese government gave many versions of the truth from time to time so that everyone remains confused. Sometimes creating confusion helps, the enemy becomes lazy as they do not have perfect information to act.

It has been researched by virologists, as we stated earlier briefly, that Spike protein or S- protein goes into the human cell, since 2005 research has been going on in Wuhan on this. In nature it does not happen this way, S protein does not bind on the virus, it has been designed that S-protein sticks in the virus and penetrates human cells so that it can transfer and kill 'humans to humans'. S-proteins have affinity towards human cells and bind with cell walls. It is like two train wagons connected by a locking chain. Now when it all became public the Chinese Communist Party CCP wants virus samples to be destroyed. Now China is censoring all the information. Why did China ignore the virus threat for six weeks when the world started learning about it- it appears they did on purpose for it to explode and travel the world over? They waited so that the disaster could not be controlled once it went out of proportion. It appears they were buying time for the virus to take an 'ugly shape'. There is enough media news in America that if they knew 4-5 weeks ago thousands of people would have been saved. Imagine, telling a small girl of 5 years of age, that her dad could have been alive if Chinese told us six weeks ago, how she would feel, her life and her future is destroyed. Now all her life she will live with this trauma of having lost her dad due to a virus attack on her loving dad. We must restate and overemphasize such stories as it creates decades of loss to families and nations.

The "Bat Woman"- Shi Zhnegli- presented many papers of Bats from 2005 onwards in the last 15 years, often discussed in our book, is the center of the controversy. She is involved in research that works on creating 'synthetic virus'- meaning made by humans artificially. She has done experiments on primates to establish similarity with human beings. Why is it that this lady has done so much research on creating viruses and why has she been rewarded by Chinese government? Why would Chinese government be so much interested in funding and encouraging this research which could kill thousands and infect millions world over? How does China stand to gain from it? What is the motivation of this research for the last 15 years since Wuhan lab was established. This seems like doing research on nuclear reactors so that you can use them to harm the human race. Now if we look back, close to 7.5 million people infected by Coronavirus as on June 10th in the world in less than 3 months and close to 400 thousand people dead, most outside of China, where it was created, it appears simple to understand that this was perhaps done on purpose to damage the world as knowledge was created over decades of work.

One writer from the Wall Street Journal while discussing the spread of Corona by China thinks that the Chinese government has some mental challenges at the top level. He states "China is the sick man of Asia"- as reported in Wall Street. There have been Concentration camps in China of more than 10,000 people where people from organizations such as 'Falun Gong' have been suppressed. It appears Chinese people are very good, very hard working, very sincere but the communist government is evil. That is why so many people from China flew and bought homes in the Bay Area and even in Fremont, where I live, in the last 10 years after the 2008 recession. The Chinese government looks at America as their major enemy and they will do anything to destroy America, its economy, its people, and its prestige, even though America did not do anything wrong with them and helped them grow after joining WTO in 2000. It appears it gives sadistic and vicarious pleasure to Chinese government and makes them feel very happy when people in America suffer. It is monstrous like a dragon.

In order to fight the panic, the government is showing it is doing something, therefore quickly it files a patent for a vaccine called Remdesivir by Wuhan Lab of Virology to show they are saving lives. Did the Chinese government ask them to do it? Thousands of people were dying in China. The Chinese government does not know what to do? The research journal Nature published an article on Cell Research by Zhengli Shi et al that this drug when used with Chloroquine helps save people in clinical trials done in Beijing in a hospital. The research paper and patent filed on Jan 27th when 81 people have died and close to 3000 impacted in China. The paper claims that Remdesivir and chloroquine effectively inhibit the recently emerged novel coronavirus (2019-nCoV) in vitro. Is it that China wants to build a vaccine quickly and then sell their own to the rest of the world after learning from Gilead? History confirms, everything they learn from the outside world as a result of technology transfer they end up making it themselves so that instead of importing it they export it so that they do not have to spend foreign exchange but actually earn it and keep their economy strong. This is how China built a strong reserve surplus in trade running in trillions of dollars. There seems to be some foul play here and needs investigations from external entities.

The Chinese government and Communist party has created confusion and there is chaos where the virus came from and is the Chinese government wanting to divert attention to the market whereas it actually came from the lab. The government maintains that the virus came from Wuhan Sea Food market but two researchers have done extensive research, as stated in the last chapter, who were mentioned earlier also - Xio Botao- from South China University of Technology and Lei Xiao from Wuhan University of Science and Technology. These researchers found that the origin based on facts cannot be the Wet market, the Wuhan seafood market, Wuhan Virology lab, or maybe directly from bats to humans. "The Possible origins of CoronaVirus"- Now this paper is not available and it appears that the communist party asked the researchers to remove the paper and not press for their claims or they could be in trouble. In China no one has the freedom to think and say what they want, the hard working sincere Chinese people are scared of the Communist party and could be eliminated if they do not listen to the party. These researchers claimed that around 90 kilometers of Wuhan there are no Bat species available and they were never sold at the seafood market. They even suspected anyone who came in contact with the bats might have been exposed to their urine or blood and contracted the virus from there. The Chinese government put censorship on this paper and got it removed from the internet.

The kingpin and pivot of this whole controversy is 'Shi Zhengli' who has been working on bats for 17 years, as mentioned earlier, and goes to caves hunting for these bats. She is the top researcher who published multiple papers on 'synthetic viruses'. Hybrid or Chimera virus which has S-protein and can infect a normal human cell and kill it. In 2018 she even presented a paper on this in Beijing. It appears that she was working on creating this virus in the lab and testing it on mice where the missing link between the bats with coronavirus and their transmission into human beings was being studied for the last 10-15 years under her leadership for the program. Shi ZhengLi was even heard saying in one of the conferences, as stated earlier, that " maybe the virus came from our lab?" It appears she knew what her masters wanted but wanted to keep this a peaceful mission. She probably got confused: are we doing this to save human lives by creating vaccines or are we going to use this as a human bomb? Then she was silenced by the Chinese government. It appears that the Chinese government created some confusion here and the world wanted to know what was actually happening in the lab? It also appears her life is in danger as she might spill the beans. There are a lot of 'hide and seek' games played here.

This is further captured in the interview with the two noted virologists, researchers, and PhDs in the field of virology with The Epoch Times, Dr Sean Lin and Judy A Mikovits- both talked that there is significant evidence that virus did not come from market but chances are high it came from the lab. Dr. Lin talks about how viruses can now infect quickly and multiple organs which is not possible with natural SARS virus. Judy states that the S Protein in the Covid can penetrate the human cell and kill the tissue, which cannot be done organically in Bats SARS coronavirus, which means it cannot come from the Wuhan seafood market and chances are it was designed in Wuhan lab. The findings from both these scientists points towards the lab as the source of origin. So many studies done separately hint towards the same source, then why does the Chinese government not explain or accept it and take responsibility for it. Apologize and fix the problem. We discuss later in the book on how 'Corona Bonds' or 'Corona Tariff' can be used to solve the problem.

As discussed earlier briefly in the book, just before the outbreak the Wuhan lab published two job ads on Wuhan Lab website and job boards in December of 2019 that they are working on a cutting edge technology where corona virus from bats and their human interaction is being studied and they are wanting to find scientists to help them on research on conduct quick research on viruses that can transmit to humans. What was the need for these quick ads in succession? When we look back we see that they had developed the sequence for the virus and wanted to increase their work based on funding they had received to get better results quickly to ascertain the research findings. Imagine you have a restaurant and your sales are going up , you would like to hire more waitresses to serve customers, likewise, it appears that the lab had done a breakthrough research and wanted more people to help it scale and benefit from it. In other words, build more viruses that can transfer from humans to more humans.

Virus could also have been transferred directly from animals to humans as mentioned earlier. Research labs have been found to be prone to virus leaks all over the world. Scientists have been attacked by bats, there has been contamination between scientists and bat blood and bat urine. There is a history of leaks from labs all over the world therefore the chances of it getting leaked from Wuhan lab are similar, higher, and then maybe it went to the Wuhan market. This is also one of the possibilities apart from synthetic construction of the virus or transferring it from bats to animals to humans, and finally humans to humans. There is confusion and chaos as to what really happened? No one knows what happened? Or is it that the Chinese government knows but are not telling the truth. I have tried in this book to build and reconstruct the top around 15-20 possibilities that could have happened. Right now on the web you will find 100 stories but a lot of them have no teeth.

As the world opinion started building against China and the Wuhan Lab, The Chinese Government put YanYi Wang, a virologist from Wuhan Lab, who was promoted as Director General for the lab in 2018 and also as Deputy Director from Wuhan in the Chinese political party Zhi Gong party. She put up an Important Notice on Prohibiting Disclosure of Information on Unknown Pneumonia. The Top Military Expert was put as in charge of the lab and no one was allowed to share any information with the outside world. The evidence at the lab seems to have been destroyed. The Researchers who were working on CoronaVirus have gone missing and no one knows what happened to them, where are they? Are they even alive? or the Communist party killed them? or put them in isolation in some jail. The family members of these researchers must be approached to understand what happened to them and if they need outside help in sorting this problem as no family member wants to lose their near and dear ones in a conspiracy to kill innocent people at home and in the world. There is still confusion about a lot of these folks going missing and not surfacing to tell the truth. The world wants to know the truth from them. There is chaos and confusion owing to this sudden disappearance of people. How can people in a civilized world disappear? This is against basic human liberties and freedom. And how can such a country be Superpower#1 and rule the world. How do you see the future of our kids if this continues? We all need to worry about this.

There is a lot of information that went viral on social media that YanYi Wang sold the experimental bats from the lab and leaked the virus into the market. The news on twitter on Feb 17th 2020 and from GlobalTimes and many other media outlets, states the link between Wuhan Lab and Wet Market and mentions that is how the virus ended in the Wuhan Sea Food Market. This story adds another dimension to the complexity and further complicates the reality. Did she really sell them? Did she sell them so that virus inside them goes to the market and replicates? Did she sell them because it was useless dead and just sitting there. No one knows the truth.

Did Shi Zhengli the 'bat woman', discussed many times, who is supposed to be the Top Virology scientist from Wuhan Lab run away from China as a part of the panic that happened after the accident? She does not feel safe in china anymore and the head of Yanyi Wang has put pressure on her. She feels threatened that she might be killed by Chinese Communist Party. It is rumored that she defected from China and went to the US embassy seeking asylum in the USA. It appears that Chinese government has created pressure on her either to lie or hide something that they do not want to be known to the world. There is something she knows which she feels is not safe for her and she might lose her life if she stays in China. The Chinese government is asking her to do something about Virus that she is not comfortable with. Maybe they are asking her to create more of those viruses and intensify attacks or biowarfare on the world. We do not know what is going on. But rumor is spreading very fast and there is chaos as to what China is trying to hide from the world about the 'Bat woman'. Mystery surrounds this important researcher.

The Chinese government has hidden the information about what happened to Huang YanLing, a researcher from Wuhan Institute of Virology, as discussed earlier also, her name and picture has been removed from the website of the lab while all others are still there. She is suspected to be 'patient zero'- she disappeared and went missing, did she die of the Virus? Did the Chinese government hide her body, or she is still put inside some jail in China? The Chinese government has to tell the whole world what happened to her and where is she? Maybe if she comes out in the open if she is alive and can tell us what exactly happened. Maybe we can ask the Bat Woman Shi Zengli in a zoom call what really happened? There has been chaos, misinformation and Chinese government has either purposely kept the information secret because they have something to hide from the world, or they were inefficient in handling the accident. They must come out clean from that situation and reduce the confusion and chaos.

As briefly mentioned earlier, when the problem happened in Wuhan Lab in January of 2020 The Chinese government in order to keep situation under their control appointed Chen Wei, an immunologist, and a Jiang or a Major General, who had earlier worked on 2003 SARS virus and Ebola virus as the head to make sure that information does not leak out and she conducts the cleaning up and maintain control of the lab. She actually took an untested dose of Corona Vaccine in Feb when it was being patented along with Gilead company. Why did she do that? Was she scared the virus would kill her? Did she know the virus was very dangerous? Right now she is actively involved in the Vaccine development program and seen with a vaccine in her hand under the Chinese flag. There is confusion and chaos why Chinese government got into this hush hush operation and tried to overrule Yiyang Wang who was at the helm of affairs and silence the 'bat woman' Shi Zhenli who is now trying to flee China and take asylum in the USA.

When China went back to and revisited the deaths due to Wuhan they realized some people who died or got infected were not reported and the actual numbers might be much more than originally claimed. This further created a credibility issue with what the Chinese government is sharing with the world is not correct data. Why are they hiding things? What is the truth? How would huge cities like Beijing and Shanghai have less than 70-80 cases reported and only 5-10 people died, this is unbelievable. There was chaos, misinformation, and lack of information in the aftermath of the Wuhan accident. Or was it that the Government thought if people outside came to know that lots of people died here but China stuck to the same number, is not a good idea, let us show, we did some more work, and found there could be some more cases- but just a few more? One article states millions were lost in China? Millions of phone owners went missing and did not pay their bills? Why? Is that true ?

The Chinese response after the accident in the lab was one of chaos and confusion leading to giving out wrong information and creating distrust with global countries. It started from having no idea of what is going on, to panic, to miscommunication, to hiding facts. They even retorted to military operations, killing people if required to hide information. They did not share information, groups were not allowed, global inspectors were not allowed, lab was closed down and evidence was destroyed. They did not allow the global media to enter Wuhan after the accident. Army arrested people who acted as a whistleblower, and even doctors, nurses, hospital staff, etc were not treated nicely. There was fear, anxiety, scare, and uncertainty and millions of Chinese citizens went through a grueling experience which they might not forget for lifetime especially if they lost a loved one during the crisis. This can be compared to be worse than Tiananmen Square for at least people from Wuhan and comparable to Hiroshima & Nagasaki bombing or the German concentration camps where people were killed brutally. We do not know. Confusion, chaos, conjecture surrounds everything that Chinese government does. This is like World War III

Chapter 6

Spread The virus Globally

Wang Wei shouts at all his army men and administration folks "Close Beijing, close Shanghai, Guangdong, etc. close nearby places, close all planes going internally domestically, stop all trains, block subways, stop trams, stop buses going out. Allow only international travelers from Europe, USA to leave 'safely' via international flights". Local people in Wuhan were put into quarantine- one scientist from Australia said that the conditions created are like Wuhan itself will become a 'breeding place' for the virus if people are blocked and asked to stay in that place only. Little did the research community globally realize that this could be a part of a well thought, designed strategy to export the virus, via travelers who would be asked to leave China for Europe, and the USA. This possibility cannot be ruled out. It could be part of the evil design of the Chinese government.

There are clearly Four stages of Corona growth in almost half a year, the spread and the journey of the virus so far from December 2019 till June 7th 2020 as this book goes into printing and publishing. Corona spread globally and infected 7 million people and close to 400 thousand people are dead till June 7th. In my assessment this has happened in four phases of 'Globalization for Corona'. Phase I was a local outbreak in China called the 'Start phase'. Phase II was Europe where it was 'thrown' out of China to European countries. Phase III was the 'Grow' America phase where it infected 2 million people and killed 110 thousand people. Phase

IV is the 'explode' phase where it spreads to Brazil, Russia, and India. Continent wise Only Europe, America were targeted initially and now South America and Asia are also on the virus hit list- with countries of Russia and India badly infested. The continents of Africa and Australia were not targeted much as they do not contribute much to global GDP and if you do not have GDP or market- what will you destroy and what will you rebuild?

Phase I was China from December 2019 to mid of February 2020 called as the 'Start Local' phase when from nowhere suddenly people started getting exposed to Corona. It had a total population reach of 11 million in Wuhan and a total extra 15 million people maximum in 3 other areas surrounding Wuhan. Economic impact maximum could be $1 trillion only. Goal was to minimize the local damage. It started from the Wuhan lab most probably. It went to the Hunnan seafood market from there. Then it went to Wuhan metro area. And some neighboring areas. Finally it did reach Beijing, Shanghai but in a very controlled manner where less than 100 people got impacted. In this phase infections reached a total of 85000 people and led to 4500 deaths in China. The first phase can be called the 'prototype' phase, where testing, understanding, feeling the virus in the human body, seeing what it can do and what it cannot do, figuring it out how it compares with older 'battle tanks' like SARS, Ebola, MERS, etc as a part of biowarfare- most from them produced from China in last two decades only/ Also the big question was how many people it can reach quickly (speed) and how many maximum it can kill (lethal). Once this was clear it was time to defuse the bomb globally.

China perhaps focused not to spread the virus internally because they knew it would create havoc and devastation internally and destroy China's economy. They were very 'Hush hush' about the accident when the virus spread in Wuhan not letting anyone know and probably quietly confided and took the WHO on their side. They did not stop flights going to New York and Europe but stopped all flights for Beijing and Shanghai- why?. They did not inform the world that there might be potential virus spread as we had in Wuhan, why purposely they underplayed Wuhan and kept saying 'It is just a flu'. They knew it was not just a flu. They tested it on bats, snakes, and other animals and saw thousands of animal populations dying in their own land. They saw SARS, Ebola, MERS causing damage and killing people globally. They knew the virus was deadly, lethal, and much faster than earlier ones created by China SARS MERS etc. but did they purposely hide it from people? This was like version 3.0 of the Virus much like the F35 fighter jet from the USA with latest features in the latest and most advanced version with a higher price tag.

The main festival is going on in China, this is around 20th of January, the new year celebrations are going on, most people travel around this time, people are hearing stories about cases in South Korea, Japan and Thailand but not that much about Wuhan. They heard about virus spreading to Beijing and Shanghai and few cases reported from there, but the city of Wuhan is not informing the media what is happening there. The 'group of 8 people' were told not to spread rumors about the virus or will be arrested- after a lot of tension this group was not sentenced or punished and charges dropped against them. They were charged for spreading the rumor and misinformation- actually they wanted people to know as they feared the Government might not disclose any information about the virus to the global community. If whistleblowers were listened to global spread could have been stopped. Renowned Professor Xu Zhangrun from prestigious TsingHua University from China was suspended and found missing after condemning President Xi Jinping, his wife received a message about his welfare.

As the virus was spreading inside China, many theories were propounded to divert attention of the people away from China. The Chinese government said it could have come from the USA when athletes came for October Military games or even from Italy.

One popular and well know doctor Dr. Giuseppe Remuzzi, Director of Mario Negri Institute of Pharmacological research in Italy said he heard from General Practitioners from Lombardy that they had reported a very strange and very severe pneumonia in old people in December or even late November in 2019 much before the virus outbreak in China. This suggested that the virus came from Italy and not China. The news spread like wind and led to 500 million people downloading the information about the origin from Italy. Later the doctor denied it and said that Chinese government and media is purposely twisting his words to divert the attention of their innocent people away from the malicious intent of the government.

By the Jan end, China had reported 80 deaths already by now and 3700 cases are tested positive. By 27th January cases were reported from a lot of other neighboring countries such as Taiwan — and in Thailand, Australia, Malaysia, Nepal, Singapore, France, Japan, South Korea, Vietnam, etc and far away countries such as the United States, Canada and Mexico. The virus was penetrating in China vertically and horizontally spreading and expanding its reach outside of China in neighboring countries and also touching ground and landing in far-away countries.

On January of 25th more than 100 people died in China and 37 infected globally. First 'human- human' case was reported from Germany on January 28th where a person contracted it from a colleague. In Vietnam a person acquired from a family member, in Japan a bus driver who had transported people who came back from Wuhan, tested positive for Corona.

The Chinese government worked very hard to ensure that they Stop spread in Wuhan China and do not let it expand to Beijing and Shanghai. Now China is desperately wanting to export the virus to America and Europe. China engineered, manufactured, and exported the Corona virus and gave America and Europe a run for its money. It exported a $ 5 Trillion problem to these countries with more $5 trillion potential at a total price tag of $10 trillion.

A teacher in Wuhan Ben Kavanagh from Ireland was caught in the quarantine and was interviewed by the lady from the TV channel Channel 4 news on Chinese new year. He states he used swimming goggles and two pairs of masks because doctors and nurses got infected through eyes. They covered their mouth by wearing masks but could not protect their lives. It is Chinese New Year day in Wuhan having a population of 11 million people and the streets are deserted. He says stay local and stop the disease from spreading. Ben says there are on January 12th a total of 4000 reported cases of positive Corona infections in Wuhan as of today and each of these persons is further infecting 3 other people. The city has raised the Level 1 alert. They have sent 6000 taxis to pick up people. Wuhan has become the epicenter of Coronavirus. From here Hongkong got 5 cases, South Korea, Japan, Thailand, USA, Australia also reported active cases. The Hong Kong government stop trains and flights to and from Wuhan. On the same day 31 cases were found in the UK but they tested negative. There are so many cases reported that the administration decided to build new 2 hospitals in Wuhan to attend to so many cases. French and Americans are evacuating their citizens and this is how Corona is exposed to the world. Ben gives a lively description of what he is seeing, hearing, and believing being in Wuhan.

The Phase II of Corona was 'Throw Global' phase, started perhaps Mid of Jan 2020 to mid of Feb 2020 spread globally from/ by China and first it went to mostly Europe and little bit in Iran. The population target for this was 500 million people in Europe, Iran, etc. leaving Eastern Europe not much impacted. The economic size it could potentially damage was Europe which has a GDP of total 20 Trillion dollars. The countries impacted were first Italy, then Spain, then Germany and then France and then UK. Italy was perhaps the first one to get impacted and the virus spread like wildfire inferno there killing older generations first.

Wang Wei says to his lieutenants "Wuhan to Italy and Europe flights must go out quickly". By suspending travel within China on Jan 23rd, it appears Chinese government is wanting to desperately spread the virus globally outside China. Italy and Spain were the first ones to get the virus much before New York got. More people travel to China from Europe and vice versa due to the proximity as compared to the USA. There is more business travel between Europe and China. China mass manufactured and exported the virus all over the world starting from Europe and in Italy. The factory of the world changed its strategy and became the human factory and started exporting humans Chinese and International people back to their homelands to expand and grow the virus at respective places they go. They first want to send it to Europe. Italy and Spain are the first places to receive this virus. Little did these people know they had a virus inside them.

It is now March 8th and this article from New York Times "Europe, with eye on Italy Coronavirus Quarantine, Plans Next Move " gives a very good depiction of what is happening in Europe. It specifically talks about Italy putting quarter of its population of 15 million people in quarantine has created a problem of unity in the European continent. Italy is the hardest hit but France has seen 1000 cases and Germany has seen 900 have also halted public meetings and emergencies are being declared. Italy's decision will stop German car manufacturers from getting car parts and create a recession in the European economy. European bank decided to inject cash and asked 3500 workers to work from home. Tesco, British retail chain, is seeing a shortage of soaps, wipes, and pasta. Italy has failed in controlling the virus. Germany stopped public gatherings of 1000 people or more. France lost 19 lives and moved to Stage 3 of security. Students numbering 300000 are at home. Spain has seen 13 deaths and 500 cases and stopped the Barcelona

Olympics. Francois Bricaire, France Academy of Science says- "we are in a world where such viruses will be seen more often and frequently but we do not have to react in this manner". Before Corona Europe has growth of Zero now it will go negative. Volkswagen will not get parts from Italy. Britain with 273 cases is still evaluating the measures. Germany had the soccer game with 54000 people where 200 cases were reported. Europe is in turmoil and heading into recession.

The phase III of the growth called 'Grow Global' was The Unites States of America- USA and around Mexico, Canada etc. from mid Feb to March 2020 end where it started later than Europe but picked up very fast. The target population of America was 500 Million people. Total GDP impact potential was $24 Trillion. New York was the first one to get impacted but soon other parts were getting affected. New York became the epicenter of Corona in the USA and from there it spread all over to Chicago, Dallas Texas, San Francisco, LA, etc.

The first case was reported as Virus travels to America a 30 year old man in Washington tested positive on January 21st, his person had travelled to China. Los Angeles, San Francisco, and New York receive direct flights from Wuhan. From January 17th these airports started screening as per instructions from CDS and 100 people were sent to verify each traveler. South Korea and America had reported the first case on the same day but it appears America has now more than 2 million impacted on June 7th but Korea managed it very well and the virus could not spread there as much as it did in America. The second case was reported in Chicago in America when a 60 year old lady came back from her trip from Wuhan, on January 24th.

Wang Wei tells Zhang Wei - "Wuhan to New York flights must go to stop local spread without delay". New York gets 50 million visitors each year. It is the most visited city in the world.

It has a very high density of population like London or the UK. These visitors crowd the city all the time. Time Square, Statue of Liberty, Manhattan Stock exchange gets thousands of tourists every day. If you drop the bomb in New York it will create the most havoc and death in America because no where in America such a high density and high number of people live. New York has the highest density of population per mile in America-27000 people per square mile. Moreover due to the presence of the pacific ocean the temperature never rises and ocean wind keeps blowing to spread the virus quickly. Forbes article states that the virus spread from New York to most states in America as it is the hub of the USA. Now it is expected that due to protests arising from George Floyd's death, people are walking in groups without masks and not observing social distancing norms- this will create further spread of Corona and might create a second wave.

American President initially thinks this to be a small thing and gets dumbfounded when he is told this can kill millions of Americans. One estimate says more than 2 Million American will die in this biological warfare. Then he gets revised estimates that no matter what happens between 100 thousand to 200 thousand Americans are going to die, till today on June7th 112 thousand people have died in America. The President got worried and started finding our ways to tackle the virus and reduce fatalities in his country.

This fear of virus attack and spread is not new or known to America. Bill Gates, the founder of Microsoft, back in 2014 did a TedTalk and explained that if we run simulations to understand how quickly the virus can spread, he even compared the next virus being comparable to Spanish flu in 1918 which killed 40 million people. He said this virus can be so dangerous that it can cost more than $3 trillion globally. He suggested working hard to avoid the spread of the bio war based "germ war". George Bush, Barack Obama also had spoken about this potential threat. We could have avoided this current global spread from China if we were prepared from our side in America and in Europe and did not take China lightly.

In the beginning when the virus reached American soil the hospitals did not have enough beds. Patients were found queuing up in front of hospitals coughing and feeling feverish and were shivering with cold. There were not enough doctors, nurses, equipment, masks, ventilators. There were so many uninsured people- who would pay for their treatment? America shutdown its economy as they did not know how many were infected and could die potentially. As businesses closed, a growing number of people were losing jobs and job related health coverage. There was a growing concern that hospitals might bill the patients if they are uninsured as someone had to pay the cost. The government is coming out with a law to reimburse hospitals all costs to provide care to corona patients. People standing in queue were scared if they will even get treated. Because people lost jobs as home owners they were struggling to make payments as they did not have jobs. The world there was in chaos.

America also witnessed information and intelligence failure at such a crucial time when people were dying in thousands each day. In New York and other cities in America, It has been found that 20 of the FBI surveillance wiretap applications were not working during the initial part of the corona crisis. There was an overall security breach and the government was not able to tap that. Corona was spreading but the authorities are not able to understand things and communicate effectively. The Foreign Intelligence surveillance court head Mr. James Bossberg stated that there are "further reasons for systemic concerns" and possible compromise. "Is it that someone is trying to thwart communication and force them to underutilize American intelligence".

Businesses were asked to close down their doors. People were losing jobs everywhere and by May 1st in America alone 30 million people were jobless claiming unemployment benefits. The industries that were impacted badly- Automobile industry, airlines, hotels, and small businesses were adversely hit. The virus was growing everywhere and along with it the scare was increasing, people were scared and did not know who will die next in their family and friends. Moms did not kiss their kids anymore. There were no more warm hugs. Family members were staying away from one another although they were in the same house. Married couples and boyfriend-girlfriends had stopped dating as each thinks the other person could be an asymptomatic carrier. No one trusted anyone anymore. It could be in anyone and everyone around you. These are crazy times never seen before. They are redefining how people behave and interact with one another.

The Phase IV of Corona growth is called the 'Explode Global only'. That is the current phase from mid April to June end 2020 as on June 7th 2020 Brazil, Russia, and now India are impacted. The target population here is 2 billion people- largest but least in terms of economic size of 5 Trillion globally as China itself ($14 trillion USD) and Japan ($5 trillion USD) are not included. Japan was impacted first due to The Star Cruise ship and its proximity being closest from China. Japan fought hard and won the battle with Corona initially only due to the mask wearing habits of the population and overall health conscious population. These Phase IV countries did not see much problem initially but when the world started getting normal suddenly these countries saw the spread. It appears that China decided not to spare any continent so the virus even travelled to South America and impacted Brazil and Peru. Likewise it went in Asia to Russia and now is exploding there too. In India it has suddenly picked up in the last 10 days in May end and June first week only.

Brazil is now second after America in number of cases 750 Thousands and soon in deaths 40 Thousands also it will cross the UK that had the highest deaths 41 Thousand after America .The country did not have many cases till very recently but due to ignorance and neglect the country avoided taking measures and now the number has suddenly swollen it has more than 40000 deaths as on June 10th. After Brazil is Russia being third in the number of 500 Thousand or half million cases but around 6500 deaths. Now India is having 300 Thousand cases which is 8000 deaths now putting in fifth spot. India had 10000 new cases in 1 day on June 10th. Virus is changing its complexion now. Something that started with G7 now is turning in direction, tone, and color to Brazil, Russia, and India. Corona has moved from G7 to BRICS (Brazil, Russia, India, China, South Africa) and now destroying their economies. Wall Street reports that "Worse than a war zone- Corona has battered the city of Mumbai". Mumbai with a 20 million population has seen 20% of all deaths and cases from that city alone- it is like the story of New York. Dharavi, a slum area, is badly affected, in one room ten by ten 5 people live- so how social distancing will happen.

World War III has been launched. Almost all the 213 countries are involved in the war. They are fighting the Corona weapon sent from China. Most economies have come to a halt under the lockdown. There is a pandemic spreading all over the world. The stock markets are down. Unemployment rate is going up in each country. It is estimated that 1 billion people will be impacted globally in one way or the other. As on May 31st more than 6 million people are infected with this virus globally. People are dying. More than 2 million people are impacted directly and 30 million jobs are lost in America alone. Production has come to a halt. There is a complete standstill and lockdown. All over the world 7 billion people are impacted in one or the other way. Never in the history of humankind this has been experienced before of this magnitude and scale. China has defeated the whole world.

As I said earlier also, I am already 54 years old and I have never seen anything like this before. I was asking my father in law who is 85 years old and he said he has also never been exposed to anything like this in his lifetime. People are stuck. People are scared. People are frustrated. There is gloom and sadness all over the world. The hustle and bustle is gone. There is a tremendous amount of uncertainty surrounding the world as no one knows what to expect next. No one knows what is going to happen next. People are staying home scared of deaths as if some bomb is going to drop on their heads or some fighter plane, missile, drone will suddenly appear and kill many people like in a world war. China has won the game and spread the virus globally but more than that they have spread the fear and scare for China and its legacy heralding to the world of this new world order.

From Phase I to Phase IV now Corona has spread globally and is present everywhere in the world in 210 countries all over the world by may 1st 2020. Is that a great job done by China, to humanity, and spreading it or helping it spread all over the world? It has infected more than 7000000 or 7 Million people and more 380000 people are dead, more than 1000000 have recovered from the infected virus. More than active 2000000 cases and more than 1000000 as per worldometers.com 50000 cases are serious and could lead to fatality. Five countries are more than 70% of the cases till May1st- USA- 64000, Italy-28000, UK-27000, Spain-25000, France-24000. Germany initially was getting lots of cases but controlled it very well and now has only 6500 deaths. Virus first destroyed the G7 and now it is destroying the economies of BRICS- the only exception being China which is laying bricks for growth power and supremacy.

Chapter 7

Europe & America surrenders to Corona

As of June 18th 213 countries are impacted by Corona . A total of close to 8700000 or 8.7 million cases are reported, more than 450000 i.e. Four hundred Fifty thousand people are dead. The highest deaths are reported from The US 120000 dead, followed by UK 40000 deaths, Italy 34000 deaths, France 29000 deaths, and Spain 27000 deaths. It appears that the United States and Europe have surrendered to Corona and had no idea what to do in its initial phase of attack on their mother lands. The mighty Europe that ruled the world for centuries and the USA which ruled for the entire 20th century were made to surrender to an invisible enemy. The safety, security and the consequent survival and growth- is a very important question for them and about them- today. The world dynamics has completely changed in less than 90 days.

In the US more than 120000 people have died till now out of 1.9 million positive cases till June 4th, the trend does not look good, and it is expected that the USA will have close to 150000 deaths when this comes to a close in a month or so. The mighty USA has bowed in front of the Corona. A nation that does not bow to the latest drones, missiles, and nuclear arsenal from known countries has been tamed by an invisible enemy. The American pride has been seriously jeopardized. The notion of American supremacy, technological excellence, creativity, resourcefulness has been seriously undermined.

Because the government closed the economy, businesses went close and lost revenue, they still had to pay rent and salary to employees, the government had to run a $4 trillion stimulus PPP (Pay Package Protection plan) for businesses and for Individuals who lost employment at these businesses- totaling to about 25 million people being out of work. The state of New York was worst hit with 1/3rd of all cases and deaths. The US got behind and incurred huge losses, there was a huge economic loss expected to be 15% for the second quarter of 2020, the unemployment that was lowest in 50 years at 4% is suddenly the highest at 16-17%. Companies are filing for bankruptcy- for example JC Penny filed bankruptcy and just decided to close more than 200 stores. Soon government counties will run out of money as people will not be able to pay mortgages etc.

Due to people dying in large numbers the US in the initial stages declared National Emergency and closed all states. Now as on May 20th all 50 states have reopened even though the highest number of people around 2000 are dying everyday in America. Nation has to balance its priorities between saving lives vs getting jobs for its citizens. India helped the US by providing chloroquine which was expected to reduce the deaths from the virus. The US and other countries are asking for a China probe on the sources of Corona. The role of WHO is being questioned and suspected to be doubtful. A total of 2909 people died in a single day on May 2 called the 'deadliest day' in the USA. People are working from home, kids are studying from home- The higher education plan, Mckinsey reports, will change the delivery model completely in days to come and people may not like to go to brick and mortar Universities any more.

The US has been so upset with the Corona virus that on the very first chance at a global platform it has expressed its anger over China and its dangerous designs. US- China feud erupted at the World Health Assembly on May 19th, as per Times of India report.

The US claimed that China played with the virus and created the problem for the whole world. President Xi Jinping announced $2 billion to fight coronavirus and send doctors and medicines to developing countries. Whereas America said it is going to withdraw its funding and membership to WHO as it failed to deliver its goals and aids and sides with China. It appears there is a direct fight for supremacy and wherever America wants to withdraw their support, China is more than willing to grab the opportunity and jump on it. Trump declined to address this assembly of 194 member states due to the Corona problem and Xi Chinese Premier grabbed the opportunity to address and had the opening session. The US used to give 533$ million to WHO funding of a $6 billion total budget for WHO and China used to give only 80-90$ million till 2018-2019 but now sensing the opportunity to be world leader China bumped it up and later on even promised to give $2 billion which is 4 times the US contribution. At this virtual event about 100 nations demanded investigations into the origin of Coronavirus. It appears by paying $2 billion China is trying to cover up its mistake and bribe its way into WHO leadership and its activities.

After the United States, the worst impact of Coronavirus is felt in Europe with more than 150000 deaths. Europe combined has more deaths than America. In the USA 110000 are dead, In Europe more than 150000 people have already died. Country wise highest is UK 35000, Italy 32000 ,Spain 27000, France 28000, Germany 8000 as on May 20th. Europe has been mostly closed for business in the last 2-3 months, only now countries are opening up to save their economies and not to miss the summer rush. Why is it that eastern Europe has less of an impact on Corona as compared to the West? Why just five countries in Europe have more than 60-70% of the cases. The United Kingdom seems to be the epicenter of Corona in Europe. Beaches and nightclubs that opened up recently, after Corona incidence dropped, are now struggling to get the tourists and people back. WHO warns there could be a 'second wave' in the EU area.

Europe has come out with a "Contact -Tracing" App to monitor Corona in Europe and are encouraging everyone to use that app. Suddenly Sweden is into the limelight and a lot of new cases are reported from there also. With Brazil, Russia, and Sweden- the world has lost further trust in Corona and uncertainty has increased about its future. Germany and France announced a 543 Billion Euro as a stimulus to boost their economies. Europe has a $1 trillion plan to revive the continent, Europe's most important electronic show is still not cancelled which is due in Sep from 3-5 The IFA and as of now will happen in Berlin in a physical space like before but we will see how this goes. Germany recently had a Bundesliga football match which was played without any audience and no noise in the stadium.

In the US more people have died from Corona than died from the Vietnam War. On April 1, the United Nations chief warned the coronavirus pandemic presented to the world with its "worst crisis" since World War II, with almost million people around the world having been diagnosed with the virus. By June 4th as I write this book the cases in the USA are at 1.9 million infections with 110,000 deaths. This represents almost 1/3rd of global cases of 6.5 million people impacted so far and total 380,000 deaths globally. More than half million people will be dead globally once this comes towards the end. More than 15 million people are expected to be impacted globally and close to 1 million people worldwide will die from Corona.

More exports of virus from Wuhan came to NY and the EU initially than any other place creating this problem. It came suddenly and brought the world to screeching halt. There was no information to people and governments and suddenly people started dying everywhere in thousands. There was no equipment to fight it.

Hospitals did not have beds to deal with sudden spurt of cases. The Hospitals were not ready to deal with this calamity. The President of the United States did not take it seriously and it appears his Impeachment proceedings were going on in America- till Feb 5th and everyone was busy with that. It was only much later that America started waking up till then thousands of lives were already lost.

The concern about the virus pandemic is not new in the United States and goes back to George Bush and Barack Obama. The President Barack Obama, way back in 2014, said on Dec 2 2014 in an interview at Bethesda in Maryland, as reported by CNN and AJC, Arluther Lee from Atlanta Journal Constitution, that a potential pandemic is coming, can happen now or in five years or decade from now, and requested more than $6 billion from the congress to fight ebola happening at that time with more than $4.5 billion dollars to be spent on Ebola. He also said we have to be prepared and fully equipped with resources beforehand by building an infrastructure with an investment of more than $1.5 billion, but the republicans denied the request. Ebola, an outbreak, was happening at that time in 2014 in West Africa that ended in 2016- there were more than 28000 cases of Ebola and more than 11000 people died because of the virus, including 12 cases that were reported in America at that time. Obama was very keen to establish a Contingency fund and create 50 centers all over the USA to fight Ebola quickly- see and identify it, isolate it, and fight it locally and globally. He said 'this is so simple', it is not a partisan issue between democrats or republicans even, it is a 'no brainer', it is in the best interest of American people's safety and security and does not even require a debate or discussion in the congress. But nothing was done.

America is witnessing big problems right now, New York appears like a "Twilight zone". It appears China sent so many people from Wuhan to New York to kill its economy. Why so many direct flights were running between Wuhan and New York, it was not a tourism times, still the number of flights were more. A lot of these flights were from China than from America. Why? This is a very important question to ask. Also what was the occupancy rate of these flights coming into America. You will notice it was not 100% and not even 80%. I tried to collect that data but airlines refused to give that data. In my opinion flights were running in losses and still flying from China to America, why? American President called the Corona virus the 'Chinese Virus'. America declares a national emergency and congress passes a $3 trillion stimulus, much larger than the greatest recession of 2008 which was supposed to be the worst than the depression since 1929.

In the US, Donald Trump declares war against the Chinese Virus. We had a great economy but China ruined it. America learnt about the virus in November- December 2019 time frame but kept quiet till now. March 13th America declares a National Emergency. The Defense Production Act on March 18th is promulgated by Mr. Trump much like it happened during World War II. Trump says- 'this is an invisible enemy and it is hardest to defeat someone who cannot be seen'. But he must be able to see through the strategy of China to become the leader and the superpower #1 and beat America in the game. Trump has become a 'wartime President" as Corona devastates the US economic and social landscape.

Corona is creating another problem. Even in economic theory we talk about this problem often. When you close down businesses and people are sitting home and doing nothing, they are getting frustrated. If they hear news of people being infected, sick, or dying, it creates a negative emotion in people. They need to do something. Something to earn a living, something productive to keep them busy and contribute constructively. if no money is coming in, bad news is coming in about deaths, change in lifestyle, and people are sitting idle, it will lead to crime. Empty mind is a devils workshop. During my doctorate days I read in my economics class- "Unemployment and crime have a direct relationship". Mexico is infested with crime because there is a higher rate of unemployment there. Right now in America people are protesting and rioting against the death of a person George Floyd. One fired police officer Derek Chauvin was charged with third degree murder and manslaughter when he sat on the neck of a person George Floyd who died after almost nine minutes of gagging as he was choked to death and could not breathe. There have been riots all over America for the last 10 days due to the killing of this person. This is an inhuman act and should be punished but a lot of this is happening because people are frustrated as they have no jobs. Even Behavioral economics states that people are emotional and if they are driven by negative emotions it will create more damage. America should control this aftereffect of Corona and bring back its economy and wonderful people back to work quickly.

The world is badly impacted by the Virus. Sporting events have stopped due to requirements of social distancing. The Olympics that were to be held in Tokyo in Japan are cancelled for 2020 and moved to 2021. This has caused a huge loss to Japan. Wimbledon is cancelled. The US Open is also on the verge of cancellation. Football games, handball, soft ball, soccer, all games have come to a standstill. The whole world is in a state of flux and all old systems seem to be non-functional or have been destroyed.

China is proposing to enforce National Security legislation In Hongkong just 3 days ago around June 10th and police fired tear gas on May 24th, as China is trying to assert its presence everywhere anticipating a backlash from the world against the virus. In Honk Kong recently there have been harsh protests against China. The famous student activist Joshua Wong, from the party Demosisto, a 23 year old and a political activist, who has been thrown in jail several times on the behest of the Chinese government. The outside world is highly impressed by this young boy. He was being considered for the Nobel prize recently at a young age of 23 only. He is fighting hard against China which wants to dominate and take over Hong Kong completely. Wong said on US Capitol Hill in 2019 that China should not grab all the benefits from Honk Kong and take away the democracy of the country. The Government of Hong Kong banned Wong from contesting elections in 2019. The US is supporting Honk Kong and a US republican has filed a bill in the senate to stop China from doing so. This will aggravate the relationship between the US and China and this is largely due to Coronavirus spread by China that hurt the US so badly.

The US President Donald Trump is not afraid of anything, he is displaying courage, has demonstrated competence, can take on China head on, make quick decisions, daily conducts press conferences, and keeps track of everything that is important for the country. He will go after China once things settle down and try to destroy their economy or even attack them before the November 2020 elections. For a long time America will not get a President who can make decisions without fear and quickly by circumventing bureaucracy. He even stopped funding for WHO because he felt that they were siding with China. The USA was one of the largest donor nations to the WHO. The only Challenge with Mr Trump is that sometimes he does not consult experts and makes decisions individually, he also does not take educated intelligentsia people into account to solve the Corona problem.

China will do the same thing in World War III- in 2020. More than 8.25 million people are infected by the virus as on June 20th, 2020 and 480,000 dead. More than 1 billion people are expected to be impacted globally in terms of employment and being in a financially awkward situation. In America alone more than 2.08 Million are infected with close to 120000 deaths were reported as on June 20th. Total 25 million Americans were out of jobs i.e. almost 18% of the total US Job market or labor market. New York City alone has 25% of the impact of America's total- New York infections are close to 375000 and close to 25000 deaths on June 3rd,2020. Reports indicate that this will impact women more than men in New York and in America. During World War II as a consequence more women got into the workforce as men went to fight the war. Women started working on assembly lines. War needed more food and weapons and women helped in creating it. Something opposite will be witnessed with World War III as more women will leave the workforce to take care of kids, families, households, and improve quality of life at home.

The US economy is expected to shrink 5.5 % and lose more than 3-4 Trillion output in 2020 as per estimates from Morgan Stanley. This is the fastest shrink since 1945 right in the middle of World War II. Unemployment is expected to be 15% and the second quarter is expected to be 38% shrink. 21 million people are expected to be unemployed in the second quarter. This is World War III because everything that is happening is so unusual, on a big scale, and is comparable to something that happened 80 years ago- the world war II.

Corona is expected to have a higher impact in the USA as compared to China due to nature and structure of its society and economy. The Chinese understand this very well. Austan Goolsbee studied and reported this in an article in New York Times. China can have a better control on people due to Authoritarian nature of communist government that can enforce complete quarantine unlike the USA where there are democratic environments. In the US, there are more urban concentrated populations and such epidemic spread faster in urban areas than China where 41% people live outside of urban areas twice as much as America. On an average Americans travel on 3 flights a year vs in China it is ½ flight a year- imagine impact on the Airline industry; think about cruise ships where 3.5% or 11.5 million Americans travel vs China it is 0.7% or only 2.3 million passengers. Americans love sporting events such as basketball and the US spending would be 10 times as much as China. Spending on gyms is where 60 million Americans spend 19$ billion vs in China 6.6 million go to gym and spend $6 billion. Health spending, such as visiting a dentist, is 17% in America almost three times that of China. Even though China has four times the population of the USA, its spending is much less in certain areas. America is more social and outgoing. Corona will hurt America much more than it can damage China.

Wall Street states that the state of the US economy is bad. The Businesses are taking out Extra Credit lines to survive, the executive are taking huge pay cuts, employees are taking furloughs & layoffs, companies are engaging in stock buybacks and dividend cuts to keep stock prices higher- Ford motor co, Royal Caribbean, Cheesecake, Delta Airlines- WSJ Page B5: Apr 14th,2020 As Virus Spreads, So Did its Financial Impact? As the virus spreads in the country it is creating destruction and death along its path wherever it is going in the country. People, businesses, governments are frustrated not knowing how to react and what to do. People are dying as if a bomb was dropped every day in their neighborhood and the police or army could not come to their rescue and in sheer helplessness people are left clueless of what to do.

China does not want to lose any opportunity to make the USA weak, even now it is keeping the war active when the enemy is trying to figure out what to do. This Chinese Strategy is coming from The Art of Sun Tzu. Right now China is engaging in Cyberattacks to steal the Corona vaccine from America. It all seems to be a part of most modern Chinese strategy of creating cyber wars, biotechnology warfare rather than using missile and drone based attacks. China has already moved forward from American strategy, they have less people than India/USA in their army today, in 2019 they reduced their army strength from 2 million to less than 1 million. China is more advanced in its thinking, strategy, and warfare than America or any other country in the world today.

The article published in the Wall Street Journal on May 24th,2020 "The End of US Military Primacy" talks about the meeting that was held in 2017 and 12 ex-military generals attended that meeting. Senator John McCain was there and he pointed out that America is getting behind China and if there will be a war, America will be in a very bad situation as its system is obsolete. He even states that we will be impacted so badly that "The Future Generations of Americans are going to look back and ask how did we let this happen". The American mindset of investing in the highest defense budget in the world, people, soldiers, ships, fighter planes, equipment, which is infrastructure and investment oriented, has to change and we have to include more of Artificial Intelligence, autonomous systems, distributed networking, advanced manufacturing, digital systems.

Brose wrote this article- 'The kill chain: Defending America in the future of High Tech Warfare'. China is far ahead of America in the game and follows a "system destruction warfare" whereby they will render the US warfare strategy as ineffective. America has to have better supersonic missiles, advanced drones, less investments in defense equipment. For example the fighter plane- F35 can have the same AI enabled computers that self-driving Tesla cars have now. McCain, was a US senator and fought for US Presidential candidate several times, he states, In the last 10-20 years there are several new 100 billion dollar unicorns in America but none of them is in the defense area-why? America is not promoting new things to come in the Defense area and has lost its advantage and needs to build new generation tools for warfare.

Our kids emulate Mark Zuckberg, Bill Gates, Steve Jobs, Elon Musk, Taylor Swift, Jennifer Anniston, Justin Beiber. No billionaire or successful person or company has come out from the defense area. It appears pentagon has stifled innovation. Lockheed Martin, Northrop Grumman, BAE systems, etc are huge billion dollar businesses surviving on their relationship with Pentagon but there is hardly any new out of the box inventions are coming out. New versions of older technologies are surely coming out to earn revenue consistently and survive but disruptive technologies are not emerging. The answer lies in the question I ask the readers or my audience. General Motors and Ford have been there for almost a century - why did Electric cars not come out from them and why did it come from Tesla? America needs innovation to its defense by engaging American kids and funding their ideas.

US businesses and President Trump now see China as a threat and that 'buddy- buddy' relationship is over. In 1999 JP Morgan Chase and other lobby firms paid $100 million to gain favor from Clinton to get China to get entry into WTO. Since then things were alright with the Bush 2000-2008 and then the Obama 2008-2016 administrations, China grew its tentacles in the USA and earned huge money from exports and created a surplus and reserves. Since 2016 when Donald Trump became President things for China have become very difficult and he himself decides on Tariffs and does not listen to any one. This has created a big problem for China. China wants to eat the US pie but not share the Chinese pie with them or with anyone else. During the "Make in China 2025' launched in 2015 they decided to get in top 10 areas and recently started the 'Anke Project' that has a 3-5-2 rule, Anke means "Anquan Kekao" or English it means 'secure and controllable', companies in government business, infrastructure, technology are required to allocate a fixed percentage of their procurements budgets to domestic companies. The rule is in 2019 it should be 30% and by 2020 it should become 50% and finally by 2021 the balance 20%. This means American companies cannot even bid for business. Cisco was not allowed to bid for a telecommunications project recently. Based on this rule by 2019 a total of 180 Chinese companies in chips, software, IT, and electronics are already supporting this plan of the Chinese government. Read the article

"Why US Businesses Turned Against China", Wall Street WSJ, June 6th for above.

The US is now coming after China to counterbalance the harm done. It is trying to delist Chinese companies such as Alibaba and Baidu from New York Stock exchange. There are 500 leading Chinese companies in the USA. Even large US companies are now Chinese owned companies. Even companies such as GE have investments from China.T he US senate passed a bill recently blocking China to buy equity in troubled American companies. During the Corona crisis China is trying to buy more US companies when mankind faces the worst crisis after World War II. For example WH group pork company from China has made major inroads into US markets by buying US companies. The US is blacklisting Chinese companies. Due to poor quality of masks sold in the United States, 66 Chinese companies are now barred from selling face masks in the USA.

The United States has realized that it has to get aggressive with China if it has to survive and retain its #1 position, or have any say in global affairs. The US has asked China to release Buddhism 11th Panchen Lama, a young child who was 6 years old and put into captivity by Chinese government in 1995. The US wants to know where is he, and he should be released and shown to public. He disappeared suddenly and after a long time the Government of China declared he is in their prison. In the meantime, few days ago, the US Commission on International Religious Freedom requested for appointing a special coordinator for Tibetan border. The Chinese government appears to kill the Tibet Buddhism by both these actions and America is now requesting that China must inform the world why it is trying to curb religious freedom in China. In other words USA is now trying to meddle in Chinese internal affairs to build pressure on them and counter the balance between the two nations. The United States in Jan 2020 passed a resolution in congress changing its stance on

Tibet and accepting its existence. This has been done to control the spread of China as an aftermath of Coronavirus. The US congress passed the "Tibet Policy & Support Act of 2019" challenging the supremacy of China in the region. This has lessons for India who has to deal with bullying China all the time.

The US always maintained a neutral position on Taiwan and Hong Kong. Now the US must start taking interest in these nations. Balance of power has to be maintained between the two nations for world peace. Right now the balance of power has shifted completely towards China and China feels it can do whatever it wants. China has to be questioned for each action. Chinese expansionary strategy has to be checked by some power in the world. We have to live in a world where there is peaceful coexistence. The US recently approved Torpedo sales to Taiwan. All over the world the US has to take interest in a positive way. A big brother is required in the world if the younger brother is forcing himself to everyone in the global family. At global regional and local level associations have to be formed to control and check ambitions of China towards smaller and beleaguered nations. Small nations are suffering- they have taken debt from China, have China build their infrastructure, and now China is involved in policy making of those countries. Fair and reasonable growth is acceptable to all but tyranny and oppression will not be tolerated.

The USA took away the special status of Hong Kong this week on June 8th, as published in a WSJ article; "Hong Kong braces for US Trade cuts". This will hurt the city significantly. Goods trade between US and China in 2018 were $450 Billion exports from China, $150 Billion exports from USA leaving a shortfall of $300 Billion dollars for the USA. Roughly 7% of the transactions are re-exported on both sides from Hong Kong China recently passed a security law which impacts Hong Kong adversely. As it is due to the US-China trade war in 2019 there is a drop of 15% in the business from Hong Kong. Hongkong is the main Financial hub for China. The re-exports from both sides are going to be impacted negatively due to the US decision. Now the US is trying to get even with China. Why all steps of the US now appear that they are sure that China purposely created a problem for the USA. The US would not have acted this way if they were convinced this was an accident and happened by mistake. President Trump and Mike Pompeo have already said this was a deliberate attempt to destroy America's economy.

In the US the impact of Coronavirus is expected to last a decade as per WSJ article June 2nd "Economy Setback Seen Taking 10 years to End". The economy will contract 7.9$ trillion cumulatively or 3% of GDP. It will reach the previous forecasted levels by the fourth quarter of 2029. There will be scars due to the painful shock caused to the economy due to Corona lockdown. This is a huge issue and can impact one generation in America. Why did China do this to America when America helped it stand on its own, they even do not trust that Chinese are giving right information about the origin of the virus. Pew research indicates that Americans do not trust the Chinese government at all and 84% of Americans distrust China about the outbreak of the virus and 49% say they have zero trust in the information..

The US wants to distance itself from China. Now it has understood the Chinese game that the government of China is playing to destroy the US economy and its strengths. India has come to the rescue of the US and is trying hard to lure 1000 US companies that are present in China today. The US government should make a plan and in the next 1-2 years either completely move out of China or remain there with minimal investments. And it should be a level playing field for both nations. The US should not dole out any advantage to China and should have an export surplus with them or at least break even. US businesses should be allowed to compete in China alongside with Chinese companies. A democratic government should be set up in China which helps the local people rather than communist government and its henchmen that are greedy and dictatorial.

Lack of vaccines killed so many people. When people died from SARS, MERS, Ebola that time the vaccine should have been ready. Remdesivir was approved by FDA as a vaccine on May1st to fight the virus. When thousands of people have already died. This drug was supposed to be used for Ebola many years ago. Why was it not created then? We could have saved so many lives then. Right now if 31% people have been found to respond positively to the drug in clinical trials then it is possible this drug can be commercialized and solve the Corona problem. Many other vaccines are being tested everyday and the next 'vaccine war' has already started between the US and China. There is a race to win this Trillion dollar war- whoever wins this war will recover all the money they lost in Corona from sales for next decade. So this seems to be a blessing in disguise to opportunistic nations.

It is not just America, China perhaps focused on the G7 nations with this bio weapon targeting. The economy of Europe is in big trouble right now. The EU is trying to get a stimulus of $2 trillion dollars to revive the economy. Germany and France are planning their own packages to rebuild their economy. Europe already has an aging population, immigration is an increasing burden on the economy, lack of growth opportunities, not much innovation happening there. There is also a political and economic divide between the 25 members. The EU that grew for two decades is now facing decay and decadence in the last couple of years and even 2019 was not good for them with Brexit talks dominating Europe. Corona has further complicated this complex situation and thrown the EU economy into recessionary mode. Most countries will declare recession after six months, because by definition recession means two quarters of negative growth- Corona happened just 3 months ago, in next 3 months, we will see Europe declaring recession officially.

Italy is on the verge of getting hammered. There are more than 225000 cases confirmed and close to 32000 deaths already reported as on May 16th 2020. Italy had one of the world's best medical system which was completely thrown in disarray by Corona. The Corona started in Italy on January 31st when 2 Chinese tourists in Rome came here from Wuhan and imported the virus into Italy were found positive, then 1 Italian man came back from Wuhan a week later tested positive. By Feb 10th it was 16 and then by 21st Feb there were 60 cases in Lombardy. Next day alone there were 60 cases in Italy. Flights stopped into Italy from January 31st. A total of 60 million people were put in quarantine by March 8th. There was a lockdown and Italy had the highest number of cases on March 19th at one time before America took over on April 11th. After being closed for two months it is going to open on June 3rd for tourists.

The first case confirmed positive in Spain was a tourist from Germany on Jan31st. Total deaths as on May 16th are 27000. In Spain deaths have increased over the period of time. The community spread of the virus started mid- Feb and a total of 15 strains of the virus were reported. By March 13th all 50 provinces had reported a case. The country declared Lockdown on March 14th. In the next 10 days by March 25th there were more cases reported dead in Spain than in China where it all started. This was a major concern. On 2nd April close to 1000 people died in Spain in 24 hours which was the highest at that time. Later in the US 3000 people died in 1 day otherwise 1000 was a big number.

The United Kingdom has the highest deaths after the USA of dead people reaching 40000 and 283000 positive cases, but Brazil and Russia are catching up very fast. The British Prime Minister Boris Johnson is the first politician of national level who tested positive for Corona and was treated for the virus and put in quarantine for 14 days. The UK probably got its first case in late January, but now research indicates it was on Dec 17 and 18th only when a person from Yorkshire came back from China. The analysis of people who died, 90% of total, who died had some prior condition or illness or were over 60 years of age. Landlords are evicting people as people cannot pay rents, so the UK government bans eviction of tenants during the Corona crisis. Many doctors including an Indian Keralite Dr. Purnima Nair succumbed to Corona along with other GPs- she was the 10th doctor to die from Corona. Even UK Health Minister Nadin Dorries tested positive for Corona. The UK was criticized for attempting to infect 60% of the population in March and build the "Herd immunity", to act as a vaccine, later it was dropped. Prince Charles also tested positive in March for Coronavirus. The UK's economy is in shambles and will take a very long time to recover as it is the hardest hit in Europe. One study says the UK is seeing the worst time seen in 300 years- the British imperialism has been jolted severely.

Germany was not doing well initially in controlling Corona and Angela Merkel, the Chancellor said "Germany is facing the greatest challenge since world war ii she even compared it with "German reunification". The first case was reported on Jan 27th from an automobile parts manufacturer. There were 9000 deaths and 185000 infections as on 4th June 2020 as reported by Robert Koch Institut (RKI)- that tracks data in Germany. Initially Germany was quite impacted and stood fifth after China, Italy, Iran, and Spain. Then they controlled the spread by adopting many measures. The impact was so profound that Merkel said "We are facing a 'historical task' that will 'change life in our country dramatically and forever". However, Germany fixed the problem significantly- Article published in Financial Times- "How did Germany get it right?" In six weeks Germany declared Corona was under control by April 17th. Recently Germany announced a $146 billion stimulus to revive its recessive economy.

In France as of June 4th more than 150000 cases have been infected and close to 30000 people have died. Recently after dropping again close to 100 deaths have occurred in 1 day. Corona came to France as early as late 27th December 2019 but some reports show Jan 24th as the first case that was reported in France and in Europe when five people had come from China. Recently in June a software application was made to track and cure Corona and it has been downloaded 600000 times which is a good sign. Recently France has decided to open its borders with Spain. The main spread happened during the 'Christian Open Door Church' between Feb 17-24th where 2500 people attended the prayers, it is calculated that half the people almost 50% got the infection from there and this led to the whole problem later on.

Therefore, we see that Corona has humbled America and Europe and both are in serious situations right now comparing this to World War II, so it is evident that World War III has devastated America and Europe equally. Half of the world's GDP of $40 trillion from America and Europe has been put under a flux. China has defeated the G7 nations and won the war.

Chapter 8

India & the Rest of the world be Devastated:

In this chapter I present how the rest of the world apart from the USA and Europe has been impacted by Corona. In doing so I table India as an opportunity for the world in this crisis to shift the world's factory to India and make a case for that.

The flow of the virus in the last three months across 200 countries suggests that China was ready to make sure that not only the USA and Europe are in trouble, as they control half of the world GDP, but also the rest of the world must be Devastated with Corona. The Communist party general Wang Wei says to his colleague Zhang Wei - "Not just America and Europe, but the entire world (ROW) must bow and salute to the CoronaVirus and the dragon".

The five countries initially impacted most by Corona were the 'rich man's world'- USA, Italy, France, Spain, and UK. More than 93% of cases initially occurred in these five countries in the beginning. Then it dropped to 70%. This also explains how this virus was designed to engage in warfare with specific target countries to spread globally. Then the virus evolved. Later on, countries such a Brazil, Russia, and India started having more cases and rapidly things started changing and countries went up and down in suffering from Corona. The truth is no one knows where we will end up. The destination is not known, the journey is going on. Maybe Brazil will have more cases than America? But for sure the world is devastated and China has a lot of explaining to do than being belligerent because this will define the future of their global diplomacy and success.

India has till June 18th had 400000 positive cases putting India in 4th place with 13000 deaths. India with the second highest population of 1.3 billion people had a big responsibility on its head when the Corona crisis started but it appears India has done a good job considering the constraints and limitations it faces. Indian PM announced 1 day lock down, an initial Curfew, had four lockdown phases 1.0 , phase 2.0 phase 3.0 and 4.0 in four stages and now has started unlocking its economy 1.0 on June 1st. India earned a reputation of a global Samaritan by sending chloroquine to America, and is now getting ventilators from the USA. Corona has had a lower rate of infection in India. India has fought well and has become a world hero. Indian PM deserves a 'big thank you' and appreciation for handling the crisis. All Flights coming to India were cancelled. People were asked to stay wherever they were and suddenly the nation went into a lockdown. Life came to a halt.

In India the industrial city of Ahmedabad has seen a spike in Corona cases as migrant laborers moved out of the city and moved back to their countryside locations. Mumbai seems like New York may be due to the high density of population there. Delhi has seen a sudden spurt in the last one week ending as on June 4th. One report from Indian Express says that 50% of the Indian population can be impacted by Corona by December 2020. India with 1.3 billion people and the second most populated country in the world will face havoc if this happens.

Indian economy has suffered as a consequence of lockdown. Barclays expects that Indian economy will not grow at all in 2020, it was going to have 5% growth but due to Corona now it may not grow at all or even experience negative growth of 0.5%. This can create a 330$ billion dent and huge impact on the economy. World Bank states that 5 million children will be impacted severely and will be undernourished and malnourished.

Mr Modi, the Indian Prime Minister, who is a very popular person, came on National TV and asked its people to not come out of the house and said to draw a line 'Lakshman Rekha', meaning a boundary you cannot cross. The country witnessed complete lockdown and it was very successful as per Indian standards where it is difficult to enforce laws stringently due to multiple vested interest groups and political parties trying to sway people in different directions to create a public sentiment and reduce the strength of the opponent.

India witnessed during the lockdown poor people seen walking out on the streets wanting to reach their homes hundreds of miles away as they could not afford to live in the capital of the country. There are rumors that the virus will not grow much in India due to heat and higher temperature. MIT research indicates that the virus grows more in cold climates and if we see the growth of the virus it has been restricted to 5-6 countries. Initially more than 93% of infections were in 5-6 countries dominated by the US and European countries.

Also, there is another theory that Indians have a higher immunity towards viruses and hence India may not get as impacted as planned. This stems from the fact the overall hygiene levels in India may not be as stringent as in other countries hence the population adjusts quickly to any immune system imbalances that might be introduced.

Modi the Indian Prime Minister and head of the federal government does a great job of controlling the spread by having a nationwide lockdown. They are not willing to surrender to the Chinese virus. Mr Modi does a marvelous job of coming on national television during all four lockdown phases and humbly requesting Indians to have lockdown and participate in the national cause. He celebrates that with clapping hands and blowing steel plates with spoons from people's homes to showcase solidarity. Then suddenly after 2-3 days he comes back on Television and announces a 21 lockdown here. The Chinese design does not seem to be working here in India. The country enters Phase 2 of lockdown on April 13th. It is extended for 3 weeks till May 3rd but might be relaxed by April 20th depending on the situation and spread in different parts of the country. In successions India witnesses 4 rounds of lockdown covering more than two months time period.

China must get India because after the US 21 trillion dollar economy and Europe 15 Trillion dollar market, India is the third largest market with a 3 trillion dollar growing economy. Japan and Germany will not grow as much and India will be the third largest economy in the next 3-5 years with $5 trillion output. India is like China 30 years ago- the population levels are similar, If India starts growing it can beat China in the game. India has ambitions to take away the manufacturing from China and become a $5 trillion economy in 2025. If it does well and doubles itself in 7 years by 2027 it will hit $10 Trillion and by the same logic by 2032 it will be $20 Trillion quite comparable to the economy of the USA. In the short run India will not only be consuming maximum masks, sanitizers, beds, thermometers but also ventilators when more and more Indians will be getting impacted by the disease. Wang Wei says" If we create a virus there, scare people, and then sell virus defeating products- India could be #1 in terms of items sold and revenue generated for Chinese companies".

India showcased its strength and commitment to Corona by making PPE indigenously. Indian government ordinance factories are going full speed to not produce bullets and guns but manufacture face masks, hand sanitizers, hazmat suits, ventilators, PPE etc. ICMR- Indian Council of Medical Research and Ministry of Health has been involved closely with the Government of India to ramp up measures to fight Covid19. Defense public sector undertaking Bharat Electronics Limited is manufacturing ventilators and DRDO Defense Research and Development Organization is manufacturing protective gears for medical practitioners and hand sanitizers for patient care.

The Indian Armed forces are keeping 28 hospitals ready to fight the virus for patients who need treatment. Government has given emergency powers to the Army corps to procure equipment and provide medical facilities to quarantine patients. To add more beds for potential patients, each zone in the Indian railways is ready to prepare a rake of 10 coaches by converting non air conditioned coaches into an 'isolation ward' to treat Coronavirus patients. The Center has directed all states to confirm a fixed number of hospital beds in private and public hospitals to fight the expected number of cases if the virus explodes.

Hospitals and medical education institutions such as Universities and colleges have been asked to keep the facilities ready to fight sudden increase in the number of cases or deal with quarantine cases. The capacity exceeds the patients active at all times.

AIIMS, The leading All India Institute of Medical Sciences, which is on the forefront of medical education, treatment, and research has created 'special task force' to deal with sudden spurt in Corona bombings. The war must be fought and won. The Ministry of Health has ordered production of 10,000 ventilators in addition to 1200 ordered earlier to be able to respond to the increase in Corona spread. The Indian Air Force has created nine quarantine facilities to fight the Corona War. The Defense Organization DRDO has supplied 20,000 three- ply face masks and sanitizers to Delhi Police. DRDO has teamed up with a private player to produce five layer N99 masks. The whole nation is involved to fight the deadly virus and defeat it.

Post Corona India will emerge as one of the largest exporters of medicines and vaccines. It is cheaper to produce medicines in India due to cheaper labor cost and constant supply of laborers who are willing to work for a much cheaper price. Also, it is faster to conduct clinical trials in India on a very large sample size as compared to the USA where it takes years and billions of dollars due to stringent FDA regulations.

Corona will bring Indian culture to the forefront of the world. India and Indian lifestyle will come center stage in the world milieu. Due to Corona being found in wet seafood wild markets of Wuhan, the people will move away from such types of non-vegetarian food items and Indian style vegan food system of vegetarianism will grow in the world. Indian 'satvik' food habits will grow worldwide and 'tamsik' non vegetarian habits will change worldwide. The Indian culture arising from its mythology and its philosophy of 'contentment' will spread as the aftermath of Corona will take people away from material pursuits or 'maya' 'mithya'. Those people who saw deaths in their family and friends will never be the same again as they do not know what lies ahead. They also do not know that if Corona can happen again. Now people will be scared to learn that biowarfare can kill anyone any time and will live in a flux. Indian system of 'Ayurveda' and 'Naturopathy' will grow as the world will eventually realize that no vaccine can save them and the modern doctors have not been able to find any cure for influenza or common cold in the last 100 years.

The lot of ordinary simple hard working people in China could save themselves from Corona, unlike in America, because they used 'naturopathy' by inhaling and exhaling hot steam air from their nostrils to kill or pacify the virus. Even Chinese habit of drinking green tea may be helping a lot to curb the virus. Based on what we saw in China- Yoga and Pranayam will be in great demand in the western world to not only cure physical ailments but also treat mental diseases. Overall the Indian value system and culture will grow. In India we wash our hands before eating, we also wear a mask called a 'gamcha' or 'angocha', we also engage in social distancing- and not shaking hands but saying 'namaste'. A lot of these things will be adopted in the western world in the next few years as we learn new behaviors to fight viruses.

Overall India has done a good job of preventing Corona from destroying their economy till today on May 18th as i write this book. Earlier, decades ago, when I used to be here, it was very difficult to get things done in India due to liberal democratic institutions, state level regional parties, and prevalent corruption. Now it appears when Mr Modi calls the nation people are glued to TV sets waiting to hear to their leader with confidence- it appears that corruption is not anymore the driving force at top level, specially in the current Modi government, all government officials and ministers have to remain over board and help the public or they would be thrown out of the system, and we saw that during Corona crisis.

The only bad thing observed was people walking on streets of Delhi to walk 500 miles with family on bare foot and reach home far away. On the one hand we have such poor people and on the other hand rich people, some of them corrupted by the system. I would be very happy to publish a list of corrupt officials and ministers to bring justice to those Corona victims who have nothing to eat and these corrupt officials have accumulated thousands of crores of rupees and bought islands in Australia and stashed cash in Swiss banks. I would encourage the honest to step out and expose them by publishing their names on Corruptofficals.com. I would also request the Indian Prime Minister to get the list of people from Swiss banks and publish on my website as he committed when he became the Prime Minister. He even said he will give thousands of rupees to each Indian by bringing ill-gotten wealth. What is he waiting for? The Corona victims and migrant labor who walk on Delhi streets empty stomach with their wives holding 2-3 month old kids need that money from your ministers and corrupt government officials. Please honor your comment and prove you are not corrupt and not hand in glove or spokesperson of Adani- Ambani type of business houses. Poor Indians need your help and build a 'world factory' to uplift masses and remove poverty from India and redistribute wealth from corrupt to ordinary migrant laborers around 140 million.

There are two types of power that we as societies or economies can command. One is a power that you get by creation or innovation. Building new innovative products and services like FAANG in America Facebook, Amazon, Apple Iphone, Netflix, and Google has more than 70% of the total US stock market capitalization. Well, some other countries might just copy the FAANG Model and create their own and not allow foreign companies with the same business model to enter and grow in their countries. I would not call them innovative and would rather call them 'copycats'. Some country leaders go by the 'nuisance power' that instead of creation can only destroy and probably destroy the whole world. I would like to put China and Chinese communist party leaders in that category. Wang Wei and Zhang Wei represent that mindset in Chinese government. They're often seen in their innuendo stating- "we will destroy and no one can do anything about it". America and India in my opinion want to be creative and innovative economies whereas China wants to build its might with the 'nuisance power' it now commands and Corona is just one example of that nuisance thrown at the world.

Another important distinction is in the 'Leadership style', America and India like to motivate their citizens and keep them happy so that they can win their hearts during election time. In

America you can be rich without knowing any powerful guy in the political arena and make it big like Barack Obama. In India today you can be a Tea Seller but rise to be the Prime Minister of the country. Indian Prime Minister's 90 years old mother does not live with him even today in his palatial house made by British monarchy before independence, but instead lives in an ordinary house 500 miles away.

In China you have to be close to Communist Government or you could be killed the next day. This dictatorial style of leadership has governed China and is deep rooted in the minds of the leadership. In India and America the largest and oldest democracies have to go back and win the trust of the people. Both the countries have their constitution starting as- " We the people........ Give ourselves". This 'negative governance' was evident when the Chinese government tried to crush the Chinese people during the current Corona crisis by making arrests, by playing down their own hard working honest people. China has used this style of leadership to destroy the world with its dictatorship by throwing Corona at the whole world without caring for the consequences. At some point India and the USA have to work together to install a democratic government in China.

The Indian economy has not been hit as much by Corona as US or Europe but certainly it has been adversely impacted and the government just came out with a 300 billion dollar stimulus, which is 10% of their economy or GDP, of $3 trillion to boost the economy that came to a standstill due to the lockdowns 1.0, 2.0, 3.0, and now 4.0 as on May 18th 2002. Barclays says in its study that there are only two countries that might emerge successfully from this Virus attack- China and India. For India there is a great opportunity to cash on the negative publicity that China has earned. Today 123 countries asked for signing a document to allow them to enter China and investigate what actually happened there and how Corona was born and sent all over the world.

Suddenly the world does not like China and the fulcrum has shifted towards India. The world needs a 'new factory' and that could be India. For India this is a big win because it lost out to China in the manufacturing sector earlier in 1980's. A lot of its population depends on Agriculture which does not produce as much results for the economy. The economy needs a shift from agriculture to manufacturing and this could be that opportunity for India to catapult its economy to #3 in the world in the next 3-5 years, right after the US, China, and being the third one there. In 2020 and beyond a lot of manufacturing will shift from China to India and India will become a hub for US & European Fortune 500 companies that will shift their plants to manufacture in India. Global travel to India will increase and Indian rupee will become stronger. Also language affinity will also help in building manufacturing base, China people spoke Mandarin, India people can speak Hindi and English and many other local languages.

The world opinion in the future will keep turning away against China. Countries will start blocking China and Chinese products. This is an opportunity for India. If I were the Indian Prime Minister of India I would ask all my ministers to hop on a plane along with their secretaries and top management to go to all G7 countries and make a presentation to all of them in the next 30 days- "why they should move manufacturing out of China to India and show how India can help them". This will include a comparative analysis of how much its costs in China and how they can 'make in India' and "make it in India Corona Free"- the world needs to move away from China and this is the best time for India to showcase as a hub for manufacturing and the world's reliable factory and a friendly nation. After 60-90 days people will forget things and get used to routine life which China will exploit.

Indian marginal farmers are very poor and often commit suicide and due to Corona it is expected that in India 100 Million people are moving back into abject poverty line of $3.2 per day, as set by World Bank due to current scare, as per Economist latest article, India On Lockdown- "Impossible Sums: The Fight Against covid-19 brings dizzying costs and unexpected Benefits". World Economic Forum WEF reports that 139 million migrant workers are there in India that depend on work to get paid daily so that they can eat and sleep. The Corona crisis has hit them very hard.

The Indian government in the short term can do contracts with Oyo type hotels that are lying empty at the moment and make the migrant labor stay there for 2-3 months till crisis is over, also a payment system of direct transfer by using 'Paytm' type companies can really help solve the 'hunger and food problem' for these migrant workers. In the long run the Indian economy has to move towards manufacturing- "Make in India, Corona Free, sell anywhere" is a great vision of the Indian Prime Minister and the right time has come to cash on it and bring out 100 million people out of poverty. Indian government can give tax holidays and single window clearance to all companies that move out of China in the next 100 days or maximum 180 days because after that the world will experience onslaught from China and its aggression. China knows that and will be patiently waiting for that opportunity. Corona brings a mixed bag for India unlike other countries where it is just a sad story. For India it is the lifetime opportunity and for the world too. It is a win-win for both.

India may not get as impacted by Corona as G7 nations due to many reasons including the 'herd immunity', that Mckinsey reports, in its March 30th, article " Epidemiological swing factors for Covid 19, - our latest perspectives on Corona Virus", where less possibility of the spread is there in India due to higher immunity created by dealing with extreme environmental conditions. McKinsey reports 66% or 2/3rd of population to have the 'inherent immunity' to be able to avoid being infected by the virus and India like Africa seems to qualify in that list. However, having said that, inheritance cannot help you if you violate social distancing norms and go and shake hands and hug everyone on the street. India has been careful on this front by and large, considering the fact that it is the second largest country in terms of the population and the overall hygiene still needs to improve a lot. This will help US and EU companies once their manufacturing comes here, any future Corona from China, may not impact their plants and supply chains as much as they would do in their homeland.

Corona therefore, it seems, can do more good to India and to the world from India- than harm, it appears as a blessing in disguise. With the Y2K problem in 1999-2000 when all computers were going to crash when the date changed to 2000, Indian software engineers worked on it and became popular globally- this brought India from nowhere to the center stage of the world economy. When I went to America, Indian economy was nowhere, it was around $200 billion and I landed in California which was at that time a $2 trillion economy and 6th largest economy of the world.

Corona brought some new opportunities for India to shine again, the advantages to India for example- Indian rivers are now cleanest and air pollution has reduced drastically. Similar trends are seen world over in saving the environment. In a normal time air pollution kills 1.2 million people in India right now levels of Nitrogen dioxide are down 85%. Suspended aerosols are the lowest since it was started to be measured 20 years ago but the problem is that with all these good numbers the unemployment rate has shot up from 8% to 26% in April according to the Center For Monitoring Indian Economy. Nomura bank calculates Indian GDP will fall from a limp of 4.5% to painful -0.5%. Almost 20,000 people die in India in car accident and 30,000 due to tuberculosis, crime rate has fallen- rape in Delhi is down 83%. So it appears, overall, despite some issues, Corona is a wonderful opportunity for India to have a India 2.0- after software work, and lead as the manufacturing hub of the world. Corona taught us that India and Delhi being most polluted is a 'man-made problem' and hence men only can solve it. This is a great learning for the governments worldwide to save earth from pollution.

Amid a pandemic China picked up a border fight with India at the end of May 2020, when millions of people are infected with viruses all over the world, hundreds of thousands are dying, is it a sad time for the world, is it the right time for China to pick up a border fight? Chinese troops have put 100 tents that India regards as its territory and instead of fighting Corona the Indian government is busy preparing for its defense. Are we humans with hearts and get impacted by sadness around us when people die or get sick, or we do not care and just try to control humans all over the world. Sdnand Dhume, WSJ article, writes: "By throwing its weight around, Beijing is unnecessarily making enemies". In the US, Australia, and Taiwan sentiment against China is very low- right now they should understand human behavior and just keep quiet for some time till things change and then the world will move on, have patience, and say sorry, instead of doing that they are becoming belligerent and hostile. That is why all "Quad plus' democracies are after China. Indian Minister for Infrastructure said recently- India should turn 'World's hatred' towards China as an opportunity to shift companies and production from China to India. I think, in my opinion this can really help India lift millions of migrant laborers out of poverty.

India and the USA take pride in having the largest Army- is it worth it in the age of Corona? Indian Army is now #1 in the world with 1.4 million people and has the largest volunteer Army. India even exceeded the USA in terms of people where the US has only 1.3 million. China decided in 2019 to reduce its army size to half and has less than 1.0 million people and at the same time pushed for modernization into cyberspace and modern warfare techniques as reported by The Print on March 17,2020. Can anyone guess the reason for that? It was done because China knew by making investments in Biotechnology they can spend less and have

145

more impact by creating Biowarfare. Therefore what they did not tell the world we are going to shift money from the army and get people, equipment, scientists, bats, etc to Wuhan lab and invest money in building bioweapons than arming our soldiers with weapons. This strategy is also evident from the 9 point strategy taken from the Chinese classic of SunTzu ``The Art of War' '. Another popular fable "Stratagems of the Warring States" is also behind the current Chinese strategy. It says do not invest in the traditional army or soldiers spend in game changing technology- which now we know is biowarfare and Corona. Why would a country cut its army to half in just one year? It means they found something worthwhile they know can have more return on their investments but they told something else to the world to divert the attention from the truth- modernize and focus on cyber and airspace. Let us ask China how diversified is their portfolio in investing in modern warfare techniques- bio, cyber, etc- much more they invested in those areas as compared to creating Coronavirus.

World manufacturing can go on in India for the next 20 years and keep prices low due to idle and continuous supply of cheap labor available in India thereby keeping FORTUNE 500 company's products cheaper and balance sheets more profitable. Historic migration of people is happening as we speak in India due to the Corona crisis. Due to lockdown businesses closed down and laid off these workers. More than 10 million people are walking on streets for 500 miles to reach back home to their villages. This migration of labor in India is the worst since 1947 when 15 million moved due to the India and Pakistan division done by British who left India in that year. This is the largest migration of humans and people in the world, as per Giridhar R Babu, from Indian Institute of Public Health. WSJ titled "India Urban Flight Risks Virus Spread", May 29th. The World Economic Forum quotes there are 139 million migration workers in India as of 2017. These people work as construction workers, waiters, cooks, servants in people's homes, drive cabs like Uber and Lyft which is more popular in India, etc. They work and earn money on a daily basis and get paid daily in cash and send a major part of this money to the village they came from. This has helped India bring millions out of poverty. Corona created this problem for India; these migrant laborers lost their livelihood. On the other hand, this is an opportunity also for India, as the world sentiment is against China, and India can bring Chinese manufacturing to India and get all these people jobs in factories.

As per Statsitica, that tracks sectoral distributions over time, Agriculture provides 17% of GDP and employs 43 % of people in India. Industry only has 25% of the workforce and Services has grown to 32%. Indian manufacturing sector should grow big time. This Corona problem can help move people from Agriculture to manufacturing, I wrote the same thing 15 years ago in my first Book and in my doctorate thesis in 2006 from San Francisco that India cannot go directly to services. The reason China grew in manufacturing was because Chinese were not very good in English, otherwise the Indian story would have never happened at all and China would have ruled the software/IT sector and none of the companies- HCL, Wipro, TCS, and Infosys would have happened. Likewise, a lot of Indians living in farmlands and working in fields do not have the skills that can be met in the services sector, but they can do well in the manufacturing sector, where speaking is less important and working with your hands is more important. And that is the place where millions can find work. It can actually consume 140 million Indian migrant workers and wipe out unemployment and poverty from India. Chinamike reports China has 120 million factory workers today in 2020 as they moved to services a few years ago, India has a comparable workforce to take on this task. If one unit employs 100 people we need just 1.4 million units all over India preferably in UP and Bihar as it is poor and can provide cheaper labor for a long time.

After putting the whole world in trouble due to Corona, China experienced an increase in exports by 3.5% in April as compared to April 2019, as reported by the Economist on May 10th. China is not experiencing as bad a situation at all as seen in the USA or Europe, India and the Rest of World (ROW). Not only India suffered downward trend other important economies such as Japan, Brazil, Russia, Iran, Australia, Canada, and Africa did. Let us analyze them one by one quickly.

Japan, the third largest economy in the world and the most technologically advanced country in the world has been humbled by Corona. There are 16000 cases reported so far on May 18th and there has been 750 deaths. Corona arrived in Japan pretty early on 16th the first case was reported it came from Wuhan, later cases came from Europe. The Diamond princess cruise ship was the major starting point of the Corona problem. The reason not many people got impacted in Japan is because they already have a culture of wearing masks in trains and public places. Due to sudden spurt of cases 'Emergency was declared on April 8th" . Japan fought Corona in a different way and put patients in hospitals and had robots to greet them. Even rich and known people got impacted badly by Corona- Aya Yumiko the famous dancer lost her savings due to Corona.

Japan even offered aid to sex workers during peak of Corona crisis. Tokyo Olympic games for 2020 were postponed for the first time in modern history of games creating a big dent in the economy. Japanese are ignoring staying home as men find it very hard to be at home and help the lady in household work. The government announced a 20% stimulus of $1 trillion. On Apr9 th Japan announced it will pay its firms billions of dollars to leave China and relocate to India. Mr Tasuko Honjo, Japan based Nobel Laureate from 2018 says Corona is not natural. Japan is experiencing a 'Coronavirus divorce'- empty apartments are being given for free rents to save marriages. Emergency was removed as cases hit 1/7 of the peak on May 15th. Osaka reports Zero new cases today first time on May 18th. The premier Shinzo Abe has just declared that Japan is entering a recession for the first time in 4& ½ years. Japan is all set to approve Remdesiver as the vaccine to fight Corona.

Brazil initially was not much impacted by the virus and the first case was reported on Feb 26th. Jan 28th was the first incident reported from a student who came back from Wuhan. But it has recently, around May 15th, shot up like crazy and passed Italy and Spain in a number of cases and now has a total infections close to 250000 and 16000 deaths. After the USA, UK, and Russia it is the 4th largest in suffering. The reason is that the Brazilian President Jair Bolsanaro has been criticized for ignoring and avoiding the lockdown. Now Brazil is the hotspot and Corona runs wild in that country.

This all happened due to ignorance not only of the people but the apathy of the President. Now there is a shortage of beds and hospitals suddenly. When people asked the President about this he said 'so what', in a single day Brazil lost 881 people who died. The deaths are rampant, the hospital system has collapsed and the health minister resigned recently. The anti-lockdown President is held responsible for this crime of killing his own people. The good news is that a 99 year old world war II veteran survives Corona and comes back alive from the hospital.

Russia was initially saving itself from Corona but now in the last one month lost that focus and control and now there are 290000 active cases, was second highest, till Brazil saw a sudden jump in cases, and Russia has seen 2700 deaths till May 25th. The first case reported in Russia was on Jan 31st two Chinese citizens who were actually cured and did not die of Corona. Russia also on Feb 23rd reported some cases from the Diamond Princess cruise ship. Even the Prime Minister of Russia tested positive. The election for Putin was postponed due to the Corona onslaught. There are rumors that Putin is joining hands with China in this World War III and supporting China. It is said in Russia there are more deaths and now they are #2 because they have under reported cases. It is said they are Doctoring death toll like it might have happened in China. Russian economy is in big trouble as oil prices have come to a rock bottom and at one time oil futures were trading in the negative as economies world over came to an abrupt stop.

In Iran as of June 3rd there are 160000 confirmed positive cases for Corona and 8000 people reported dead. Iran is also hit hard by sanctions raised by United States President Mr. Trump on top of the Corona crisis. The religious practices also created a scare of increase in cases as people would collect at holy places and congregate creating social distancing issues. The Friday prayer offerings were also an issue. Lot of people who visited the holy sites for example some Indian pilgrims got stranded till they were evacuated by their governments. One Iranian doctor was released by the US recently. It is seen there is a sudden rise in cases being reported again and there is a fear there could be a second wave expected in Iran.

Australia has close to 7000 confirmed cases and total 100 deaths from Corona till June 3rd. It appears Australia had a "win over Corona" and they did not let Corona get over them. The way they handled Corona is a matter of pride for Australian health department. Australia has been so vociferous in denouncing China and saying China created a virus and exported it to the world. They also said it is a man-made virus from China. This angered china a lot and the relations between the two countries are adversely impacted right now. Chinese own many businesses in Australia and the government there moved quickly and changed FDI laws so that Chinese companies do not start buying their companies and s\assets at cheaper prices. Australia joined the United States in condemning China for creating this problem for the whole world. Australia has already entered a recession due to Corona for the first time in 18 years.

Canada has a total of 93000 positive cases reported and total deaths of 7500 as on June 3rd. The first known case of Corona was on January 27th when a Toronto based man had come back from Wuhan, his wife also tested positive the next day. There are lots of international students who are stranded in Canada. International students are major revenue earners which is impacted heavily right now. The Prime Minister of Canada, a highly proactive man, Justin Trudeau has been fighting hard to protect his country from Corona. In fact his wife Sophie tested positive for Corona but came out of it. Life is mostly virtual as schools and colleges are closed.

The Supreme court of Canada is having its hearing and doing "virtual cases". Canadian parliament also went virtual on May 17th. Due to sudden increase of cases in neighboring US, On march 21st Canada closed its border to USA fearing spread of Virus from America- this happened for the first time since Canada was created in 1867. In one strange case in Quebec 31 residents of a retirement home were found dead. Montreal was the epicenter of Corona in Canada. It appears Canada did a better job than the US in fighting Corona. Lots of Trump vs Trudeau comparisons were made by the media. National Microbiology Lab in Winnipeg has been known to be involved in virus research and has some relationship with China. The two states Ontario and Quebec have most reported cases as they are the most populated states in Canada.

Africa as a continent with 1.2 billion people and 54 countries seems to be ahead of the curve and able to fight it out. There are positive and active cases close to 150000 infected in Africa as a continent with 4500 deaths and it appears it has done comparatively a good job with Corona. Feb 14th was the first reported case of Corona in Egypt and in Nigeria. South Africa, Egypt, and Nigeria were the most affected countries in Africa. Most cases arrived from Europe and America than China. It appears China only wanted to damage the rick G7 world with this virus. Media reports indicate Africa will have 27 million people falling into abject poverty due to Corona Tribune reports. World Economic forum WEF reports that Africa is the "least affected continent", even though it is the second largest continent on earth. Africa has 1.5% of world cases but only 0.1% people are dead. WEF reports that WHO studied the reasons and states that Africa has a long History of dealing with polio, measles, Ebola, yellow fever, and influenza. I am thinking Corona for some reason spares poverty stricken areas, similar observations are from migrant laborers in India. Due to prevalence of Tuberculosis, Malaria, Cholera, and HIV in Africa it is expected that people are already immune to fight these diseases and have antibodies already inside them to fight it out as a possible reason for lack of spread. It appears that the theory of 'herd immunity' applies here to Africa much like it applied to India.

Chapter 9

Are Most economies destroyed in the World War III?

Global recession is under way as per latest IMF reports. The world might have lost 10% of its GDP. China stopped the unstoppable growth America was witnessing for 128 months as reported by the National Bureau of Economic research. The unemployment rate that had come down to 3% the lowest in 50 years went up to 20% highest in 100 years- all in less than 90 days. The World Bank reported on June 9th that it is the 'worst downturn in 50 years'. Global economy to shrink by 5.2%, never before so many countries entered into a recession combined, even during the Great depression and two World wars- never seen this before. The World Bank expects the US to drop 6.2% in 2020 and redound to 4% next year 2021. Europe this year 9.1% drop and next year 2021 gain 4.5%. China growth in 2020 is expected to be 1.0% and 6.9% in 2021. Around 70-100 million globally will fall below abject poverty of $1.90 a day. "Global Economy Seen Shrinking in 2020 by 5.2%" WSJ, Josh Zumbrun. Australia is already facing the first recession in 30 years.

It is interesting to quote this article in this context from the Wall Street published on April 28th in the editorial section, titled - "The Century of Bioweapons" written by Walter Russell Mead. He says that if 20th century was about physics where scientists learnt to split the atom and created atomic bombs - make a bomb and drop to kill people, the 21st century is about biology where scientists learnt how to engineer the biological cells and create 'bioweapons', if you look at the start of this century you will notice that trend- SARS 2003, 2009 H1NI, 2012 MERS, Ebola 2016. It comes after every four years. He says this has been there in ancient ages also in 1000 BC, and then when Mongols came and used it in 1346. Even in World War II Allied and Axis powers used it and Japan used it against China in 1946. This Covid 2019 is just an extension of the same philosophy and there is nothing new. The world has to get used to it and be prepared for this uncertain future and loss of lives and peace like in any world war- therefore it is termed World War III by Dr. Sam the author.

The output of the USA is expected to go down by at least $5 trillion in just 2 to 2 & ½ month of Corona's expected lifecycle. In Wuhan it took 75 days or 2& ½ month for things to become normal from the start. Wang Wei says" We are going to measure how successful we are in expanding this Coronavirus to all over the world". China's focus is to destroy the rich world or G7 that produces almost half of world output and is the most advanced and developed part of the world. G7 has the highest net worth per capita. The USA has close to $1.8 trillion GDP each month. Two & half months are significantly lost from March 13th to June 1st, another month from June 1st to June 31st is also expected to be gone as the nation tries to recover. Japan has also come under trouble- thanks to Japanese culture that people there always wear masks that Corona did not grow in Japan as much. Japan now does not like manufacturing anymore in China. Japan has rolled out a $2 trillion dollar stimulus package to revitalize its economy and announced $2 billion to companies that want to move its companies out of China and hopefully to India.

The US economy is expected to drop by 37% in the second quarter of 2020, lowest seen after world war II in 1947 as per Wall Street journal IHS Markit's first quarter tracker shows 4.8% drop in

GDP, the biggest since 2008. Fed dropped the rate to almost Zero percent. Government gave a stimulus of 2.2 trillion dollars. Second quarter is expected to be worse, which means the US economy is officially in a recession, as the official definition of 'recession' is two quarters of negative growth. 26 million Americans filed for unemployment claims. Starbucks reported the first quarter 2020 drop in sales for the first time in 11 years. Personal consumption fell 7.6% steepest drop since 1980.

UN World Food Program Chief Arif Hussain told the Time magazine that the world is facing an 'unprecedented' time like the great depression of 1929 where due to Corona 265 million people are expected to go hungry all over the world. The supply chains failed, farmers had to destroy their produce all over the world, because they could not move it to the markets of consumption due to the lockdown. In 1933 President Roosevelt had to deal with the similar situation where people had no food to eat on one hand and on the other hand food was lying and decaying in the farms. The IMF predicts that the great lockdown could be worse than the recession of the 1930's when farmers had to destroy the milk, eggs, and live stocks. "The Grapes of the Wrath", John Steinbeck's novel of the great depression- if you read that book you will feel like you are in the 2020 Corona crisis where farmers world over are stuck in a limbo.

At the recent G20 virtual Summit it has been decided to spend $5 trillion and do 'whatever it takes' to bring back their economies to the forefront again. Indian Prime Minister Mr Modi was applauded for his contributions to curb Corona. Role of WHO was questioned and there were bickering between USA and China over the problem exported by China to the rest of the world. Corona destroyed the world peace and harmony and created World War III.

The US Congress is extremely concerned about the role played by WHO in this crisis and asked the Director General Mr. Tedros -

WHO helped China disseminate incorrect information and propaganda downplaying the damage from the COVID19 virus, delaying ordering the global public emergency. The committee feels that WHO is serving China rather than serving the world and the US contributed 517$ million to WHO. China under reported cases from Corona and WHO kept supporting China's efforts. China initially said- the virus does not spread 'human-human' and WHO supported China's claim. One month later WHO declared it spreads from Human to human. The Chinese government said it will jail any doctor who spreads wrong information about Corona's spread of 'human- human' disease. The delay by not declaring an emergency by WHO led to 10,000 infections worldwide and 1000 deaths in 19 countries. WHO delayed travel restrictions from and to China - in doing so 430000 people took direct flights from China to the USA. These direct flights got Corona into America and Europe. China kept covering up and provided wrong information and WHO kept praising the efforts of China. The US officially decided to cancel its membership to WHO on June 1st 2020.

The WHO said that the Corona virus may never go away. It will stay as an Endemic for a long time. The world has to get used to it. Smallpox was cured by 1948 but it took 30 years for WHO to eradicate it from the world. Also it says Corona can come back anytime. There are some relapse cases reported in China, South Korea, and other countries. No one knows what will happen as this is a new virus and there is no history and data available to understand its future behavior. In this virus age the predictability of any outcome cannot be assured. The world should have learnt from Ebola and SARS and built a vaccine at that time as a precautionary measure instead of waiting for 2020 when it completely shook the whole world and brought the whole world to a stop paralyzing its apparatus for faster recovery.

FBI Wiretap Requests show Persistent Flaws- WSJ article Apr 1st Wednesday, the FBI has been referred to as Federal Bureau of

Inaccuracy when it comes to handling the intelligence and its failure during the early part of Corona crisis. In the early days of Corona America was in chaos and no one had any idea of what was going on? The FBI that was supposed to keep things under control was in a panic mode and could not disseminate information correctly as people started walking into hospitals and started dying. Wrong information was reaching wrong people at the wrong time creating unnecessary confusion, delays, and deaths. This could have been avoided.

The US economy has seen 25-30 million jobs lost due to Corona in the last few weeks, this is the worst than 2007-2009 timeframe, some say comparable to World war II. The unemployment rate for the quarter has hit 16%. The US economy is expected to take a long time to fully recover. On top of Corona the current riots due to the killing of African American man George Floyd by a white policeman has stirred the whole nation and further complicated the situation. Looting and arson happened after George's death creating problems for businesses and tarnished America's image globally. My friends called me and said- is this what happens in your America.

This pandemic could have been avoided in America if due precaution was taken. Information on the virus pandemic was available for a long time. President George Bush had warned about the potential pandemic as early as 2005. He said if not properly and proactively handled it can spread like a forest fire and become an inferno and can impact hundreds of thousands of people. Interestingly, Dr. Anthony Fauci who is now heading Covid 19 team, was a part of the audience who heard that speech from the then President of America. President Bush even requested to set aside $7 billion and create a website pandemicflu.gov to prepare a 3 pronged strategy to identify, fight, protect American lives, and prevent such a potential pandemic from spreading all over the USA.

Wang Wei is pleased with the developments in the world and states "The world is supposed to come to a standstill. America and Europe are destroyed. Last time it was like this in world war II when everything was gone. We have taken revenge from America and Europe for the ethnic domination of the world for more than a century".

Corona spread and cases are not stopping at all. The world over 8.5 Million confirmed cases are found in 213 countries as of June 3rd and close to 400K yes 400000 people have died globally. The world looks like a place full of pain, suffering, and valley of death. America, Europe, Brazil, Russia, India all have lots of active confirmed cases as of today on June 3rd.

The US tops the list with 1.9 Million cases and close to 110K people dead. I live in a place called Fremont, it has a population of 200K people, so in my calculation half of Fremont is dead. Everyone is wondering how so many people can die in the US alone. This has never happened before. How could China do it? How could they focus on the US and how they created a virus that killed most people in the USA? This possibility cannot be ruled out.

Europe is destroyed significantly- Italy, Spain, Germany, and the United Kingdom are in turmoil. Can you imagine the UK is expected to have the lowest GDP since the last 300 years? This is even worse than World War I and World War II for the United Kingdom. Earlier Italy was having highest number of casualties but then UK suddenly saw a spurt and now is #1 in Europe area, with 39000 dead out of 275000 cases, Italy is # 2 in casualties where the virus killed 33000 people as on June1st. These people died out of a population to close to 233000 people infected by the virus. France stood #3 in Europe with 30000 people dead out of 190000 confirmed cases. This was followed by #4 by Spain which has 27000 people dead out of close to 120000 people impacted. The #5 was Germany close to 8500 people are dead out of close to 185000 reported cases of Corona. Brazil was nowhere there but it appears negligence by the President resulted in 30000 people dead and 530000 confirmed cases. Russia also was not impacted earlier but cases went up even though it has the lowest deaths of 5000 out of 425000 confirmed cases.

When the world is in trouble, China experienced growth in its industries. Vehicle sales in china rose 4.4% in April as compared to last year, as stated by The Economist on May 14th. On the online business side Chinese companies are all doing very well right now-Tencent- 26% rise in quarterly sales, and made $4 billion profit. The Video service increased to 112 million users, and the online music business gained 43M users. As per Wall Street June 2nd, the world lost output but Chinese manufacturing grew in May. China exported the virus and destroyed the world in World War III but saved its economy- Beijing and Shanghai were not touched by the virus- how is that possible? No one understands that and it indicates that there is some strategy here that was played onto the world, keeping in mind China's history of virus for the last 2 decades. One restaurant owner in China has this poster on his wall, as TIF post reports from China, states - "Congratulations to the United States for the Corona Virus and we wish the Pandemic lasts forever in Japan"

New York with 370000 confirmed cases and 24000 dead is the worst hit city with 25% cases in America being in the Top #1 city of America infected people with Corona and dying from Corona. This is many times more deadly than 9/11 that killed 5000 people. New York city looks deserted. Times Square looks like dead with no life- the most happening place in America is suddenly lacking life. The Statue of Liberty is standing there with no one around it questioning if there really is any 'liberty and freedom' left or all are getting in the clutches of the virus. The hospitals appear like slaughterhouses. One person commented that he was not breathing properly and went to the hospital. The doctors and nurses

159

there told him to run away as the hospital instead of helping him out might become the cause of his death. The doctors, nurses, and hospital administration looked very stressed out, worried, under slept, overworked, and seeing very little success with severe cases. Hospital staff is also impacted and dying.

The Economist reports that the world will run on 90% going forward. It means 10% Global GDP will be lost. "The Life after Lockdowns", states that a plunge in 10% of GDP for America would be the worst in close to 80 years since World War II, that is why the author calls this as World War III. There is expectation of a second come back of Corona and in Germany and Danes when they opened shops there, not many people came there, much against the expectations of the city and businesses. Boeing claimed it will take 2-3 years to see the same level of air travel as in 2019. In Europe the largest five economies have 30 million people or 20% of the workforce without a job. The Economist states that as an aftermath of Corona people will not like governments and businesses, and there will be less free enterprise and more regulation about security, safety, health, hygiene, hospitals, health care system in next decade than ever before in the 90% economy, where resources will be scarce.

When Corona reached America and entered Wall Street in Manhattan, the stock market crashed and some compared it to the crash drawing the great depression of 1929 or 2008 crisis Stocks suffer their worst Quarter in 12 years as per WSJ Article- Apr 1st Wednesday. Unemployment rate hit the highest in America for the first time in 12 years. Most of the States are impacted adversely. The Political and economic upheaval Corona has unleashed could last forever. Life will gradually come back to normal but it will leave scars that a lot of people will never forget like 9/11 did or World war II did to the world, it altered the course of human history. Eventually the stock market did come back and from March 25th it started its journey back and now is just 20% down from peak. In fact, people are asking this question, how can so many millions of people be unemployed and still the stock market is going up? There seem to be two Americas within America- the rich America and the working class Americans, both are completely opposite, while ordinary people suffer, the rich become richer. Richer 5% control the balance 95%-this may again be not an economic democracy.

Szlezak et al in their HBR article written on March 5th :"What Coronavirus could mean for the Global Economy" analyzes the impact of Corona on the world economy. They see this as more of a 'real recession' caused by 'wars' etc. that can create a dip in the economy but do not equate it to a 'policy recession' where interest rates are kept higher, they have actually gone down substantially, not compare Corona causing a recession such as the 2008 one to a 'financial crisis' which is gradual and has long term effects. They also talk about three different types of recessions 'V-U-L' shaped recessions and estimate Corona will be more like V shaped where sudden drop will happen but it should come back quickly. In U shaped recession output is lost and comes back slowly. In L shaped output is lost structurally and the economy adjusts to a lower level on a permanent basis. They even compare Corona to other flu such as SARS, 1968 H3N2(Hong Kong Flu), 1958 H2N2(Asian Flu), and 1918 Spanish Flu. I see a L shaped situation also as some output will be lost because of change in peoples' habits and behavior globally.

The Corona virus will have three types of impacts on the economy and leave behind different legacies- indirect hit to confidence in wealth effect, direct hit to consumer confidence, and also create supply side shocks by creating disruptions in distribution channels. Corona can leave a Microeconomic legacy- like the 2003 SARS that created online buying and growth of Alibaba in China- same way Corona can leave e-learning and e-delivery legacy; also the need for smartphone based public health tracking system. On a macroeconomic front Corona is expected to leave a legacy behind for fragmented decentralized global value chains. Political legacy- it might leave a legacy of distrust in handling the crisis and impact US elections.

In Japan, which is the third largest economy in the world, we have witnessed 17000 cases and less than 1000 deaths till June 4th. More than 61 companies have filed for bankruptcies since the Corona virus erupted. They declared an emergency. The habit of wearing masks in normal circumstances helped them keep it low lying. They have kept $2.2 billion dollars for Japanese companies to move production back from China. Japan and China historically do not enjoy a good relationship. China exports around $148 billion of products usually which has taken a hit by 50%. Japan introduced a $1 stimulus package to revive its economy.

The Tokyo Olympics that were scheduled for 2020 from July 23 to August 8th and 205 countries were going to participate in it, having 11091 participants in total performing 339 events had to be cancelled and moved to exactly one year later. Japan had made a lot of investments into preparing for the Olympics, now that whole investment has gone down the drain and has to wait for a year to give any returns. The only other times the Olympics were cancelled were World War I, World War II, and that is why I say there is no reason not to call this Corona attack as World War III. Japan has rolled out a $933 billion Corona plan or 20% of the output of a close to $5 trillion economy to deal with drop in output and employment. The national emergency declared by Japan, stated earlier, to fight the Corona war, was then removed when things became stable. Other world level games are also impacted. Wimbledon has been cancelled and we are not sure if the US Open will happen in August- it has been going on for 139 years now. Century long events came to a halt for the first time.

The United States will try to move away from China. Manufacturing will either be insourced or near sourced. Reshoring will also happen and manufacturing will come back to the USA. Canada and Mexico will have more trade with the United states in the future. India can replace China as a manufacturing hub. China exports $2.5 Trillion of goods, if you shift all this to India, it makes Indian economy a $5 .5 Trillion economy straight away. The US President is banning Chinese companies from doing business in America. The US also stopped the Honk Kong pegging to the dollar, thereby impacting the Chinese currency and exports. I also suspect a lot of manufacturing with go back to America or two reasons- one spread of nationalism created by the furor of Corona and two- so many Americans will lose job that we need a system to get them back on track, as many restaurants and retail stores will close down as people will order food and items online.

The world will start detesting China but like after world war II the United States grew despite the fact many countries did not like it, China will grow and become world leader. China says if the last century belonged to the Statue of liberty then this 21st century belongs to the dragon. After the dust settles down to Corona and the world comes back to normalcy, China will have a better deal in the world, they will have more resources, better economy, better technology and better preparedness than America or Europe to build the future for themselves. The world will no longer be the same palace as it was for the last 100 years, this century will belong to China and they will get it no matter what people think, countries do, it does not impact them. Right now when people are dying, they are claiming land in India, Nepal, Sri Lanka, Pakistan, Hong Kong, South China Sea- they are determined to get what they want. Human death and suffering does not mean anything to them, as if they are not human beings themselves.

Some countries in the world never liked the rise of the USA and always blamed them for dominating the world, creating wars, and supplying arms but now that focus will shift to China. China will have that envious position and have an economic surplus, products that it can sell very cheap to America, Europe, India, Japan, Germany etc. While the USA and Europe will be busy dealing with after effects and shocks created from Corona, China will ascertain its leadership in the world. Most countries will have no other choice but to accept Chinese leadership, only few would be in a position to challenge it and question it. At the end of the day it is all economics, in a rational world all politics is economics.

Josh Jumbrun from IMF publishes an article on WSJ and does a comparative analysis of 2008 recession and 2020 recession. He says that 3% of the global GDP will be gone in the 2020 recession. The world has 90 trillion dollar GDP from that 3% is gone or $2.7 Trillion will be lost. In 2008 only 0.1% drop was there. He says 90% of countries will experience a drop vs the great depression of 2008 when 40% countries experienced it. China's economy is expected to expand 1% or 150 Billion dollars as compared to last year's 6% of 800 Billion. So when the world is shrinking China is expanding. Different studies from different sources suggest the same conclusion. The dragon has arrived. On the other hand the American economy is expected to shrink by 6% or close to $1.2 Trillion in 2020 vs 2.5% in 2009. The EU is expected to shrink by 7.5% compared to 4.5% of 2009. Even at the end of 2021 the IMF expects a 4% shrinkage in the world economy. In the first quarter of 2020 itself banks are experiencing a big drop in their margins. The too big to fail American banks witnessed huge drops- Goldman profits sank by 46%, Citi by 46%, and Bank of America by 45%

Even if the government opens up the economy, the workers will not be willing to come back to work after the Corona crisis is over. There will be a lot of fears for at least 6 months till Dec end-2020 has disappeared from the exciting world calendar. It came and it went. People would not like to take a plane and travel to their far away offices even if companies want them to do so, people would not like to stay in Hotels, or eat in restaurants. There will be structural change in the global economy. Human interaction is not going to be the same anymore.

McKinsey, predicts some trends, based on studies of the Impact of CoronaVirus and reports that it is too early to predict what will happen in the future but there will be a 'new normal' and the old normal will never come back. It talks about five trends we need to watch- 1) there are many places where the Covid19 is getting worse- for example in Brazil as on May 16th, so we do not know how this will unfold. 2) reopening the economies is good for business activity but we do not know if it will help in the long run-there might be a relapse as we saw some cases in China. 3) it is all about testing, tracing, and quarantine - it does not matter how much it costs but human life is very important and we must improve our success by testing more. 4) The R Number or Reproduction rate of the virus is important to understand how fast it will grow but we need to be open to understand new trends- as we cannot compare what we have seen in Hubei and New York and cannot generalize it 5) innovation and clinical trials will help solve problem- hundreds of companies are testing the vaccine, drugs, equipment etc and are collaborating to win the race to fight Corona. New models will emerge on sharing of data, business models, a new normal, and we must be able to separate truth from noise and get more data points to get results to understand patterns.

Not only will the economy shrink due to reduced economic activity but also there will be structural change and some economic output will be lost forever as people will become inward looking, reflective, less social, more isolationist, and the 'family system' will grow. Dating places will reduce, bars will not get the same number and type of people for years which will reduce their business and viability- lot of them will close down. The world will move away from 'conspicuous consumption' as seen in the recent past, Adam Smith capitalism will take a back seat. People will become more religious, more self-contained, read books at home, watch TV, spend time with family, do Zoom calls or Skype calls with friends. The world will be a completely different place. Corona changed it forever. I expect a 5% loss of global GDP around $5 trillion owing to this- that is why I say the 80-90 trillion world will have $5 trillion loss not because people cannot afford it, it is simply that they will not want to buy products. Why will you buy expensive Chanel perfume if you are sitting home whole day and working and buying items from home online. Game ticket sales, airline tickets, movie tickets, hotel stays will go down for at least 2-3 years till it comes back. World will need a stimulus to come out of it and even then it will never be the same again.

Mr Nicolin who leads Ansell, a personal protective equipment company, reports price gouging, in an article on Wall Street on April 30th - "Mask Maker Confronts Surge in Demand", he mentions that the demand has gone up many times, quality has gone down, and Chinese suppliers are charging 20-50% and sometimes 500% higher prices and sometime the equipment supplied are highly inferior in what they can deliver. There are 25000 companies in China that are now selling these masks and other protective equipment. The world is suffering and China is busy making money by selling masks and other PPE. The cost paid for all PPE by each country must also be recovered from China, all costs hospital bills, doctors, nurses - extra pay, etc associated with Corona have to be paid by China. I have suggested some options and formulae to recover the money from China later on in this chapter.

The world economy suddenly came to a screeching halt. I could not even believe it. Till yesterday there was so much excitement and suddenly the world became a sad place, no movements, people locked in their homes, listening and watching on TV thousands of people dying all over the world. This all happened due to China and China should pay 'world retardation tax'- the world lost its momentum and investments made by companies in latest technologies ran away from AI, Blockchain, Quantum Computing etc. World will never be the same place again. If the world does not make these governments responsible you will keep getting Corona again and again as people like Kim Jong Un from North Korea will now take advantage to gain global mileage. Even small nations will be tempted to destroy a large population or a large country. Now with the biowarfare you can be a very small country and cannot contribute much to the world but can destroy the world because you got a 'virus', a bioweapon- nuisance value will be more important than positive contribution. China must pay $10 trillion dollars and the United Nations should help get the money collected and distributed to countries. Or simply nations should stop paying China for its exports done since Corona happened and all pending bills must cover up for the costs. This is a very important issue that must be dealt with seriously and I have given a formula to create distributions for the country and people later on.

China is losing respect in the western world and it will be hard for China to serve these markets in the future as it did in the past. WSJ states in this article "Regard for China Recedes in the West". Europe and America both are relooking at China with a threat. Mr Trump had signed a trade deal for $200 billion for exporting American goods to China but now he does not feel as excited and the thinking has changed. Same is observed in Europe where 45 years of relationship is in jeopardy. Western world feels that China withheld the information and delayed quick response to the crisis and did not give timely information to solve the problem. China is pointing at the H1N1 flu of 2009 that had originated in America and is trying to justify its position on Corona but is not able to convince them.

Two top athletes from China rebuked and denounced the China Communist Party. WSJ article on June 11 th 2020 claims. The Retired soccer star Hao Haidong World cup player and his wife

167

ex badminton world champion twice Ye Zhouyinkg. The couple said from their home in Spain- "the communist party should be kicked off the stage of history", they said they have always been disillusioned by the party and termed them as very unprofessional. Guo Wengui, a fugitive businessman who lives in New York, states that the party is highly corrupt and works in tandem with top businessmen in China. Guo combined with Steve Bannon, Donald Trump's adviser a 'China-hawk' launched a campaign to create "New Federal State of China' and replace the current government. On The 31st anniversary of Tiananmen square movement, they recently proclaimed the declaration of independence from communist party in China. This movement is gaining momentum and support from more than 7 million people on social media. Chinese government has to be careful or may be thrown away from power.

The Chinese defense industry is growing rapidly and will soon overtake the American companies. Last couple of years ago in the top 100 defense companies none of the Chinese companies showed up in the list but in 2018 for the first time in Top 15 there are 5 Chinese companies. For Example AVIC- Aviation Industry Corporation of China is fifth in the list with $ 25 billion in revenue ahead of General Dynamics and BAE systems from USA and UK. It is just trailing behind Raytheon and Northrop Grumman. It makes China's fifth generation J-20 fighter and H20 Stealth bomber planes. Business Insider reports, this is something completely new as the US never had a competitor who is as big as China, earlier Russia was there, but its economic power was never as strong as China has today. It already leads the world in many areas and PLA if it wants today can destroy the whole world. China can destroy countries and control their economies and even directly rule them if not stopped.

World War III must be declared by the United Nations. WEF must be involved or a new organization created to get damages and liabilities settled as WHO and UN seem to have lost its relevance.

International court of Justice In Prague- World War III beneficiaries must fight a lawsuit against the perpetrator, trial must go on, for negligence, hiding information, delaying information to the West. China must pay 20 Trillion dollars as claimed by the US attorney in his lawsuit, spread over the next 10 years to all victims who lost lives and economic output. 10 Trillion Economic output loss and $10 trillion for families of victims who lost their lives globally. The formulae is Benefit to be given to recover loss = LXE= 30 years tax paid, GDP lost immediate + Long term. Loss of life (L)+ Loss of employment (E)+ loss of business (B). Whatever amount countries have paid to businesses, unemployment benefits, insurance on lost lives, etc. must be covered by China. It should be left as an option. If the United Nations fails to recover this money then the governments should stop funding the United Nations. WEC can do this job on behalf of governments for each country.

Another way is that the WEF or United Nations can create 'Corona bonds'- equal to loss of GDP for each country and China buys those bonds. That way the countries that lost output and opportunity will be able to get money. That money can be used to revive and revitalize their economies. It should also pay for loss of life and each family member must get some fixed money from that bond purchase by China. We can also impose a 'Corona Tariff' of 10% for example on all Chinese exports till the loss in GDP is compensated for each country. China must own the problem and pay for it otherwise any country can create a virus and destroy world peace. This World War III needs to be dealt with seriously.

Chapter 10

World war III is Over- New world Order

Wang Wei tells Zhang Wei "When we close this project World War III and are in the last phase in 2022 to 2025, China would have surpassed the US as the largest most sophisticated and technologically advanced nation on earth with the highest GDP and market size". The Project will close only then as a part of "Made in China 2025" initiative. A world dominated by China, Chinese culture, language, technology, companies, brand, and systems awaits human beings. There is no other choice. The writing is on the wall. People can have different opinions and stories about it but once you read what I have to say in this chapter, and if you already do not know it, your eyes will remain wide open for next few hours, if not more.

The economy of China is expected to grow at 7-8% each year to add more than $1 Trillion each year to achieve 'Vision 2025' or "Made in China 2025" and now with Corona it can be achieved earlier in 2022 to become #1 in the world. Everywhere China is dominating the game-Cars, Aero planes, renewables. China is the highest car producer and consumer in the world, as per investopedia. Out of 100 million cars made in the world 25 million or 25% one fourth are made in China and 86% consumed domestically. US is now #2 with 12 million cars. Japan, Germany cars are more of exports but China consumes them means if no one buys their cars outside China, it will still sell. India comes sixth in the list. China consumes almost double the number of cars than the USA since 2018. Even in the airline business China places the highest number of orders for the planes. Boeing and Airbus will come in losses if China stops their order. The number #1client for airplane companies is China. Xiamen Airlines of the Govt of China in 2019 placed orders for 380 Boeing and 863 Airbus planes as per Bloombergquint. China makes its own Aero planes- Comac flew its own planes ARJ 21 and Chenghu Airlines C919, by 2021 China wants to go commercial, as BBC reports, and start operating in Africa and South America, and sell their planes half the price of Boeing. Read on to see that in renewables it is also a similar story.

Once blamed for polluting the world with factories and chimneys and making cheaper bad quality products, now China is the hub in renewables- Wind & solar energy. China wants to change the game and instead of providing cheaper and bad quality products- The "Made in China 2025" is targeted towards making the best products with very high quality unmatched in the world in every sector including the energy sector. The program 2025 has 3 phases by 2025 become a leading brand in 10 key sectors of technological advancement, phase two sell your best and most expensive products to the entire world by 2039 and last phase establish supremacy by 2049 that completes 100 years of China that Mao started a century ago. In renewables China is now #1 leaving America and Japan behind, as reported by Nikkei Asian Review. China's solar energy capacity soared to 700 times in a decade by 2018. China now accounts for 30% of the world's renewables now leaving the US at distant third with 10%. China leads the world with solar panels and 70% of the world's solar panels were made in China in 2017.Japan gets only 8% of its energy from renewable sources, which does not sound like the most technologically advanced country as compared to China.

In the Tech Cold war between US- China, China seems to be catching up very fast. Artificial Intelligence (AI) space currently

China is number 2 right behind the USA, it is fighting very hard to gain advantage over the US by 2022 it wants to take over the USA in patents, research papers, and market value of its AI companies. Tech republic reports that China has 18000 AI engineers as compared to 29000 in the USA in the space of AI. Allen Institute observed after looking at 2 million research papers that 50% of top papers cited China is going to beat the US in 2020, in top 10% research papers cited by 2022 and top 1% of papers cited by 2025. Brookings Institute says whoever wins in AI by 2030 will rule the world in technology. Clearly, in most latest technologies China is giving the USA a run for its money and beating it in their own game.

In the blockchain technology space also China is winning the game with the USA. University of Arkansas finds that China is leaving the US behind in Blockchain technology adoption. China CNIPA filed more than 2200 patents as opposed to 220 by USPTO. China plays a game in patent filing also. US patents are filed globally for 53% of the patents but China only filed 4% of US patents. The US takes 20 months to approve a patent whereas China takes less than 6 months to approve a patent- are we losing the race due to bureaucracy? Most people thought China was more bureaucratic than America but this incidence does not indicate and support that assumption. While China is dominating with its top patent filings from its companies as top 3 filers- China Unicom has 54 patents, Alibaba got 51 patents, NCHAIN filed 37 patents whereas The Top 3 companies from USA side are IBM with only 34 patents, Accenture barely 23, and Mastercard just 9 of them.

In defense technology also China is not behind America. China's J-20 Stealth fighters compare well with American F22 in most features. It is priced at 100$ million as opposed to 330$ million for F22 from America. New Chinese aircraft carriers are 6 times more powerful than America has. China has more warships numbered 300 than America has. China buys more planes than

America. Comac Chinese Aircraft company, as described earlier, set up in 2008 is going to give challenges to Boeing and Airbus in the coming years. China is investing over $1 trillion in 7000 new planes. CNBC reports that China needs to invest $3 trillion in aircraft business over next two decades

China spends one third 220$ billion on Military as compared to $660 Billion by America but has the largest military personnel on earth 2 million people in PLA- People's Liberation Army. That also Chinese reduced in 2019 as they shifted their focus to biowarfare which is very cheap. USA has 20 times nuclear warheads 1350 vs 45. China is defensive on this aspect and does not spend so much, now we can see they have a different strategy, let America waste its money on Nuclear heads, and we will do biowarfare quietly without anyone knowing. Let America shout about their 'nuclear triad'- ballistic missile submarines, nuclear bombers, and ground based missile silos but we will not invest heavily into this. It is not about investment, it is about being smart.

China became the World leader in patent filing beating America for the first time in 40 years. Innovation used to be the baby of America while China was the world's factory. When did China become a leader in innovation? What happened ? Why suddenly so much innovation is coming out of china. Huawei filed 4411 patents, as UK Telegraph reports, taking the top spot in innovation for the third year in a row. Tsinghua University in China today produces more PhD's in electrical and electronics engineering than top American universities. America lost its innovation capability, partly because America tightened its immigration policy and did not let the human capital travel freely into its country during the current administration. China filed 430000 patents as compared to 310,000 from America as per WIPO. America is no more #1 destination for innovation. Thanks to China's zeal to dominate the world and desire to snatch America's sweet spot. Today's world leader in Innovation is China.

'Made in China 2025' was the strategic vision of Chinese premier Li Kequing finalized in 2015, they had a vision of a decade later- what will happen in 2025. How They have a vision till 2049 for a century of growth. China will move away from being a 'cheap factory of the world' to being a globally endowed 'technologically advanced powerhouse engine' of the world. The strategy was to get into the 'High tech' industries which were mostly under the purview of foreign companies then. China decided to increase its footprint in industries such as Pharma, automotive, aerospace, semiconductors, IT, and Robotics .China wanted to compete with America and Germany and was willing to spend $300 billion in this initiative. It appears the bio war was also discussed around this time, as Interestingly around the same time Wuhan lab BSL 4 for Corona was established.

China created the virus, exported it to America and Europe, thousands of people started dying in these countries, whereas Wuhan comes back to normalcy and there are no deaths reported any more. The manufacturing has started again. Actually, China started making the highest number of 'face masks' to sell to the rest of the Corona stricken world. So they even profited from the Virus they created that killed thousands of people globally. It appears like many decades ago, people used to say, oh- America will first create a war and then sell arms to both the sides, and profit from it. Something similar is being seen with masks, hand gloves, ventilators, PPE. Even the gambling place Macau has started again and when the whole world has torn the world apart, Chinese are playing Black Jack and Baccarat in these casinos. China is now determined that with the successful implementation of this plan it will overtake America even before 2025.With Corona and biowarfare, the Vision 2025 is working out, as seen by Li Kequing, great for them. Wang Wei shows satisfaction on this, tells Zhang Wei " that day has come in our lives that we can proudly announce we are world leader #1".

While New York Times Square wears a deserted look, Paris and Rome look devastated, Tourism has already started at the Great Wall of China and local Chinese people can visit there. The restaurants in Wuhan are open again while everyday restaurants and retail stores are closing in America and in Europe in the April-May 2020 time frame. The 'factory of the world' is open in Wuhan to manufacture not only Corona items but also other products and services. The small businesses are open while SBA in America ran out of funds to keep businesses alive by declaring a $350 billion package. The Airlines in China have opened up for domestic flights whereas United, American, Southwest, Virgin are negotiating bankruptcy with respective governments. In this entire story do you sense where the Chinese suffer much like American or European are experiencing right now. If China had accidently created this problem then they would be suffering equally, actually much more, because their population is more than double the size of America and Europe combined. Why 80- 90 people only got impacted in Beijing and Shanghai and more than 100000 in NewYork and London, Rome, etc. There is definitely something fishy here.The two & two do not add up.

Companies are doing well in China right now. Don Weinland and Sherry Fei Ju from Financial Times from Beijing report that Mr. Yu Xiaoning owns a mask making company- The company is named Dawn Polymer, a Chinese company that makes masks and has gained 40% market share in Masks in China in less than 2-3 months, gained 417% stock valuation up to $1.9 Billion. With 40% market share Don Polymer is doing brisk business by selling masks to people who are scared, infected, positive, or dying in America and in Europe from Corona. In Jan alone 2020 the company made 9000000 masks, 10,000 ventilators made and shipped to all over the world. There are five companies in China that are trading at high values as stock markets are down 30-40% in America and Europe. Business is hot in the online education, video streaming, and remote working space in China. The companies in this space are selling like a hot cake not only for the domestic market but for exports to all over the world. Tianjin Teda which makes filtering material for face masks has seen stocks jumped 90% in Shenzhen, Jiangsu Wuzhong, Shandong Dawn Polymer stock gained 89% in Shenzhen stock market. The companies that make drugs for Corona treatment- Porton Pharma solutions, Jiangsu Wuzhong saw a rise of 64% in Shanghai and Shenzhen stock exchange. It is interesting to note that the drugs made for these pharma companies were endorsed by Li Lanjuan, a leading expert from a panel from the National Health Commission, a close associate of Communist Party. In the booming video collaboration and chat market- even 'Bizconf Telecom'- a video conferencing company is doing phenomenal business and saw 68% gain in stock price.

China has global ambition to take on the world and own 5-10% equity of all Fortune 500 companies all over the world. They have bought companies in the UK,USA, Europe, Australia, Canada, India- all over the world. Since Corona happened China is buying companies by hostile takeover bids by putting their own people in the Board of Directors the moment they have the highest equity stake. U.S., Australia, and Japan were among countries that have blocked Huawei from their 5G plans. China's four largest internet companies — BAT and JD.com — have invested US$5.6 billion in 48 U.S. tech deals over the past two years.

China has been buying Australian farmlands, coal mines, airports, water supplies, infrastructure, hospitals, milk companies for almost a decade for now by investing $150 Billion, as per KPMG, in the name of Free Trade agreement ChAFTA. China got the port of Darwin for 99 year lease. In the last five years China scaled up investments in Australia and in 2018-2019 close to 50% of foreign investments came from China and it became #1 trading partner for Australia. Last year in 2019 FIRB allowed China

Mengniu Dairy company to buy Australia Baby food company Bellamy's for $600 Million. Right now China is busy applying to buy distressed assets of Australian companies in aviation, healthcare, freight sector that are suffering from drop in demand due to Coronavirus where 3500 cases are reported as on April15th. Australia is witnessing a recession after 30 years. Right now Air Qantas Freight is one of the major targets as it laid off 20,000 or 2/3rd of its staff due to Covid.

Getting alarmed with all this the Australian Foreign Investments Review Board FIRB made a decision last week only to stop hostile takeover of their companies that will be cheap and vulnerable at this time due to Corona. They said all foreign companies have to apply to the board and wait time to get a response has been increased from 30 days to 6 months. Richard McGregor, an analyst at Lowy Institute, says " vultures are found in many forms and a lot of them are expected from China and other countries to conduct a predatory purchase of our troubled and vulnerable assets". Andrew Hastie- an MP from Australia states that due to Corona- "authoritarian countries will like to snap up the distressed business and assets and we have to stop them from doing so". The same trend is seen in most other countries where China is dominating.

China companies are already doing good business in India. smartphone companies such as oppo, vivo, home appliances- media, automotive- SAIC,Haier- electronics, Healthcare company fosun. After Corona in April only, PBOC increased its stake in leading Indian bank HDFC by buying stocks and raised its position to 17.5 million stocks worth of holding on March end 2020 to the surprise of everyone. People Bank Of China (PBOC) now owns 1% of the bank with a value of 395$ million (3000 crores). The government of India got immediately concerned about this and changed its FDI policy that any country that has a natural border with India has to go through a government approval route and will no longer have automatic approval through single window clearance. They also defined that certain sectors of the economy are prohibited from participation from Foreign Investors- space, defense, atomic energy, etc.

Ananth Krishnan, Visiting Fellow, Brookings India, writes in his article "Following The Money: China Inc's growing stake in India"-China has been steadily increasing its investment in India from 2014 onwards and currently they stand at around $26 billion. In the tech space, the "big three" BAT companies — Baidu, Alibaba, and Tencent — as well as the e-commerce giant Jing Dong or JD.com, have led the investment push in the U.S., where the volume of deals peaked in 2015, reaching almost US$10 billion. Alibaba and Tencent now have been the two biggest investors in India, together participating in funding rounds that exceed US$3 billion. You will be amazed to see that most digital smart futuristic Indian companies are actually either already owned by China or are moving in that direction.

Alibaba investments in India

1.Paytm- US$680 million 2015 via affiliate Ant Financial 40% stake in One97 Communications, parent company that owns online wallet (300 million users).

Additional US$177 million by Alibaba in 2017 further raised its stock in the company.

2.Snapdeal- US$500 million with SoftBank and Foxconn, e-commerce company

3.BigBasket-US$146 million +US$50 million investment,online grocer. 2017

4.Zomato- US$210 million investment in restaurant aggregator and food delivery app

5.Xpressbees- US$35 million in the logistics firm

6.TicketNew-US$17.3 million.entertainment,news,media Alibaba, online ticket platform

7.Dailyhunt- News aggregator app got funding from Chinese tech firm, ByteDance

Tencent's Investments in India

1.Ola-US$400 Mil ride-hailing app

2.Flipkart-US$700 Mil e-commerce platform

3. Dailyhunt- $25 million, Indian news aggregator

(ByteDance,news aggregator China, Jinri Toutiao & popular video-sharing app, Douyin)

4.Hike Messenger- US$175 million fund-raising

5.Practo- US$90 million injection in healthcare startup, additional US$55 million round

6.Byju's-US$40 million, education space,learning app, US$11.4 million next funding

7.Swiggy- US$1 billion, food delivery space, joining Naspers funding round

8.Dream11 Fantasy- US$100 million, plans US$200 million in online gaming

9.Gaana- US$115 million funding round into the music streaming service

10. NewsDog- leading a US$50 million round in aggregator app

Xiaomi has made US$500 million investments in India spread in smaller amounts in more than one hundred different startups. Some of the investments made are as follows:

1. ShareChat- Shunwei Capital, US$8.5 mil. in social media app US$32.5 million.

2. Hungama entertainment- Shunwei's, US$25 million funding round entertainment space

3. KrazyBee- US$8 million round in lending platform

4. ZestMoney- US$13.4 million,

5. US$3 million in a used car seller app,

6. US$1.5 million in the Bengaluru-based Mech Mocha Game Studios

7. US$1 million in another Bengaluru startup, the video app Clip App

8. US$4.3 million funding round for self-publishing platform Pratilipi

9. US$5 million funding round for vernacular knowledge-sharing app Vokal

10. US$5 million investment in medical startup myUpchar

11. US$50 million round for e-commerce platform Meesho

Chinese company TikTok- Douyin's English-version in 2019, grew to over 300 million users in India. UC Browser-Alibaba-owned, is the most widely used mobile browser in India, news aggregation space. In 2018 in all 44 of the 100 most downloaded apps in India were made by Chinese companies

Factories are back in business in China, BMW factory in Germany is closed but in China it is open and employing local people, Chrysler is open, Foxconn is open and making phones and TV sets, Tesla in Fremont is closed but in China it is open in March 2020 and making cars at great speed- Tesla stock went up due to that. This piece may actually help America a little bit but Americans lost jobs in Fremont car factory and car dealerships.

China has a 70-80% business resumption rate and companies are back to life with double speed. The largest city Beijing has 21 million people, less than 100 cases and only 8 deaths, and shanghai 20 million people living there with only 80 cases and only 6 deaths- how come they are untouched by Corona crisis? How come Corona travelled from Wuhan to New York and London, Paris, and Rome and not to Beijing and Shanghai is a question every reader should ask again and again. This clearly indicates there is some relationship between the locations of Corona spread and the Chinese government.

In 2019 for the first time 129 Chinese companies are there in the global Fortune 500 list and the number of American companies is lesser at 121 only. According to Geoff Colvin, While American companies account for 28.8% of Global revenue of Fortune 500 in 2019 and China accounts for 25.6% by next year Corona will help to change the game forever. This has happened for the first time since World War II that America is being challenged and being replaced by China in most areas of significance. Chinese companies have a bigger market and higher revenue than American companies because they serve 1.4 Billion companies internally and externally billions of dollars. On the other hand, American companies are not allowed freely to do business in China- so companies like Google, Facebook, Apple, Netflix,etc that are growing everywhere in India and the world are actually struggling in China. Their pie is kept smaller. This is by Chinese design.

China's economy has a GDP of $14.14 trillion dollars and the USA has $21.44 Trillion dollars in 2019. On Purchase power parity basis, Investopedia, the leading portal on investments and economics, reports on Top 10 economies of the world in 2020, China has $27.31 trillion is already ahead of America $21.44 and bigger by more than 30%. On Straight terms China is determined to cross the US economy by 2025, Corona will help achieve that goal faster. The gap is shrinking by the day and China seems to have a perfect plan which is meticulously executed without failures. Sometimes execution is even inhuman but as long as it brings growth, Chinese government accepts that.

The whole world has been destroyed in World War III and now the Chinese companies can dump the cheapest products all over the world via online channels such as Amazon, Alibaba etc. China is emerging as #1 country in the world as 2500 people are dying each day in America and Europe. In future they will be able to copy more products and sell worldwide. Once American and European companies file for bankruptcy due to the Corona problem created, China will fill the gap and provide cheaper products as people cannot afford expensive products that USA and Europe makes especially during a recession. In April alone 560 companies filed Chapter 11 bankruptcy in America and the judges were scared how will America recover if this continues. Imagine JC Penny filed for bankruptcy recently- but a lot of those suppliers will still be in America via some Chinese company. JCrew, Neiman Marcus, Hertz, Pier1, are some other similar companies that filed bankruptcy and business will shift to some other company. This is the perfect design of this game played by China on the world.

The Chinese companies have copied the American model and made their companies such as Alibaba, Tencent, Baidu, We Chat highly successful. The companies such as Sinopharm will dominate in medicine area around the world. Xiaomi will dominate the world in consumer electronics. Geely a car company will make new energy electric vehicles at half the price of Tesla. Huawei which was banned by America will be leading the world in semiconductors, telecommunications and consumer electronics. Baidu is expected to drive AI and autonomous vehicles globally. Jack Ma the equivalent of Jeff Bezos from America who created Alibaba will dominate e-commerce. Another company Tencent will rule the e-commerce space. Megvii, a relatively unknown company, will feed future AI based business models. A lot of their growth may not come from USA and Europe right now but Africa, South Africa, South America needs these companies to get basic products at cheaper rates that China can only provide as compared to USA & Europe.

China devalues its currency constantly to increase exports from China by making Chinese goods cheaper in America and Europe. The Chinese 'currency weaponization' is its trade war tool which seems very effective. Kathy Lien from CNBC reports that on August 5th, 2019 that China devalued its currency and made it lowest in 11 years against the US dollar plunging US stocks by 800 points on a single day. This was to help Chinese exports but Mr. Trump started imposing tariffs on exports, this has created a cash flow problem for China. USA giving incentives and sanctions can reduce free movement of the currency markets and 'weaponize' its currency creating opportunities for controlled trade instead of free trade. China weaponizes its currency by keeping it lower to help exports.

China has embarked on the "Project of the Century" "Belt and Road " program Or BRI- Border Road Initiative in 2013 which covers 70 countries in Africa, Europe, Asia. China is building infrastructure on this route. Centuries ago China used to dominate the world trade via the Silk route. Xi Jinping the Chinese premier, wanted to emulate that again after thousands of years. This project will give direct access to world markets for China- they can sell their products and services directly into these markets. This road passes through 70 countries and connects them in terms of sharing resources. Forbes article states that It covers 60% of the world's population, 30% of world GDP and 75% of energy resources of the world. China wants to cover 137 countries through this road. It is speculated that China wants to control Europe, Asia, and Afrcia through this huge project. It is expected to be for $1 trillion and some estimates state it to even worth $8 trillion in investments. China gives loans to countries to build the infrastructure and when they default China takes over their assets. Srilanka, Pakistan, Africa and many countries are facing this problem. In Africa China invested more than $300 billion towards this program.

Africa has to pay more than 300$ billion to China due to this program of BRI. Sri Lanka accepted development of infrastructure from China, tools loans from them, and could not pay for it, so they defaulted, they ended up signing their port for 99 year lease to China and 15000 acres of land around it. Zambia has a similar problem where they could not pay such loans as the loans rose to 100% of their GDP and they had to offer their copper mines in return for the loan repayments. The 'debt trap diplomacy', as Felix Chang from Foreign Policy Research Institute refers, says will only bring most countries under the vicious designs of China .China is now becoming the "world's loan shark" as quoted by New York Times in 2019. There are predatory 'hidden loans' that countries are not able to understand till they get into the actual implementation of the projects. In Pakistan the BRI program put a squeeze in the economy of the country and they started defaulting- it changed from an economic boosting program to a military deal to help Pakistan from India. Pakistan signed infrastructure projects of $60 billion but less than 30% through into the loan program, could not pay for them, defaulted, and is now standing at 19$ billion in interest only, also Pakistan asked them to set up factories in lieu of loans owed for $1 billion, in fact Pakistan went ahead and took an emergency loan of $2 billion from china for development activities and to set up Chinese factories. Also an emergency bail out loan of $2 billion was also taken to fight the balance of payment crisis- so China has made inroads into the inner working of the country now.

The Chinese Virus has struck with unprecedented scale and ferocity with exponential spread. China will achieve 6-8% growth easily once Corona destroys the other economies and can even touch 10% growth rate- this means adding more $1 trillion each year. Once Europe and America is destroyed they will need ready made products at cheaper prices as their economies will not have the resources to produce it. They will end up becoming consumers for these products and services from Chinese manufacturers. The Corona design will ensure that no matter what America and Europe does they become a net debtor and look up to China all the time for support. This is a Machiavellian strategy masterminded by Mr Wang Wei, as he says to Zhange Wei- " No matter what they try to do, they are going to be a net loser, and we will be a winner, so we have beaten them in this game of Chess, by calculating all their moves, and having a ready made solution for all possible scenarios, America is doomed".

The size of Chinese economy will grow faster in 2021 China will overtake America as the largest economy in the world by 2022-2023. Once that happens the currency markets will be redefined and the US dollar will not any longer be the leader. The Bretton woods conference rule created in 1945 will change forever. The Chinese government vision 2025 - "Made in China 2025". 'De-throning the US dollar', an article published on the Economist, states that China is trying very hard to promote its own currency exchange system like CLIPS but it has nor been successful till now. Chinese currency became a reserve currency in Oct 2016 and has 11% SDR Special Drawing rights in the basket of currencies globally. In the future most transactions will be online and digital currency is expected to replace paper money, bitcoin or crypto currency has a lot of future but it is early for that right now. Because China has four times the population Of USA, and more people are buying online and say using bitcoin in future or some other currency that digital currency will become #1 in the world just because of the number of transactions. With Corona the world has become more conservative and trying new things such as bitcoins etc and taking more risks has been pushed away to the back burner.

There is another dimension to China's growth In the new world order, not only China will dominate the world, internally Chinese men will have more share of that growth than the woman who will suffer more. As a result of Corona quarantine people stayed home and instead of having a happy married life got into bullying relationships that ended up being divorced. The increase in Divorce rate will impact women more in China, reduce their employability, bargaining power, financial position, and social standing. Same trends will be visible in Japan, New York, Los Angeles, San Francisco, and Chicago. Women stand to lose due to Corona globally.

In the new world order we will have to all get used to being lied and being cheated by China. It is not uncommon for China lying and misrepresenting facts and bribing WHO, UNO, University professors in America and elsewhere to get what they want. China has not been transparent about the number of deaths, according to one report 21 million phone subscribers disappeared in China during the Corona crisis. Is China underreporting the whole Corona fiasco they created to avoid blame game? How can Beijing and Shanghai be not impacted at all by Corona. The US Congress has asked WHO Director General to provide information why he supported China in hiding the crisis and showcasing China as a nice country when it had sinister designs to hurt America and Europe. China has built its relationships with its stakeholders and can manipulate them as they chose. This will make it difficult to solve global problems such as climate change, de-escalation of arms, de-risking countries from future virus attacks, etc where building global consensus is very important.

Forbes correspondent from the Middle East Khouloud Al Omien writes an article "Are we witnessing the awakening of a new world order? She argues that once all this is over will we go back to the world as it used to be and business as usual or the world will be completely altered forever- and there will be a new turning point. She points out many new trends will emerge but #1 finding is that China will become stronger than the USA. The world will many new things such as have more automated production systems, more work from home using technology, decrease in business travel, governments will introduce more e-services like Dubai did, more investments in health care, enhanced government trust as they try to help people and businesses, social behavior change towards more giving, improved environment by reducing carbon emissions, more shift from brick mortar schools to online education systems, etc. The list looks good and interesting to me.

But the big question is - Will America let this happen? China hegemony will not be tolerated by civilized economies. Even now that the world economy has been destroyed by spreading Coronavirus- will America jump back as the savior of the world. The way it bounced back from the 9/11 and 2008 recession-will it emerge back to serve humanity with all humility. Will it have the resources to dominate again or China would have grown its tentacles like an octopus into the world markets. Will the dragon replace the Statue of Liberty as The global symbol of growth, peace, and prosperity. We will see. Time will tell us.

The world is expected to shrink in economic activity, the US is expected to have a 20% loss in GDP in the second quarter of 2020 and is expected to hit 10% unemployment rate for 2020. On an annual basis it will be 5.6% GDP loss or more than $1 Trillion, worse than the World War II of 1946. There will be a structural change in the world wide economies and I suspect very few people would like to take a flight, go to a Foreign land- see the wonders of the world, stay in a hotel. This behavior shift alone will impact economic loss of potential of $5 Trillion as per my calculations. This could be a permanent shift. China wanted to capture the world but they did not realize human beings work on emotions- the success of America and Europe is not economic hegemony but freedom and care for its citizens. How will China keep growing its economy if the world economy goes in recession and people do not buy its products and services? Exports still form 20% of China's GDP and in case of World recession it will mean an impact from the $3 trillion export kitty.

As China grows. The World Will Shrink in 2020 and in 2021. According to my calculations, as stated earlier, to further reiterate and drive my point, China created a virus with a price tag of "$10 Trillion CoronaVirus"- called Corona and dropped the bomb like America did on Hiroshima and Nagasaki in 1942 World war II. Well this bomb was not just dropped at one place but this bomb hit everywhere in 213 countries in 75 days, and $10 Trillion is lost as a result globally. Now China wants to help in rebuilding those countries, sell their products, build their infrastructure, buy their companies, run their governments, export some from their billion plus people there, and pick up troubles assets at throw away prices. The losses expected, as per my calculations for each country, are as under:

2020-2021 Loss Report -10 Trillion in World Economy

(based on GDP rank globally in 2019)

1.USA- Loss $4- 5 Trillion

2. China- Gain- $2-3 Trillion

3. Japan- Loss $1 Trillion

4. Germany- Loss $500 Billion

5. India- Loss $400 Billion

6. UK- Loss $500 Billion

7. France- Loss $300 Billion

8.Italy- Loss $300 Billion

9.Spain- Loss $250 Billion

10. Russia- Loss $250 Billion

11.ROW- Loss $500 Billion

World TOTAL- $6 Trillion Loss Approximately

Structural change/potential loss-$5trillion-Total loss/impact $10Trillion Approximately

If we analyze the above data, in nutshell, while the world moves back 10$ Trillion, China moves forward and will gain GDP and size and become the largest world economy in 2022-23 much ahead of their vision of "Made in China 2025". No study as of now measures the permanent impact of Covid 19 on human behavior and its impact on drop in consumption and hence needed production on the supply side to match it but I can tell you that it will be humongous and will shift the world focus. The only thing that can stop this from happening is if the whole world got together and stopped buying Chinese products the chances of which seem less. Mr. Trump recently invited G7 members for a meeting and included India, Australia, and South Korea in that list but kept China away- this is an important event that might shape things that will happen in the future. China got highly angry with this Trump initiative and showed its strength in the South China sea, Hongkong, and Taiwan.

It appears that South Korea, Australia, Japan, and Singapore did a good job of recovery from Coronavirus- putting their country back to work- and seems to be good model to follow, as reported by World Economic Forum- "How The Fourth Industrial Revolution Can Help us Beat Covid19". The report says using AI and Data Mining to understand the spread of Covid helped Taiwan, South Korea, and other countries to contain it in a timely fashion. It says AI and leadership are the key factors for success. As on May 1st there were no new reported cases of Corona in South Korea. The South Korean way of handling the situation by reducing the impact of the virus on society and economy can be learnt and applied in the future. We can have a model built to be used for future reference with more predictability. Although, there has been a recent episode in South Korea where people went to a bar that led to 90 people being infected. This happened in Mid May 2020 itself so we are not sure if the South Korean model is the best one but it appears they did do a good job and contained the spread of virus and did not let it impact its economy in a big way.

As per IMF report China and India are the only two countries that are expected to grow in 2021 due to the impact of Corona. China will grow 1.2% in 2020 and 9.2% in 2021 adding more than $1 trillion to its output where the US will lose more than

$1 trillion in output. India will grow 0% in 2020 but in 2021 it is expected to grow 7.9%

Future trends

In the future trends we will see that Taiwan & Hong Kong will see unrest as America will try to establish its lost position and recover from China. Balance of power has to be established and America has lost credibility in the international markets due to its vulnerability to get so much impacted owing to a small virus. The United States is even considering severing its ties completely with China. Mr Trump even talked about a 'Reshoring fund' of 25$ billion to bring back American companies from China to the USA. Chinese companies are being banned from doing business in America. Indian celebrities met recently and requested people on TV to boycott Chinese goods as China creates border skirmishes with India in the Leh area.

There is a large social and civil unrest expected in China like the one that happened in Tiananmen square in 1989. The way Chinese government handled the citizens of the country during the Corona crisis has enraged the public, and they are not going to sit quiet. The lady called 'Fang Fang' spread a lot of word against the ills of the government. She could be the next person to challenge the government if Western powers back her up. In China the success of the country is just apparently a government success-the people are not engaged in the political process at all. In America an African American lady named Karen from Chicago Tribune, recently interviewed President Trump and asked very pointed questions to undermine the President on Black Lives Matter movement in America- in China no one can dare question the Communist Party leadership like this- it is dictatorship. It must collapse. It does not help the people. People are mere spectators of China's government activities. Organizations like Falun Gong, a spiritual cult group, are getting active, they have been banned by China two decades ago, but now suddenly it is picking up in the movement in China. Five Eye can support such an action.

Yuval Noah Harari the noted historian analyzes what happens after Corona- How it will change the world order in coming years and decades.

Biometric devices and bracelets will become popular. They will also be dangerous as the government can know where you went, whom you met, and how it relates to epidemics, political campaigns etc. He states that the new police will be 'soap police' creating more awareness for cleanliness and better personal hygiene. Earlier policing was more about chasing thieves, but modern policing will also add one major function if not move completely from such a behavior to 'soap police' checking health hazards of people in local communities and public places. Technology will be used in the future to understand body temperature and blood pressure by using mobile applications and communicate to hospitals and authorities. This can help as well as create privacy and security problems. Imagine insurance companies selling insurance plans based on real time data from these applications that track health levels of different population segments.

World needs a Global plan to run the future. It is required but it appears that Corona will leave a fragmented world. This will reduce travel and globalization and more nationalization. The scars of Corona will remain for a very long time and shape the future of the new world. Donald Trump has invited world leaders for the G7 meeting, and included India, Australia, Korea in that meeting but excluded China in that meeting. Maybe he has some plans, but we do need a unified world, not a fragmented world. While nationalism is always good and in World Wars it gets more impetus but we live in a global world now. America needed Chloroquine that India provided. There might be many such synergies. Only 2 countries make Aero planes: France and the United States- it is duopoly- do we want to lose what the theory of 'comparative advantage' proposed?

Earlier the US stood for humanity and if you look at 2008 financial crisis or Ebola crisis in 2014, the US led the world. Now the US cares more about its own people than the world. We need global leadership. Recently there was a meeting of G7 nations, America decided not to lead, and China came forward as a leader, they could not reach any conclusions in this meeting. This is another problem that the world is going to face in the future. If we do not create good strong leaders bad will dominate. Does World need a world leader? Who that country should be? How democratic that country is? Are they dictators? All these questions have to be answered. In my opinion, the world does need leadership, and the world does need a constructive consensus on issues rather than being selfish, all the time. A new organization is needed to replace UNO.

A lot of people in the western world -America and Europe will not come back to work. They witnessed the worst thing in their lifetime that now dissuade them from working. I have this friend David who lives in the Bay Area, i was talking to him, he said he wants to retire now, he is actually 63 years old and had plans to world for another 4-5 years but now the family decided to downsize, cut their needs, but chose to lead a minimalist life. I asked David- do you not have bills to pay or are you not ambitious anymore as I used to see you always being busy, travelling and doing something or the other. What David told me made me open my eyes wide and think about the ramifications of the conversation with him. He said- "Sam, I do not need to work anymore, me and my wife, we sat down and planned out everything, we saw so many people dying, we lost interest in everything material, what is the purpose of life, to keep chasing money, and one day suddenly some stupid virus will come from stupid country China or wherever and you will die?" This is the beginning of an end, I could totally relate to him and could generalize this to so many baby boomers I personally know in America- I think a lot of them will do the same thing. There will be loss of interest in economic activity in the western world. Not to mention mental diseases will increase, more drugs, narcotics, and people will be smoking more weed and doing more cannabis stuff to ease out tensions that Corona created and scars it will leave behind.

Due to Corona many US and European companies are asking their employees to work from home. They have even told the employees that they do not have to come to office to work for 2020 and some even 2021. Some companies have decided to give away their rental office leases to save millions of dollars and now they are floating these units in the market. Some other companies are going to sell the real estate or even rent it out and make money out of it. After six months or so, they will fire employees WFH and hire people in India, Vietnam, Philippines, etc. as those people can be hired for one fourth the price of an American employee, this is not good for America and Europe in the long term- more jobs will be outsourced. Employees should insist on coming and working from office or demand rent from their companies to utilize it for office purposes, now this will further aggravate employers and give more reasons to shift jobs to cheaper locations. Americans & Europeans have to also think of the big picture- car sales, gas stations, office restaurants waiters, buying groceries, picking and dropping kids- all these activities keep the economy growing. The economy must be kept alive and all its sectors must function as before. On the other hand this will surely help countries like India, Philippines , Mexico, Canada etc.

In days to come people will not like to travel, as said earlier, as easily as they did in the last few years. 2019 was probably the best year for airlines, hotel, cab companies- when they look back in

2020-2022. The travel was very easy- book a flight, get an Uber, reach your destination hotel, or stay in a B&B. I met a couple in San Francisco who managed their entire trip from Europe in less than 2000 Euros. Not anymore, people will be very selective about how they travel, where they travel, and when they are putting themselves at a risk. It will take at least 2 years for the hotel, airline companies to get back to business as it was before the Corona crisis. Not only Corona created social distancing, it shifted the behavior of people by telling them travel may be actually risky and there are many other options available. People would like to do Zoom meetings and avoid travel. Some people will leave their jobs because they require travel. New job openings- people will negotiate if they have to travel or not before they accept the job offer. Companies will also accept it as the result obtained might be similar and the cost saving higher as economies will suffer retarded growth for at least 1-2 years.

Technology firms in America are having a good time during the corona crisis, the new trend is that work from home- Zoom, Go To Meeting, SKpye, Slack. WSJ reports that "The Tech Companies are suddenly heroes for now" Food delivery companies such as Doordash and Grubhub will grow are doing good business right now. Facebook had lots of people leaving in 2017 but now they are coming back. Instagram and snapchat are experiencing growth. Because people cannot go to stores- Amazon is getting more visitors and more sales and stock went up big time when all was going down. It appears all internet based online ecommerce companies are going to win the Corona war in the new world order. Same thing is witnessed in China, India and other places. Laid off Americans and Europeans can find jobs in these companies.

Recently American companies such Google, Facebook, Twitter, Sales Force, etc declared work from home for the entire 2020 or some even for 2021. Right now it is a welcome step and I discussed this earlier also, but beware this will eventually lead to more outsourcing. People in America and Europe have to learn to come to office and work from there otherwise if they can work from home, their jobs will not be safe, I am repeating this to make my point well understood, because they can be done from India for 10-20% of the cost. Most Americans and Europeans are requested to drive to their workplace and ask their employers not to give away their offices. Human Face- Face physical interaction must continue to keep America alive.

China GDP is still going to be positive. They said they will not set a target in May Conclave but it is a lie. They already set a target but did not tell the world because the number is very high and will attract negative world views, how can China grow when all countries are in shambles? You will see this in Dec 2020. China will report a growth of 6-8 % for 2020 while American companies Hertz, JCPenney, Jcrew, Neiman Marcus file bankruptcy. What China says and does are two completely different and 'diametrically opposite' things. If they have to go right they will tell the world they decided to go right. The world will believe them. Then they will laugh at it internally and as Wang Wei says" Why did they believe in it, why they are so stupid? Why do they believe in what the enemy says? They are dumb people, and that is why world needs a smart strategist and thinker nation like China as their undisputed ruler". They will actually say they are going 'right' while they intend to go 'left', so that people get confused, cannot plan their strategies and in case of disaster they will be caught 'off guard'- that is what happened with the Corona disaster.

China Marches on to be #1 in the world.

China's parliament the National People's Congress met for a Conclave on May 22nd when the world was engulfed in Corona to discuss the new world order post World War III. The meeting lasted for 10 days and 5000 thousands of people normally joined this meeting. This meeting always announces the GDP projections but this time it did not announce the GDP for next 2-3 years and formally did not declare that - what we also do not know and they did probably declare internally- The new world leader #1 is - China and The New initiatives of the World Leader #1 China. The New world order formally came into place on this day of May 22nd. We all must not forget this date. It changed the world for ever in our lifetimes. The Chinese government did not declare the GDP growth rates this time, and to me the reason is that they do have plans but do not want the world to know any more so it might have been a quiet discussion and I can bet it was around 6-8% and maybe even 10% growth rate for 2020. Congratulations and Welcome to the New World Order as an aftermath of World War III: The Corona biowarfare- China won, World Lost!!!

Chapter 11

How to deal with Corona? Getting Ready for Life After Corona Fully Equipped

This Chapter is like a User Manual on how a person can use this chapter to fight Corona and come out successfully, so it is written in third person.

Do you sometimes feel 'I feel lonely, left out, single, isolated, and sad and often feel I should go back to my country side place, or go stay with my parents". I find myself a misfit and do not know what to do with myself. Suddenly I find lacking skills and preparedness to deal with this thing I didn't even know in my life 60 days ago something will happen that will have such an impact. It has altered everything in my life. It has even changed the way I think and feel as a human being. I am struggling to feel better, pass time in a fruitful way.

How do I deal with Corona and make myself a better professional and a better human being, if not a holistic human being.

Corona will change the world forever. Social distancing will change countries, industries, businesses, cultures, and people's lives.

If you work in the following industries your life is going to be in trouble. There are good 20-25% chances that your job will be lost forever- Airlines, hotels, coffee shops, restaurants, movie theaters, etc. Think this way- if your employers require physical collaboration to get things done- they will suffer. Well that is where most jobs are in the society. Think about Stadiums- games, athletes, sporting events, standup comedy shows, etc. All this will have to wait a lot to come back to normal. There will be no old normal. It will be a new normal- 10% less than old one. These industries will experience a drop of 20-25% in demand over the next 6-12 months. Afterwards in 1-2 years also there will be a 10% drop in their business till they innovate and create new business models. Move away quickly from these types of companies if you work there today.

People will not like public places, congested places, metro trains, ferries etc. The demand for cars will go up as people who travel in buses or metro will now prefer private vehicles. People who live nearby will take a bike to work or go grocery shopping. Religion will get a beating as less people will visit churches, mosques, temples etc. Tourist places such as Times Square, London, Rome, San Francisco etc will have major demand loss. Beijing, Shanghai, Mumbai, New York, Los Angeles all these places will have lesser tourists coming over for next 2-3 years at least if not more. Birthday parties, marriage parties, anniversaries will be celebrated at home and will be less social than before. Simply put people will become less social and more home oriented.

Start shifting your career to new generation companies, the post corona world order will be completely different. Some people think life will come back to normal as it was, that is not true. Companies in the online space will grow. Companies such as Amazon, Google, Netflix, Facebook, Doordash, Grubhub, will grow. Move your career towards these companies. Learn digital marketing skills. People will work from home, eat at home, have friends come over for dinner, watch movies at home, spend more time with friends and family. The world will be conservative again once more. Build skills in this area. Start building skills that these companies need. If you spent all your life working in a restaurant or a bar- well time has come that you start thinking out of the box and start reinventing yourself. Get new skills.

A lot of people live as a single and struggle being alone and need social collaboration. For these sets of people Meditation will really help. Some people are not just meant for socializing and going out and making friends is not easy for them- even in normal times they find it hard, with post Corona, it will be harder for them, as opportunities will shrink. Due to isolation there will be an increase in mental diseases, depression, melancholy, neurotic and psychotic disorders will increase. Some people will retort to excessive alcoholism, food abuse, and cannabis or drug/substance addiction will increase. Looking inwards and meditation will help. If you close your eyes and sit in a relaxed mode for just 2-3 minutes, take deep breaths, try becoming thoughtless, it will help a lot- you will see that your mind will become more relaxed. I take 50 deep intense breaths in 1 minute of time- deep inhaling and exhaling- this helps me a lot to calm down and be relaxed.

People like me who love to spend time in a Starbucks sipping coffee and have a lot of my meetings there will change. I also love to go to bars in Fremont and grab a drink, this habit will also change for considerable time. Probably people will have coffee at home and alcohol at home. Do virtual meetings with their clients. Drive thru bars will emerge and coffee shops will also become more drive thru style. My favorite Sunday farmers market, where I go and grab food stuff, vegetables, fruits- will probably go online. I will buy more stuff on Amazon and order more delivery of food by Doordash.

Instead of GDP countries will start looking at new metrics like (GHP)- Gross Happiness Product- happiness produced each year in a country. HDI could be one indicator but right now it is heavily impacted by 'conspicuous consumption'. A country can be materially not as rich but might be higher on the happiness index. I would like to quote Philip Kotler here, who is the father of marketing management, and wrote an article recently- "The Consumer in the Age of Corona", he states that countries should look at GDH (Gross Domestic Happiness) and GDW (Gross

Domestic Wellness) than just GDP, he states 'anti-consumerism' will grow much against the wishes of capitalism that thrived till now. Kotler states there are five types of anti-consumerists now post Corona- Life simplifiers (reduce complexity and make it cheaper), degrowth activists (why grow? What for?), climate activists (claiming earth cannot support consumerism), food choosers (turn vegetarian), conservationists (conserve nature and products). He says there should be redistribution of wealth and the richest 1% such as CEO's etc should be taxed more to pay for 99% under them.

Materialism and capitalism will reduce post Corona as it has taught us the value of human life. The value of something you do not have or you are going to lose, or you might lose, or you might not have it in the future, is always going to be higher than before. We will value more what we have than chasing things in the outside world. People should develop new skills such as playing music, reading books, watching more TV, exercising, etc. To build a more holistic personality as happiness no more will come only from how many dollars you make but from how you will spend those dollars and have a better quality of life. You have to become your own friend- your alter ego has to talk to you and you have to play with it and interact with it.

We will have to deal with more Uncertainty, more complexity, and more people skills will be required at the family level. People spend more time on computers and laptops, phones, texting, Facetime than physically meeting. More friends parties will be online parties. A cake shop will have cake delivered to all people from the guest list once the birthday boy cuts the cake virtually.

Exercising will really help in keeping mental balance post Corona. I walk everyday for 45 minutes and want to increase it to 1 hour a day. If walking one hour a day keeps me healthy and away from doctors, hospitals, arthritis, heart disease, mood swing, gives me higher productivity- why would I not do that. In Fact the way I fought Corona was by increasing my body immunity through exercise. I would recommend that we spend more time exercising and getting back in shape otherwise the chances of falling prey to obesity and diseases are higher as we have not much to do. There will not be many opportunities and desire to "Go places far away". Corona and viruses like it now are the future, they can come from China, North Korea, Pakistan, Mexico and probably anywhere. In the new world anyone can easily destroy you. So equanimity of mind is the biggest asset to have.

Alcohol consumption is expected to go up as people will think more about their loss of family and friends during the corona crisis. Boredom and loneliness will also force people for alcohol. Local nearby stores will increase and people will not like to go too far away to specialty stores. Mom and pop stores will come back as they are nearby, cheap, and do not get big crowds. Some people who lost jobs can actually start a small business of coffee retailing, donuts etc. as people would like to go to the next door guy, the friendly guy who serves clean food, with lots of hygiene.

We will also have to exercise and reduce our food intake and control it to keep it low. Food companies will be pushing a lot of food on us via TV sets and delivered free to our homes as many of their physical outlets will experience drop in walk-ins. But exercising restraint and staying away from temptations will help. I lost 10-15 pounds since Corona started. I stopped drinking alcohol because I thought I should spend the rest of my life drinking alcohol and worry about how the world is going to end after world war III or do something positive and concrete to improve the quality of my life. Then I sat down and started writing this book. Obesity is expected to increase as people eat more when they have nothing to do. I recommend daily exercise schedules.

We will spend more time with Family and a selected group of people we know as friends. As a happy person we should learn to be content with our families. Talk more with your spouse, girlfriend, boyfriend, kids, brothers, sisters, mother, father, etc. It is time we spend quality time with our people whom we love the most. Time has come to show and feel loved by your near and dear ones.

Because people will be staying more at home, the divorce rates will increase. In Japan divorce rate and suicide rate both have increased post Corona. There will be more fights so people have to learn 'listening skills'. We all need to listen more and talk less. Thep problem is we all like to talk more and listen less. We have to reverse this habit with practice. Sometimes I imagine that someone came and stitched my lips so I cannot speak at all. This practice has helped me listen more and observe more. By talking too much we create problems for ourselves and believe me I am one of those only. By listening we know what is going on in other people's life. We will be more successful in life if we listen to what others are doing and how they are living their lives than telling the whole world how good I am and you all must listen to me all the time. We must also work on improving our Conflict resolution skills and respect individual differences.

We were all born great and have lived a great life. So have others. Individuals will always be different. We can be successful if we respect each other and the fact that there is " no best one way of doing things", even small things like picking up a plate and setting up dinner for the family can be done in many different ways- and we do not have to be right all the time. "My way or highway" approach will not help. I have two daughters Eva- Eti, twins, born from the same egg- monozygotic, from the same parents, lived under the same roof but they have completely different personalities. No two human beings are the same and we cannot expect them to think, feel, and live my way. I wish 'he could be a little different and behave like me', is not going to fly. He is unique and that is why you love him so do not try to make him fall in your line. Similarly, if you love a woman, respect her. Be with her. Do not force her to change- love the way she is, be happy. Do not teach her, do not question her. Accept her the way she is- that the best version of her- do not try to change it a bit. This will give immediate happiness and long lasting happiness where there are no expectations.

We will have to really work on improving our 'Happiness index'. Now that we have realized how millions got impacted and infected with Corona, and thousands and thousands of people died, we have an opportunity to be happy with what we have. Minimalist approach will help us a lot. In the richest and most advanced country America- hundreds of thousands people died, those people could have lived a happier life. You and I can lead a happy life. We do not need too much stuff. We need peace with our souls and our family members. Give away your differences with them, give them another chance. Give yourself another chance- and be nice to them. Build a happy tomorrow. Happiness will not come from outside- it will come from within us, each one of us. We need to be more happy people as a human race, and need to stop complaining about small and little things.

In order to deal with post Corona, I recommend 'Book reading', there is so much to learn, and know in the world. Books on science, fiction, history, arts, etc. Whatever your hobby is, read on that. If you do not have one, this is the best time to pick it up. With reading we do not do it because of social pressure to belong to the intellectual elite but we do it as it takes you deeper into your own existence and makes you at peace with yourself. I am sometimes not very focused and do not like reading but once i get down to it it really feels soothing and excellent. I spend 2-3 hours each day reading- in my case I read Wall Street Journal each day, the Economist, the CIO and some technology magazines. We are knowledge workers- we will be paid more if we know more, now that the job market will change and a lot of stuff will move online- we can add this skill of reading for those of us who hate reading.

People will love to have more peace and there will be an anti-China movement, as China will try to assert its hegemony over nations. World over China will be aggressively pursuing its business interests and more and more people will start acting anti- china. Chinese products will be boycotted. 'Made in China' will become a problem. People will start using domestic products and sometimes homemade natural products. Environment friendly products will grow in need. For example, instead of a plastic bag or a paper bag, people will carry a cloth bag that they can use again and again. I used to do this when I was a kid in India. My mom would take me to the market with a cloth bag.

I have been thinking about working on my guitar skills. We must pick up our hobby or pursue an old one. We are all so stuck in our jobs and families that we have no time for working on our own self and our own hobbies. It always goes to the back burner. Corona taught me 'if you will not do it now, you will never do it'. It gives a tremendous amount of happiness when we get away from work and family and do something that we like just for ourselves. Initially it looks stupid then gradually you start enjoying it. It can be anything under the sun- Playing guitar, reading books, spending more time with kids, watching your favorite show on TV. Whatever gives you the most happiness. That is your space. You must get it daily. For an hour at least.

I also figured out during the Corona crisis that "Giving corona victims" really made me feel good. I felt I was helping in a big cause for humanity. You do not have to give thousands of dollars, give whatever you can. Give 10$ or whatever you can afford. A lot of us are so lucky that we have a roof on our head and do not have to worry about where our next meal will come from but in the world there are people who must work 8 hours to earn their next meal. If we can get any chance we must give and donate to them. Giving is very powerful, it makes us feel good about ourselves. It is the opposite of taking- a lot of us are just busy taking from the society we live in but not comfortable giving it back to the society. This is your chance to do it. Post Corona let us all start believing in 'giving', there are poor people, there are people in Africa, India who need help. There are people in San Francisco in the Tenderloin area I have met many of them- they need help. Let us help them grow. Let us make this world a better place that we can live in proudly.

We can learn new technologies to stay ahead of the curve. With people working from home and having more freedom, they will have to showcase that they know the latest technologies, as work will be done remotely with less supervision, the onus will shift from manager to concerned person. In the technology world where I come from things like Artificial Intelligence, Data Science, Blockchain, Cloud computing, Data Security will have more value. A lot of people who are losing jobs due to Corona are encouraged to learn these technologies and move ahead in the knowledge economy. Agile and Project Management as a discipline will grow as companies will have more focus on getting things done faster due to more uncertainty and complexity.

AI will replace traditional jobs. It is said in America 25% jobs will go away and robots will do jobs for humans. Any job that is mechanical and requires repetitive actions can be done by a robot. After Corona companies will increase the pace of AI adoption as they will feel intense pressure due to reduced demand. This is the time to get ready for it. Now it will be faster and we have to learn AI as a technology to get ahead in life. I would recommend that people impacted by Corona, who will never get their waiter jobs, bus driver jobs etc. back can now spend time and learn AI. Also work from home means more outsourcing as companies will realize after 6 months they can get this done from India and Philippines for one fourth the price.

The good thing about learning in post Corona world is that no more we need to go to brick and mortar universities and pay hundreds of thousands of dollars to learn new things, we can go to platforms like Udemy, Udacity, EdEx, Coursera, Smarter Learner and learn things at fraction of cost, less than 5% of what we used to spend on going to a university- we can learn programming skills. This means we can learn with our own money and do not have to depend on student loans, grants, if it is cheaper and we can pay from our pocket or use a credit card to pay for it. In America, there is going to be a shortage of STEM- Science, Technology, Engineering, Mathematics talent that America needs to import from India, China. We can learn all that sitting at home online- python programming, coding, database management can be learnt at low cost and with ease online.

The post Corona age will be the age that respects 'Digital skills". We can try to add 'Digital certificates' in our profiles. Now that people will have more free time, less commute, they will focus more on their careers and add new knowledge and certifications. The employers will become more demanding for skills. The new economy will respect people more for what they know than whom they know and where they work from? The power of networks and wine- dine will reduce. More people will work from home and work from anywhere in the world. Lot of people will leave expensive places like Silicon Valley, Manhattan, Los Angeles and go to smaller places and instead of renting wil buy a home at the same price. Outsourcing will grow and companies will have more people working from different parts of the world which also means jobs in America and Europe will not be safe. The call for digital is the call for systems and streamlining and getting away from paperwork, redundancies, and whom you know.

Because people will spend more time at home, home products will grow. Home depot businesses will grow. People would like to do more barbeque, more Jacuzzi, have pools at home than going to the gym, home base gyms, etc will go up. Furniture stores such as 'living spaces' will grow. Because people will like more being at home they will decorate their homes more and have more plants at home, more curtains, music systems, new furniture, new TV, new dining table. The home will be redesigned and reinvented to suit the needs of the soul. People will learn new cooking and eating habits. Friendship in neighborhoods will grow as people can trust neighbors more than strangers in coffee shops and bars. Even dating trends will change and people would like to meet someone new nearby than far away.

We will have to improve our skills on making digital presentations, giving talks, writing on white boards, all using Video Conferencing tools- these skills will grow. Tools like Zoom, Webex, GoToMeeting, Skype, Slack, Google Hangout, etc will grow. Those impacted by Corona can learn these skills and look for new jobs in these areas.

People will become short tempered and more sensitive and emotional as when you are locked down in one place you get claustrophobic. Even if Corona dies down people would have got habituated to staying indoors and this will create a behavioral change in people. People will have to learn positive communication, mindfulness, happiness and solve their own problems themselves rather than depending on friends. people will have to learn skills of soliloquy than feeling lonely. Your best friend is you yourself. Happiness is internal. It has to be found and enjoyed.

After Corona is over, we will move away from leading a "quantity of life" to leading a happy and high "quality of life". From lockdown we will move to unlocking ourselves. Unlocking from earlier habits and patterns of behavior. It is not about how much variety we have but it is going to be about how much quality is there in each moment we live. People would cut down the number of friends they have and focus on a few good ones. "Too much with too less" is the future. We have to all reduce the number of things we are doing on a daily basis and focus on how good we are doing it.

In the modern post Corona world, there will be more reliance on video calls, emails, chats, and social media will grow. There will be more software applications on your phones that can communicate between you and your employer, your well wishers,etc.employer will know if you are having a productive day or not. By getting AI in emails they will fathom your moods also depending on what type of words you are using. Productivity tools and cyber security tools will increase in numbers. More intranets and VPN virtual private networks will be used. More and more companies will give up servers and go to the cloud.

If we listen to Music everyday, it really helps in reducing anxiety levels. If the music is from Zen or 'flute' then it also helps in soothing and healing. I have tried music a lot and to me it always helps. When I work I put music on very low sound, so that only I can listen to it. I find it cathartic and very relaxing. We all know this but I still find people who would come and start fighting with their spouse or start getting panicky about things. Life is to enjoy and have fun. What will we all do with lots of money if basic happiness is missing. This instrumental music really helps in destressing and changing gears quickly, those of us who use it already know the power of it.

We will learn more from TV and viewing will go up. Universities, learning institutes, restaurants, hotels, airlines will advertise more on TV. Movie watching will increase significantly as people become more fatalistic. Netflix stocks are going up in America. Similar companies are growing in Europe, China, India etc. Restaurants will now be putting their menu online. Doordash in America, Zomato/Swiggy in India will grow. People will have more parties at home than in restaurants. Furniture sales will also go up.

People who want to build a new career can focus more on advertising jobs on TV and desktop, mobile phones, etc.

References

Coronavirus is Germany's biggest challenge 'since Second World War' Angela Merkel says, By Justin Huggler, BERLIN, 18 March 2020 • 7:52pm

https://www.telegraph.co.uk/news/2020/03/18/coronavirus-germanys-biggest-challenge-since-second-world-war/

'Our Big War.' As Coronavirus Spreads, Trump Refashions Himself as a Wartime President,

https://time.com/5806657/donald-trump-coronavirus-war-china/

It's China's World:
China has now reached parity with the U.S. on the 2019 Fortune Global 500—a signifier of the profound rivalries reshaping business today. BY GEOFF COLVIN
July 22, 2019 2:00 PM EST
https://fortune.com/longform/fortune-global-500-china-companies/

The Top 20 Economies in the World

Ranking the Richest Countries in the World
By CALEB SILVER Updated Mar 18, 2020

https://www.investopedia.com/insights/worlds-top-economies/

WORLD ECONOMIC OUTLOOK REPORTS

World Economic Outlook, October 2019

Global Manufacturing Downturn, Rising Trade Barriers

October 2019

https://www.imf.org/external/datamapper/NGDPD@WEO/OEMDC/ADVEC/WEOWORLD

China's currency weaponization its most effective trade war tool: Pro, CNBC

https://www.youtube.com/watch?v=dGRUqxc2kw8

#CNBC

Watch CNBC's full interview with Berkshire Hathaway CEO Warren Buffett

https://www.youtube.com/watch?v=JvEas_zZ4fM

Coronavirus latest: pandemic could have killed 40 million without any action

Updates on the respiratory illness that has infected hundreds of thousands of people and killed several thousand.

https://www.nature.com/articles/d41586-020-00154-w

Quarantined Wuhan Writer Challenges Regime. By Chun Han Wong, Wall Street Journal. April 3rd, 2020.

FBI Wiretrap Requests show Persistent Flaws- wsj article Apr 1st Wednesday

Stocks suffer their worst Quarter in 12 years.WSJ Article- Apr 1st wednesday

Impact of World War II on US Economy

http://www.iowapbs.org/iowapathways/artifact/impact-world-war-ii-us-economy-and-workforce

What Coronavirus Could Mean for the Global Economy

by Philipp Carlsson-Szlezak, Martin Reeves and Paul Swartz March 03, 2020

https://hbr.org/2020/03/what-coronavirus-could-mean-for-the-global-economy

Timeline: How the new coronavirus spread

The virus has killed more than 53,000 people and infected more than 1 million worldwide. April 3rd

https://www.aljazeera.com/news/2020/01/timeline-china-coronavirus-spread-200126061554884.html

DOJ Is Told to Review Wiretap Paperwork: By Dustin Walz

Unrestricted Warfare: China's Master Plan to Destroy America, 2015

by Qiao Liang (Author), Wang Xiangsui (Author)

US economy to shrink at fastest rate since 1946, unemployment to top 15%: Morgan Stanley, Read more at:

https://economictimes.indiatimes.com/news/international/business/u
s-economy-to-shrink-at-fastest-rate-since-1946-unemployment-to-
top-15-morgan-
stanley/articleshow/74962381.cms?utm_source=contentofinterest&
utm_medium=text&utm_campaign=cppst

Harvard Professor's Arrest Raises Questions About Scientific
Openness February 19, 2020

https://www.npr.org/2020/02/14/806128410/harvard-professors-
arrest-raises-questions-about-scientific-openness

Fact Check: Truth of corona conspiracy theory behind arrest of
Harvard professor

https://www.indiatoday.in/fact-check/story/truth-coronavirus-
conspiracy-theory-behind-arrest-harvard-professor-1663659-2020-
04-05

George Bush, President of the United States, 2005, Talks about
Potential Pandemic at the National Institute of Health,

https://georgewbush-whitehouse.archives.gov/infocus/pandemicflu/

Why the Coronavirus could threaten the US economy even more
than China's

The disease poses a threat to older patients and it could be just as
bad for mature economies like the USA's. New York Times|Last
Updated: Mar 09, 2020, By Austan Goolsbee

https://economictimes.indiatimes.com/news/international/world-
news/why-the-coronavirus-could-threaten-the-us-economy-even-
more-than-chinas/articleshow/74535695.cms

https://en.wikipedia.org/wiki/Made_in_China_2025

The Hundred-Year Marathon: China's Secret Strategy to Replace America as the Global Superpower By Michael Pillsbury.

The Tribune:DRDO develops Casualty Evacuation Bags. Vijay Mohan, March 30th, 2020

https://www.drdo.gov.in/sites/default/files/drdo-news-documents/DRDO%20News%2030%20March%202020.pdf

'Pack up and get out of there,' Japan to spend $2.2 billion to get Japanese companies to exit China

https://tfipost.com/2020/04/pack-up-and-get-out-of-there-japan-to-pay-2-2-billion-to-get-japanese-companies-to-exit-china/

Forbes, Middle East, Celebrating 10 years: Are we Witnessing the Awakening of a New World Order, By Khuloud Al Omian, April 2020

$20 trillion lawsuit against China! US group says coronavirus is bioweapon

https://www.businesstoday.in/current/world/usd-20-trillion-lawsuit-against-china-us-group-says-coronavirus-bioweapon/story/399071.html

Top Cities of America

https://en.wikipedia.org/wiki/List_of_United_States_cities_by_population

City of Wuhan in Hubei

https://en.wikipedia.org/wiki/Wuhan

Wuhan Institute of Virology

https://en.wikipedia.org/wiki/Wuhan_Institute_of_Virology

Menachery, V., Yount, B., Debbink, K. et al. A SARS-like cluster of circulating bat coronaviruses shows potential for human emergence. Nat Med 21, 1508–1513 (2015). https://doi.org/10.1038/nm.3985

Butler, Declan (12 November 2015). "Engineered bat virus stirs debate over risky research: Lab-made coronavirus related to SARS can infect human cells". Nature News. Nature. doi:10.1038/nature.2015.18787.

Drosten, C.; Hu, B.; Zeng, L.-P.; Yang, X.-L.; Ge, Xing-Yi; Zhang, Wei; Li, Bei; Xie, J.-Z.; Shen, X.-R.; Zhang, Yun-Zhi; Wang, N.; Luo, D.-S.; Zheng, X.-S.; Wang, M.-N.; Daszak, P.; Wang, L.-F.; Cui, J.; Shi, Z.-L. (2017). "Discovery of a rich gene pool of bat SARS-related coronaviruses provides new insights into the origin of SARS coronavirus". PLOS Pathogens. 13 (11): e1006698. doi:10.1371/journal.ppat.1006698. PMC 5708621. PMID 29190287.

Qiu, Jane (11 March 2020). "How China's "Bat Woman" Hunted Down Viruses from SARS to the New Coronavirus". Scientific American.

Chris Buckley; Steven Lee Myers (1 February 2020). "As New Coronavirus Spread, China's Old Habits Delayed Fight". The New York Times. Retrieved 3 February 2020.

Jon Cohen (1 February 2020). "Mining coronavirus genomes for clues to the outbreak's origins". Science. Retrieved 4 February 2020. The viral sequences, most researchers say, also knock down the idea the pathogen came from a virology institute in Wuhan.

Shi Zhengli; Team of 29 researchers at the WIV (3 February 2020). "A pneumonia outbreak associated with a new coronavirus of probable bat origin". Nature. 579(7798): 270–273. doi:10.1038/s41586-020-2012-7. PMC 7095418. PMID 32015507.

Shi Zhengli; Team of 10 researchers at the WIV (4 February 2020). "Remdesivir and chloroquine effectively inhibit the recently emerged novel coronavirus (2019-nCoV) in vitro". Nature. 30 (3): 269–271. doi:10.1038/s41422-020-0282-0. PMC 7054408. PMID 32020029.

"China Wants to Patent Gilead's Experimental Coronavirus Drug". Bloomberg News. Retrieved 5 February 2020.

Denise Grady (6 February 2020). "China Begins Testing an Antiviral Drug in Coronavirus Patients". New York Times. Retrieved 8 February 2020.

Josh Taylor (31 January 2020). "Bat soup, dodgy cures and 'diseasology': the spread of coronavirus misinformation". The Guardian. Retrieved 3 February 2020.

Kate Gibson (3 February 2020). "Twitter bans Zero Hedge after it posts coronavirus conspiracy theory". CBS News. Retrieved 4 February 2020.

Clive Cookson (14 February 2020). "Coronavirus was not genetically engineered in a Wuhan lab, says expert". Financial Times. Retrieved 14 February 2020.

Butler, Declan. "Engineered bat virus stirs debate over risky research". Nature News. doi:10.1038/nature.2015.18787.

Wuhan Pneumonia: "Wuhan Virus Research Institute" in the eyes of the outbreak and fake news storm". BBC News China. 5 February 2020. Retrieved 8 February 2020.

Yang Rui; Feng Yuding; Zhao Jinchao; Matthew Walsh (7 February 2020). "Wuhan Virology Lab Deputy Director Again Slams Coronavirus Conspiracies". Caixin. Retrieved 8 February 2020.

Broderick, Ryan (31 January 2020). "A Pro-Trump Blog Doxed A Chinese Scientist It Falsely Accused Of Creating The Coronavirus As A Bioweapon". Buzzfeed. Retrieved 31 January 2020.

Derek Hawkins (1 February 2020). "Twitter bans Zero Hedge account after it doxxed a Chinese researcher over coronavirus". Washington Post. Retrieved 3 February 2020.

Stephen Chen (6 February 2020). "Coronavirus: bat scientist's cave exploits offer hope to beat virus 'sneakier than Sars'". South China Morning Post. Retrieved 8 February 2020.

"Administration". Wuhan Institute of Virology, CAS. Archived from the original on 29 July 2019. Retrieved 26 January 2020.

Yuval Noah Harari: the world after coronavirus | Free to read

https://www.ft.com/content/19d90308-6858-11ea-a3c9-1fe6fedcca75

Barclays cuts India's GDP forecast to zero for 2020

https://economictimes.indiatimes.com/markets/stocks/news/extended-lockdown-to-cause-234-4-billion-economic-loss-says-barclays/articleshow/75138567.cms

Never Taking Travel for Granted Again

Crossing the globe had never been easier, until the coronavirus reminded us of the real meaning of distance

https://www.wsj.com/articles/never-taking-travel-for-granted-again-11585245786

http://ereader.wsj.net/?publink=29c87398a

Global Recession Likely UnderWay, IMF Says, BY JOSH ZUMBRUN

https://www.wsj.com/articles/coronavirus-afflicted-global-economy-is-almost-certainly-in-recession-11586867402

Chinese mask entrepreneur reaps $1.9bn coronavirus bonanza

Don Weinland and Sherry Fei Ju in Beijing, MARCH 27 2020

https://www.ft.com/content/2b70712c-6e3f-11ea-89df-41bea055720b

These five Chinese stocks are runaway winners in rally fuelled by coronavirus scare

https://www.scmp.com/business/companies/article/3050249/these-five-chinese-stocks-are-runaway-winners-rally-fuelled

Hear what Barack Obama said in 2014 about pandemics

CNN Tonight, During a 2014 speech, then-President Barack Obama warned about the need for the US to cast aside partisan differences to prepare for an upcoming pandemic.

https://edition.cnn.com/videos/politics/2020/04/10/barack-obama-2014-pandemic-comments-sot-ctn-vpx.cnn

Australia tightens investment rules on foreign takeovers

Canberra warns that companies hit by coronavirus could be targets of 'predatory behaviour'

https://www.ft.com/content/fda7e3cf-a605-4697-9bc0-6fe91b739eb9

Govt rushes in to check takeover of Indian companies after China scoops up HDFC stake; tweaks FDI rules By: Surbhi Jain | Updated: April 18, 2020 6:09:39 PM

https://www.financialexpress.com/market/government-rushes-in-to-check-takeover-of-indian-companies-after-china-scoops-up-hdfc-stake/1932510/

https://www.investindia.gov.in/country/china

FOLLOWING THE MONEY: China Inc's growing stake in India-China relations ANANTH KRISHNAN* Visiting Fellow, Brookings India**

https://www.brookings.edu/wp-content/uploads/2020/03/China-Inc%E2%80%99s-growing-stake-in-India-China-relations_F.pdf

https://www.ted.com/talks/bill_gates_the_next_outbreak_we_re_not_ready?language=en#t-500745

The New England Journal of Medicine, "Early Transmission Dynamics in Wuhan, China, of Novel Coronavirus–Infected Pneumonia", List of authors. Qun Li, M.Med., Xuhua Guan, Ph.D.,

Peng Wu, Ph.D., Xiaoye Wang, M.P.H., Lei Zhou, M.Med., Yeqing Tong, Ph.D., Ruiqi Ren, M.Med., Kathy S.M. Leung, Ph.D., Eric H.Y. Lau, Ph.D., Jessica Y. Wong, Ph.D., Xuesen Xing, Ph.D., Nijuan Xiang, M.Med, et al.

Scientists Haven't Found Proof The Coronavirus Escaped From A Lab In Wuhan. Trump Supporters Are Spreading The Rumor Anyway.

https://www.buzzfeednews.com/article/ryanhatesthis/coronavirus-rumors-escape-lab-china-fox-news-trump

How China Is Losing Support For Its Belt And Road Initiative

Wade ShepardContributor Asia

https://www.forbes.com/sites/wadeshepard/2020/02/28/how-beijing-is-losing-support

for-its-belt-and-road-initiative/#315190322199

https://www.fpri.org/article/2020/04/lack-of-demand-coronavirus-pandemic-belt-and-road/

U.S. Economy Shrank at 4.8% Pace in First Quarter

Gross domestic product recorded steepest contraction since the last recession

https://www.wsj.com/articles/first-quarter-gdp-us-growth-coronavirus-11588123665

https://nationalinterest.org/blog/buzz/chinas-military-biggest-planet-can-it-fight-america-and-win-58862

https://virologyj.biomedcentral.com/articles/10.1186/s12985-015-0422-1

Coronavirus did not jump from Wuhan's seafood market: Here's the evidence

Is the SARS-CoV-2 a 'chimera virus' made in the lab? A virologist's warning

https://gulfnews.com/world/coronavirus-did-not-jump-from-wuhans-seafood-market-heres-the-evidence-1.1586936434717

FDA issues emergency authorization to use remdesivir as COVID-19 treatment

The drug will be given to coronavirus patients who are "hospitalized with severe disease."

cnet.com/news/fda-issues-emergency-use-authorization-for-the-drug-remdesivir-as-covid-19-treatment/?ftag=CAD-03-10aaj8j

The mysterious disappearance of the first SARS virus, and why we need a vaccine for the current one but didn't for the other

May 5, 2020 10.20pm AEST, Marilyn J. Roossinck

Professor of Plant Pathology Environmental Microbiology, Pennsylvania State University https://theconversation.com/the-mysterious-disappearance-of-the-first-sars-virus-and-why-we-need-a-vaccine-for-the-current-one-but-didnt-for-the-other-137583

1-Idea/2-Implementation/3-Success/4-Accident/5-Panic/6-SpreadGlobally/7-USA & Europe 8-ROW- India 9-WorldDestroyed 10-NewOrder

Is coronavirus part of Chinese biological warfare?

By Tehelka Bureau -February 18, 2020

New SARS-like virus from bats implicated in China pig die-off

https://www.cidrap.umn.edu/news-perspective/2018/04/new-sars-virus-bats-implicated-china-pig-die

Indian Army now world's largest ground force as China halves strength on modernisation push

While the Indian Army is bearing the burden of a large personnel driven force, the Chinese are in the midst of a massive modernisation.

SNEHESH ALEX PHILIP 17 March, 2020

https://theprint.in/defence/indian-army-now-worlds-largest-ground-force-as-china-halves-strength-on-modernisation-push/382287/

https://www.washingtonpost.com/national-security/chinese-lab-conducted-extensive-research-on-deadly-bat-viruses-but-there-is-no-evidence-of-accidental-release/2020/04/30/3e5d12a0-8b0d-11ea-9dfd-990f9dcc71fc_story.html

Timeline of the COVID-19 pandemic in January 2020

https://en.wikipedia.org/wiki/Timeline_of_the_COVID-19_pandemic_in_January_2020

There's only one option for a global coronavirus exit strategy, World Economic Forum

https://www.weforum.org/agenda/2020/04/there-s-only-one-option-for-a-global-coronavirus-exit-strategy

How the Fourth Industrial Revolution can help us beat COVID-19, World Economic Forum:

https://www.weforum.org/agenda/2020/05/how-the-fourth-industrial-revolution-can-help-us-handle-the-threat-of-covid-19/

Our Latest perspectives on Corona Virus Pandemic: Mckinsey

https://www.mckinsey.com/business-functions/risk/our-insights/covid-19-implications-for-business?cid=other-eml-alt-mip-mck&hlkid=766741fd88db489199d009e896d96341&hctky=2078426&hdpid=6889a209-b1c3-4e0e-a655-ca08f404e325

China's defense industry is exploding onto the scene as its top arms makers push past Western powerhouses.

https://www.businessinsider.in/home/chinas-defense-industry-is-exploding-onto-the-scene-as-its-top-arms-makers-push-past-western-powerhouses/articleshow/70354108.cms

The origin of covid-19: The pieces of the puzzle of covid-19's origin are coming to light

https://www.economist.com/science-and-technology/2020/05/02/the-pieces-of-the-puzzle-of-covid-19s-origin-are-coming-to-light

China Lied, People Died: Inside China's Death Labs

Video Clip, Benny Johnson

Account: Junior Donald Trump

Turning Point USA

https://www.facebook.com/turningpointusa/?eid=ARD7OAA3NaTjdDerCaupZ_ukXblMnB72ok_cxTUCJD__ZidvMCI53xQetrCX7cl1OFIse_CzQfUblFzs&fref=tag

The Consumer in the Age of Coronavirus, Philip Kotler, Father of Marketing

https://sarasotainstitute.global/the-consumer-in-the-age-of-coronavirus/

Bat Coronaviruses in China

2019 Mar 2;11(3):210. doi: 10.3390/v11030210.

https://pubmed.ncbi.nlm.nih.gov/30832341/

Inside the Chinese lab poised to study world's most dangerous pathogens

By David Cyranoski, 22 February 2017 Updated: 23 February 2017,WUHAN, CHINA

https://docs.google.com/document/d/1F0kaFxVXVXpt9pIWh169k
G4_D6XVfFDudMWM7i_-RDk/edit#

YouTubers capitalizing on public fear of novel coronavirus condemned

By Ji Yuqiao Source:Global Times Published: 2020/2/5

https://www.globaltimes.cn/content/1178601.shtml

China storms past US and Japan to take lead in wind and solar power

Beijing's pivot to renewables is one reason for trade war with Washington

https://asia.nikkei.com/Business/Energy/China-storms-past-US-and-
Japan-to-take-lead-in-wind-and-solar-
power#:~:text=China's%20wind%20power%20capacity%20soared,f
old%20over%20the%20same%20period.&text=Longi%20Solar%2
C%20the%20world's%20No.

Dethroning the dollar
America's aggressive use of sanctions endangers the dollar's reign
Its rivals and allies are both looking at other options

https://www.economist.com/briefing/2020/01/18/americas-
aggressive-use-of-sanctions-endangers-the-dollars-reign

Africa 'least affected' by COVID-19; Hydroxycholoroquine trial
suspended   -   WHO   briefing

https://www.weforum.org/agenda/2020/05/covid19-africa-hydroxycholoroquine-world-health-organization/

50 per cent of Indian population could be COVID-19 infected by December: NIMHANS Neurovirology head.

The numbers will go up from June onwards after Lockdown 4.0 ends on May 31, and there will be community spread.

https://www.newindianexpress.com/states/karnataka/2020/may/28/50-per-cent-of-indian-population-could-be-covid-19-infected-by-december-nimhans-neurovirology-head-2148985.html

Novel coronavirus is human-made, says Australia studyNew study finds evidence of a sign of human intervention in COVID-19 pandemic, Web Desk May 20, 2020

https://www.theweek.in/news/sci-tech/2020/05/20/Novel-coronavirus-is-human-made-says-Australia-study.html

'The Saddest, Bitterest Thing of All.' From the Great Depression to Today, a Long History of Food Destruction in the Face of Hunger

https://time.com/5843136/covid-19-food-destruction/

Tracking coronavirus' global spread

Since December, the virus has spread to nearly every continent and case numbers continue to rise

By Henrik Pettersson, Byron Manley and Sergio Hernandez, CNN

https://edition.cnn.com/interactive/2020/health/coronavirus-maps-and-cases/

China Rules Out Animal Market and Lab as Coronavirus Origin

Comments by Chinese scientists aim to counter what Beijing perceives as efforts from top U.S. officials to focus solely on China's role in pandemic

https://www.wsj.com/articles/china-rules-out-animal-market-and-lab-as-coronavirus-origin-11590517508?mod=hp_listb_pos1

Coronavirus may have existed in Italy since November: local research

https://news.cgtn.com/news/2020-03-22/Coronavirus-may-have-existed-in-Italy-since-November

-local-researcher-P4i2As2OAg/index.html

Coronavirus outbreak:A timeline of how COVID-19 spread around world:Global News

https://www.youtube.com/watch?v=ST-cn2JQ31M

Chinese Sporting Power Couple Issues Rare Rebuke of Ruling Communist Party

Retired soccer star Hao Haidong and his wife, former badminton world champion Ye Zhaoying, are speaking out against Beijing's leadership

https://www.wsj.com/articles/chinese-sporting-power-couple-issues-rare-rebuke-of-ruling-communist-party-11591797324

+++++++++